# A CHRISTMAS KISS

"That was cheating," she said, suddenly finding it difficult to breathe. It was such a small kiss, really, not one that should shoot desire through her like a bolt, but it had—right to her toes.

"I suppose I should have warned you first," he said without even a hint of apology in his tone.

She gulped. "Yes, that would have been nice."

He looked down at her, his gray eyes intense with an expression she could hardly read. "Miss Amelia, I'm going to kiss you."

A little thrill went through her, and she lifted her chin. "All right."

And he did, bringing his mouth against hers, a slow, wonderful kiss that made her knees instantly weak. Carson's kisses had been full of blatant lust, but Boone's was more like warm, dark chocolate spreading slowly through her. Delicious, and beyond divine . . .

Books by Jane Goodger

*Marry Christmas*

*A Christmas Scandal*

*A Christmas Waltz*

Published by Kensington Publishing Corporation

# A Christmas Waltz

## JANE GOODGER

ZEBRA BOOKS
KENSINGTON PUBLISHING CORP.
http://www.kensingtonbooks.com

ZEBRA BOOKS are published by

Kensington Publishing Corp.
119 West 40th Street
New York, NY 10018

All Kensington titles, imprints, and distributed lines are available at special quantity discounts for bulk purchases for sales promotion, premiums, fund-raising, educational, or institutional use.

Special book excerpts or customized printings can also be created to fit specific needs. For details, write or phone the office of the Kensington Special Sales Manager: Attn. Special Sales Department. Kensington Publishing Corp., 119 West 40th Street, New York, NY 10018. Phone: 1-800-221-2647.

Zebra and the Z logo Reg. U.S. Pat. & TM Off.

ISBN-13: 978-1-4201-1150-7
ISBN-10: 1-4201-1150-7

First Printing: October 2010
10 9 8 7 6 5 4 3 2

Printed in the United States of America

# Chapter 1

*Small Fork, Texas*
*1894*

As Lady Amelia Wellesley stepped from the stifling air of the train into a blast of heat such as she'd never felt before, she had a sense of deep foreboding that she had just stepped into a nightmare of her own making.

This could not be the place.

After all she had gone through, after sitting endlessly in a cramped and oven-like train car for days, after crossing the bloody Atlantic and being abandoned by her maid, this could not be Small Fork. Amelia stood on a dusty platform in a dusty, dry world devoid of all color but for the bright bleached blue sky above her, and could not believe she had reached her destination. It was impossible. Carson had described Small Fork in detail in his slow Texas drawl, and she had the images etched in her brain.

"Well, it's the prettiest little town you ever saw," he'd said. "The main street has a church with a white steeple that stretches to the sky, pointing up to heaven. There's roses everywhere and houses with white picket fences, children playing everywhere you look. And in the center of town is a park with a whitewashed gazebo where the local band plays concerts every Saturday night. All the townspeople gather 'round, and there's dancing." Those had been his exact words.

She had not seen a blade of proper grass in three days.

"Miss. Your bags are yonder," the porter said, wiping his brow with an already damp-looking cloth. "Good day, ma'am."

Horrid day, more like it, she thought darkly. The thick feeling of regret began seeping through her and she stalwartly pushed it back where it belonged, in the pit of her stomach where it had been since the day she'd lied to her brother and told him Carson had sent for her. Their manor house by the sea seemed so very far away at the moment as she stood quite alone on the platform watching the train she'd been in since Fort Worth move slowly down the track to God knew where.

Amelia eyed her pile of luggage, knowing there would be no porter to help her carry it to wherever she should go. With that thought in mind, she looked down the unpaved street and saw only a handful of buildings, and even fewer pedestrians. The architecture was vaguely reminiscent of paintings she'd seen of Spain, but without the charm of the Mediterranean as a backdrop. There was no gazebo, and certainly no church with a steeple. The only recognizable structure was a strange looking windmill, lazily turning in the hot breeze.

A trickle of sweat ran between her breasts, then moved to soak into her already damp chemise.

Carrying her pelisse, she lifted her chin and pretended she wasn't more frightened than she'd been in her entire life. It wasn't the first time in the past month that she'd had to do that, and she feared it would not be the last.

As she stepped down from the depot boardwalk and walked along the street, lifting her skirts slightly to avoid the swirling dirt, she noted a mercantile, a bank, and a larger two-story building further down, with the words "Hotel/Saloon" painted on a faded, warped sign moving lazily in the wind above the entrance. There were other buildings, but they were nondescript and could have been saloons or even homes. She eyed the town's sparse inhabitants, wondering who would be the most helpful. Sitting in a wooden chair leaning up against the wall of the hotel was an old man who appeared to be sound asleep. Other than two horses tied up outside the hotel, and a shaggy dog lying outside the mercantile, there wasn't another soul in sight.

It seemed as if the town had been plopped down in the middle of a barren field for no apparent reason. There was no river, no protective valley, nothing for miles but endless land that ended on the horizon with an odd-looking mountain range.

The mercantile seemed like a good place for information and the dog appeared much friendlier than the old man outside the hotel, so she headed there. The dog, likely as hot as she was in the sweltering heat, raised its head and gave its tail a halfhearted wag before letting out a groan and falling back to sleep.

"Hello to you, too," Amelia said, smiling, feeling a certain camaraderie with the dog. She was entirely overdressed for such a temperature, and was quite certain if she were to remove her dress she would be able to wring perspiration out of it. She'd tried her best to tidy up on the train, for she wanted to look her finest when she saw Carson again.

Amelia pushed open the doors, pleasantly surprised that the interior was lit by a series of skylights in the ceiling that gave a soft glow to the place. A large man was behind the counter, busy arranging cans on a shelf, and Amelia found herself relaxing a bit at the sight of him. He seemed so ordinary, so clean, with his pristine white shirt and dark blue vest, almost a gentleman in a world of buckskin and dungarees. Indeed, the air in the store was surprisingly cool compared to the outside temperature, and Amelia smiled as she waited for the man, who must certainly have heard her, turn to her.

When he did, she was struck nearly dumb. For the second time in her life she felt a reaction, like a physical blow, at the mere sight of a man. The only other time it had happened was when she'd first laid eyes on Carson, and she wondered if she were becoming one of those women who found all men attractive.

"Excuse me, but I wonder if you could tell me if it is possible to hire someone to take me to the Kitteridge ranch."

He stared at her with eyes the color of cold slate, as if he didn't speak God's English, or as if he'd never seen a woman before. His cheeks were slightly flushed, a man who blushed easily or spent a bit too much time in the sun, and his face was clean-shaven, unlike so many men of the West she'd encountered.

"Excuse me?" he said slowly in a Texas drawl she recognized, and his eyes did a quick and completely neutral scan of her person. His voice was low and raspy, like a person who hadn't spoken yet that day.

"I need to hire someone to take me to the Kitteridge ranch," she said a bit louder, just in case the man was hard of hearing.

"The Kitteridge. Ranch."

He was becoming annoying.

"Yes. I'm here to see Carson Kitteridge, Mr. . . ."

"Kitteridge. *Boone* Kitteridge."

Oh, goodness. That explained a great deal. Boone was Carson's older brother, and Carson had mentioned more than once that he was quite dim-witted. She smiled, completely relieved that at least something of all the things Carson had told her was true. He seemed almost startled by her smile, and actually backed up a step. Oh dear, she'd frightened the poor man.

"Boone. How wonderful to meet you. I am Lady Amelia Wellesley, Lord Hollings's younger sister." At his blank stare she felt a snag of pity for him. What a trial it must have been for Carson to care for him. "I'm Carson's fiancée," she said, raising the volume of her voice. "From England. Surely he's mentioned me. He's told me all about you."

Boone Kitteridge wouldn't have been more surprised if this exquisite creature in front of him sprouted fairy wings and granted him three wishes.

Carson's *fiancée*? It was almost as impossible as finding a woman this beautiful standing in front of him. She didn't seem real.

She wore a buttercup-yellow dress that made the air around her fairly glow as if from a light within. It had lace and beads and all sorts of things that glittered beneath his store's skylights. Her hair was nearly the color of that dress, a golden halo around her face. She reminded him of a doll sitting on a shelf, perfect, and something you really shouldn't touch, never mind play with.

And for some reason, she thought she was Carson's fiancée.

"Carson's not here," he said, full of caution. There wasn't a woman this side of the Mississippi who was dumb enough or crazy enough to agree to marry Carson. And from this girl's accent, he figured she wasn't from anywhere near here.

She smiled again, and Boone started to wonder if perhaps she wasn't all that bright. "Where can I find him? Is he, perhaps, at the ranch? I've come a very long way to see him, all the way from England, you see. He should be expecting me."

That's when it fully dawned on Boone. This girl actually thought she was engaged to Carson. For some reason she thought Carson had a ranch, and even though she was acting sure of herself, he thought he detected just the slightest bit of worry, a small quaver of uncertainty in her lovely, melodic voice. The situation, he realized darkly, was going to get a whole lot uglier for this girl, and she didn't have the slightest clue of what was about to happen to her. Or perhaps she did.

"You can stay here, miss. I'll go get him."

"If you could just direct me where to go, I'm certain I can find him myself. I've become quite independent on my journey here."

"I'll get him," he repeated, because God knew he couldn't send this pretty thing where Carson was at the moment—likely between the legs of Geraldine Turner. "I doubt I'll have any customers while I'm gone. You sit tight now. And if someone does come in, you just tell them to wait."

"All right, but . . ."

He didn't even wait to hear what she was going to say, just headed out the door, grabbing his hat on the way and jamming it angrily on his head. There was no way in hell that his brother was going to marry that girl. No way in hell.

He made his way to the saloon and pushed through the door, ignoring the surprise on George's face when he came in. The only time Boone ever set foot in the saloon was when he was looking for someone else.

"George," he said politely as he could, taking off his hat and slamming it on the bar.

"Boone. What brings you in here?"

"My brother still upstairs?"

"This got something to do with that pretty young thing what just come off the train and went into your place?" George asked, full of rabid curiosity.

"My brother."

"Yeah," George said, purely disappointed Boone was going to be so closedmouthed. "He's still here. Third door on the left."

Boone nodded grimly before heading up the steps to the hotel part of the building, though the word "hotel" was a rather grand word for the three shabby rooms George let out on occasion. Geraldine Turner was the town whore. The town whore because she was the only one, and practically the only woman living in the town proper. Most of the respectable women lived in the outskirts on the three ranches that surrounded Small Fork. As such, she was kept busy by most of the men in town, but she had a special fondness for Carson. What woman didn't?

Boone didn't bother knocking, but opened the door calmly and stared daggers at his brother, who was lying in bed well satisfied, his long hair a tangled mess around his head. It didn't look as if he'd shaved or bathed in a while, and Boone couldn't help thinking how insane it was that the bit of feminine perfection standing in his store could possibly want Carson. Then again, it was difficult to believe Geraldine, whose bloom had long since started to wilt, would see anything in him, either. Geraldine didn't even bother acting surprised, and certainly didn't bother covering up her phenomenally large breasts.

"Hey, Boone," she said, smiling in a way that Boone guessed was supposed to make him horny, but just served to annoy him. She was lying in bed with his brother, after all.

"What the hell you doing, Boone?" Carson asked goodnaturedly, putting his hands behind his head as if he had all day to loll about in bed, which was pretty much the case.

"Your fiancée's here, you stupid son of a bitch."

Carson didn't move an inch, but his face turned a deadly pale. "My what?"

"Your fiancée."

Carson sat up in bed, a look like death in his eyes. "What did she look like?" he asked, as if expecting the worst.

"Why don't you tell me?"

"No. No, no, no, no . . ."

He continued to say that word over and over, terror in his eyes, and so Boone, rather enjoying his brother's pain, proceeded to describe the fiancée. "She's blond. Pretty. With blue eyes the color of blue sage in the spring."

"Shit."

Boone set his jaw hard as he watched Carson scramble to find his clothes. Meanwhile, Geraldine was laughing so hard, there were tears streaming down her face. At least she had a sense of humor.

"Who is she?" Boone demanded, and Carson stopped pulling on his last boot and slumped back onto the bed.

"She's a lady," he said.

"Didn't notice."

"No. I mean she's a *lady*. Lady Amelia Wellesley. Her brother is a goddamn earl. Lord Hollings. What the hell is she doing here?"

Boone felt the urge to punch his brother in the face, but like all the other times he'd felt that urge, he resisted. "Apparently, she thinks you're engaged and she also believes you're expecting her."

"I was supposed to *send* for her," he lamented. "I told her specifically. Holy God. What the hell am I going to do, Boone?" He clutched his head as if he were trying to stop it from exploding, which likely wasn't far from the truth. He turned to Geraldine, who was still laughing beside him, and said, "Shut the hell up, Geraldine. You cackling over there ain't helpin' me one bit."

Poor Geraldine tried to sober up, but, failing that, grabbed her clothes and left the room, her giggles still audible as she ran down the hall.

"Is anyone with her?" Carson asked, his voice filled with dread.

"Nope."

"Well, that's one thing. At least she doesn't have her brother with her. He'd have me walkin' down the aisle before I could spit."

Boone looked at his brother with pure disgust. "I have one question for you, little brother."

"What's that?"

"Why does that girl think you two are getting married?"

Carson looked at Boone as if he were the simpleton he'd told everyone he was. "'Cause I asked her to marry me. It was the only way I could . . ." Carson stopped mid-sentence. "She's all high falutin', and it was the only way."

Boone told himself he shouldn't be surprised, but he was. "Are you telling me you lied to that girl just to get her into your bed?"

"That was the general idea. She kept tellin' me we had to wait until we was married. Can you believe it? Never had that happen to me before. I even had to go to the brother and ask for her hand. Shit."

"You were formally engaged?"

"Not *formally*. Nothing written down, if that's what you mean," he said, yanking on his boot angrily. "What the *hell* is she doing here?"

"I think she's here to get married."

"Well, she's dead wrong about that. We'll just send her on her way."

Boone knocked his hat against his thigh, unable to believe that even Carson could ask a girl to marry him just to bed her. Then again, he wondered what *he'd* do for that privilege. She was simply the most beautiful girl he'd ever seen. Just thinking about touching her was enough to make him weak in the knees.

They ignored George as they walked through the saloon and broke out into the glaring heat of the midday sun. Carson took two steps before he stopped, his skin clammy and bathed with sweat. "Oh, God, I think I'm gonna puke," he said, hanging his head down and bracing a hand on each thigh. He swallowed heavily three times, straightened, then puked all over Small Fork's only main thoroughfare. "I can't do it. You go tell her I'm gone. You tell her you couldn't find me. I can't do it, Boone. You saw her. You saw how she can look at you and drive you crazy. Oh, God, I can't do it."

Boone heaved up his brother as if he were a child, instead of a grown man who was almost as tall as he was. He shook him hard, clutching his shirt and driving his fists against his shoulders. "You got to face this, Carson. You've got to tell her to her face."

"She thinks I'm some sort of hero. She thinks I'm Carson Kitteridge, former Texas Ranger, some-goddamn-body. She thinks . . ." He began swallowing heavily again, and let out a couple of dry heaves before gaining control of himself. "She thinks I have a goddamn ranch. Hell, you wouldn't believe the shit I was telling that girl just to get up her

skirts. I would have told her I was the president of
the United States if I thought that would work. You
seen her."

Boone let out a sigh. In a small way, a *very* small
way, Boone almost understood. "That doesn't
excuse what you did and you know it. You've got to
face this, Carson. I'm not bailing you out again.
I'm not."

Carson gave him a belligerent look that was
tinged with enough guilt that Boone knew he understood. All his life, Boone had been covering for
Carson, taking his pain. Not this time.

"Hell. Let's get this over with," Carson said. He
started walking toward the mercantile when Boone
put out an arm to stop him.

"Go 'round back and clean up. You smell like a
whore and you look like hell."

"Oh. Yeah," Carson said, as if the thought hadn't
occurred to him, which it obviously hadn't.

Boone went back into the store, something tugging at him hard when she whirled around to see
who'd entered. Her disappointment was painfully
obvious. "He'll be right here."

"Did he . . . Was he . . ." She stopped, her porce-
lain cheeks turning a vivid red. He'd never before
seen a girl with skin so pale. "Thank you," she said,
finally. "Do you work here alone?"

"Yes." He started finishing the work she'd inter-
rupted, setting up cans of corn so that the labels all
faced precisely the same way.

She nodded as if interested in his one-word response. "And are you in charge of keeping this all
neat and clean? You do a marvelous job."

He stopped for a moment and narrowed his eyes.

She was talking to him as if he were a child who'd finished all his dinner.

"Carson must be so proud of you," she said to fill the silence.

Boone should have said something, but he was too busy mulling over why she was talking to him like a child.

"You have to be very smart to take care of a store all by yourself."

He finally turned, overcome with curiosity. "Miss."

"Yes, Boone."

"Are you somehow under the impression that I'm not right in the head?"

Her cheeks turned scarlet once more, two painful blotches of red. "Oh, no, Boone. I would never think that. You're very smart. Your head is perfectly . . ."

"Because I'm not stupid."

"I know," she said, as if he was a simpleton.

He set his jaw, knowing that short of producing his degree from Tulane University, she was going to continue to talk to him as if he were a dunce. He glared toward the back of the store where Carson was no doubt trying to clean himself by the fountain, because he had a feeling he knew where she'd gotten the idea he was short of brains.

Spotting a fingerprint on his gleaming counter, he took out his cloth and wiped it down. He was bending down to be certain the smudge was gone when the front door opened and in walked Carson, bigger than life, a smile on his face, as if he hadn't just been puking in the middle of the street.

"Where's my darlin' girl," he shouted, and opened his arms.

The relief on Miss Wellesley's face was almost painful to see. She ran into his brother's arms, and Carson embraced her like a man who was actually happy to see her, something that only made Boone even angrier.

"I wasn't certain you wanted me to come," she said, her voice muffled against his shirt. "You didn't write."

"'Course I did. An' here you are." Carson looked up at Boone and gave a little shrug, as if to say "See? I can't help myself." Boone's heart tugged for the girl, because he knew Carson would leave at the first opportunity. Hopefully, he'd tell the girl first. Boone would make certain of it.

"I knew you had, I just knew it. My brother wanted me to wait, but the post isn't always reliable and no doubt dozens of letters get lost when they're going across the ocean." She looked so happy it hurt.

"Amelia, this here's my brother Boone. The one I told you about."

"Yes, we've met," Amelia said, beaming a smile at Boone. God, that girl could make a man weep with that smile, it was so beautiful. Her whole face lit up with it, shining like a happy light.

"You mind telling your fiancée that I'm not a moron?"

Amelia began to object, but stopped when Carson began to laugh, doubling over in his mirth. "Oh, Lordy, I forgot I said that about you," he said, wiping his eyes. Boone never even cracked a smile.

"He isn't dumb. He's about the smartest person I know. He's a pure genius."

Amelia looked initially shocked, then swatted Carson playfully, laughing. "Is there anything you told the truth about?" she asked in mock exasperation. "I can tell you one thing, Small Fork looks nothing like what you described."

Carson didn't even pretend to look sheepish. "If I told you what it looked like, would you have come?"

Boone watched in pure dismay as Carson charmed the seemingly intelligent woman standing before him. He truly was an artist. Boone had never had that ability with women, or with anyone, if he were honest. But Carson, he could spin a tale and, even if someone didn't believe a word out of his mouth, they'd been so entertained they ended up forgiving him for the lies.

Boone watched and grew more and more angry. Because within minutes Carson had that girl believing he was glad to see her. He was making her feel like the most desired woman on the planet. Hell, he could almost fall for it, and he knew what a liar his brother was. If he hadn't watched him vomit in the street in pure panic, he would never know how Carson really felt.

"When can I see the ranch?" Amelia asked, and Boone looked up, curious as to what his brother would say.

"Well, the ranch. That's . . ."

"Another lie." Amelia smiled, and for the first time Boone thought he saw a brittle edge to that smile, and he found himself reconsidering the girl. She wasn't fooled for one second, he realized. Not one.

"Lie is such a harsh word, darlin'," he said, looking hurt.

Amelia didn't believe a word out of his beautiful mouth. Carson had lied about everything. Everything. And she almost willed him to lie about the ranch. "Well, is there a ranch?"

Carson looked over at his brother, almost the way a naughty child looks at a parent. "Why don't we talk outside. More privacy."

Before she walked out the door, she looked back at Boone. He stared at her impassively for perhaps three beats, before tearing his eyes away. He knew, she thought. He knew what a liar his brother was. And he pitied her. She wanted to slap that pity from his face. No one was going to pity Amelia Wellesley. No one.

# Chapter 2

"I can tell you're upset."

"Why would I be upset?" Amelia asked calmly. The strange thing was, she did feel calm, as if a part of her wasn't surprised by a single thing that had happened since she'd left Meremont. "Is it because everything you told me was a lie? Why would that upset me?"

"You're upset," Carson said in a long, beleaguered sigh, as if he were the injured party.

"Take me to your ranch," Amelia said, tapping her foot and crossing her arms. "And on the way you can tell me what happened to the grass and gazebo and roses and white picket fences that are supposed to be in this town. I haven't seen a tree in hours, never mind a rosebush."

Carson grinned, but Amelia noticed that much of the bravado he'd always had was gone. It was so wonderful to see him, but he'd changed in the months they'd been apart. He looked tired and beaten, older than he'd been in England, far older than his brother. She had no idea how old he was, in fact, because she assumed he had lied about that, too. His hair was not the gleaming, golden mass it had been, but hung in a tangle down his back, tied with a long string of rawhide. His mustache was too full, and the rest of his face looked like it hadn't seen a razor in days. His clothes were, well they were filthy. Maybe it was all this dust, she thought, glancing around this poor excuse of a town.

He led her behind the store, and Amelia was surprised how large it was. From the front, it looked like a tiny building, but it stretched back, much farther than any of its neighbors. It was made from a hodgepodge of materials, and had obviously been built at different times. By the time they'd reached the back, Amelia found herself in a tiny little oasis, a courtyard that was filled with flowers and grass and a whimsical little fountain. Benches were set neatly around the perimeter of the courtyard, which was surprisingly cool away from the glaring heat of the sun. Just the sight of it made Amelia feel cooler.

"This is lovely," Amelia said, nearly overcome with happiness to find a bit of color in this brown world. The back of the building was far more lovely than the storefront.

"My brother has his offices there," he said, nodding toward the left side of the U-shaped building. "And we live there."

"Oh." As lovely as it was compared to its surroundings, it was far smaller and simpler than any home she'd ever been in. Her brother's estate, Meremont, with its twenty rooms, was a castle compared to this. Even her childhood home, which was far more modest than Meremont, could fit this entire building twice over.

Carson turned her to face him, putting his hands gently on her upper arms and looking down at her. "All right. I lied. About everything. What was I supposed to do with you lookin' at me like the sun rose and set across my shoulders? You saw Carson Kitteridge, American hero—not me."

"But you *are* Carson Kitteridge," Amelia pointed out, even though she knew what he meant. Finally.

Carson let out a sigh and gazed toward the mountains in the distance. "I'm nothing," he said quietly. "I'm an actor. I've never been a Texas Ranger. Hell, I'd hardly been on a horse until I signed up for the Wild West show. Turns out, I'm pretty good at it, and the manager made me the star of the show. I fit the part. And the costume," he added with a wry smile. "Might even sign up for the cattle drive over at the Three J's ranch." He shrugged and looked down at her.

"I know you lied, Carson. Part of me knew you were lying the whole time. But I don't understand why. Didn't you know I'd find all this out when I got here?"

He looked about to say something, but let out another sigh. "I figured I'd cross that bridge when I got to it. Guess I got to be crossing the bridge now, hmmm?" He grinned and Amelia's heart squeezed in her chest. No matter that he wasn't wearing the white fringed outfit she'd first seen him in, he still had a way of reaching her heart. He laid a hand on one cheek, and Amelia closed her eyes.

"I don't care, Carson. I don't care if you're not a hero." She sounded desperate, even to her own ears.

He let out a bitter sounding laugh.

"I don't care," she insisted.

"Yeah, well, maybe I do."

She laid a hand against his and squeezed it. "I knew half of what you said was made up, anyway. Didn't you know that?"

He looked momentarily surprised, then shook his head as if vastly amused by her. "And here was I thinking I was fooling you completely."

"I'd have to be completely daft to think you rode with Custer. You're not old enough to have done that. Are you?"

"Then why'd you come all this way if you knew I was lyin' about near everything?"

She looked up at him and smiled at his confusion. "I love you," she said simply.

He looked momentarily stunned, then drew her against him, tucking her head beneath his head. "Oh, darlin'," he said, sounding almost sad. "That's what I figured."

Amelia let him hold her, loving the familiar feel of his big body even as her stomach gave a worried twist. She'd so wanted everything to be just as Carson had described. She'd pictured herself the mistress of a large rambling Texas ranch house filled with children and happiness. And servants. Yes, she'd imagined a neat little maid, a gruff housekeeper, an efficient butler. She'd pictured her life exactly as it had been, but in Texas and with Carson. If he'd prepared her in even the smallest way that he didn't even have a proper house, she wouldn't be looking with such dismay at where she was to live. But he'd drawn a picture of perfection for her, as if every fantasy she had about living in Texas were a reality.

Looking at the small portion of the building that Carson said was the living quarters, she doubted even a single servant lived there. She'd imagined being ushered into her own suite of rustic rooms by an apple-cheeked maid, as men carried her luggage into her room. In her imaginings, Carson happily introduced her to everyone. The sound of cows mingling with the familiar sound of crickets would have lulled her to sleep.

"Where shall I stay?" she asked, eyeing the house doubtfully.

Her question seemed to baffle Carson. "I don't know. I suppose you could stay at the hotel." A queer expression passed over his features, almost as if he'd eaten something awful. "No. Maybe not such a good idea. You could stay here. We have an extra room."

Amelia looked shocked. "With two single men? My maid isn't with me. I should have mentioned that. She came with me as far as New York, but she fell in love with one of the ship's crewman and asked if she could stay in New York. Of course, I said yes." Amelia, in the throes of adventure and love, had practically begged her maid to take a chance with the young sailor. It had been so romantic to watch the two of them fall in love. She'd been so happy, she wanted everyone to be in love as much as she was.

"You brought a maid with you?"

Amelia looked at him as if he were mad. Everyone knew a proper unmarried girl traveled with a maid— at the very least. It had been quite adventurous and quite improper of her to come all the way from New York on her own. "Of course, I did. How else was I to get dressed? As it is, I only have two gowns that don't require assistance to get in and out of. And they are sorely in need of replacement."

He grinned at her with the devil in his eyes. "I can help you now that you're here," he said.

Amelia laughed. "I'm sure you wish I'd let you. But no. Until we are married, it wouldn't be proper."

"As I recall, darlin', I almost had you undressed that once."

Amelia blushed, recalling that time during his visit to Meremont that she'd actually had the nerve to invite him into her room. She'd only done so when he'd promised not to touch her, a promise she knew—and was secretly glad—he'd been unable to keep. Just thinking about the things they'd done made her entire body flush. "Yes, it was quite improper," she said, but she was completely unable to retain her spinster demeanor for more than a second before laughter bubbled up again.

He pulled her against him so she was aware of his arousal, and he bent to kiss her. "I've missed you sorely," he said against her lips. With a groan, he deepened the kiss, and Amelia, sighing in relief and pleasure, felt herself falling into a pool of lust just as she had so many times before when Carson had stolen kisses.

They separated quickly when a door opened behind them.

"Carson, your brother says to get a room ready for the girl." Standing before her was an older woman with dark hair sprinkled with gray, and sharp brown eyes that at the moment seemed to be shooting daggers at Carson.

"Amelia, this here's Agatha. She's our house-keeper, and she helps Boone out in his office and the store sometimes. Agatha, this is Miss Wellesley."

"Lady Amelia, actually, though I suppose I shall have to get used to informalities. I am Carson's intended," Amelia said, slightly baffled by the famil-iarity between the two. No matter how much she adored her servants back home, none would have ever called her by her given name. It was almost un-thinkable.

Agatha's deeply wrinkled face split into a grin. "Ain't you fancy," she said, as if delighted by the dis-covery. "Your brother wanted to know if that is a good idea. I suppose the hotel won't do for *Lady* Amelia. Not with your . . ."

"Thanks, Aggie," Carson said, interrupting the older woman.

Amelia smiled, as it dawned on her that perhaps she could stretch propriety a bit since she was in the Wild West. If the Kitteridges had a housekeeper, she could certainly act as a chaperone. "This is perfect. Why didn't you tell me you had a house-keeper? Agatha will serve as a chaperone, won't you, Agatha?"

"Chaperone?" she asked haltingly, as if she'd never heard the word before.

"You shall make certain that Carson takes no more liberties with me," she said, giving Carson a stern look.

Agatha smiled. "I could do that," she said agree-ably, ignoring Carson's mock scowl, then looked in-stantly worried. "What about the night? I live down yonder with my husband." She worried her hands in a blue and red apron she wore over her faded yellow dress. "My Dulce, my daughter, will do. She's a widow and all she does is mope around the house doing nothing but complain that she has nothing to do."

"No," Carson said, and instantly, Agatha scowled.

"Why ever not?" Amelia asked. "I do need a maid. I didn't realize how much until I let mine go." She eyed Carson, who seemed adamantly opposed to the idea. "I suppose I'll have to stay in the hotel."

Carson and Agatha said "no" in unison.

"There is a *puta* there," the housekeeper said darkly, glaring again at Carson.

"What's a *puta*?" Amelia asked, and Carson nearly choked.

"It's Spanish for a lady who is, um, free with her favors," Carson said.

"Not free," Agatha said.

Amelia felt her cheeks turn red. "I understand, Agatha. Don't worry." She turned to Carson, who looked pained. "What is wrong with Dulce?"

"Nothing's wrong that a little hard work won't cure. And I'm thinkin' you'll be a fine influence on her. Dulce could use a bit of polishin' up," Agatha said, letting out a sound that was decidedly cackly.

"I never said there was something wrong with Dulce," Carson said in a placating tone. Then he spoke to Agatha in fluent Spanish, which Amelia found quite bothersome. However, it wasn't diffi-cult to tell that whatever it was he was saying, Agatha didn't much like. After a few minutes of rapid-fire Spanish, Agatha looked smug and Carson looked decidedly dejected.

"I'll go tell Dulce the good news," Agatha said happily.

"What was that all about?" Amelia asked when Agatha had gone. "I hope you know it is terribly rude to speak in a foreign language in front of someone who knows no Spanish. I didn't even know you could speak another language. You don't know French or German, do you? Italian? I'm fairly proficient at each, but not Spanish."

"I picked it up here and there. We had a bunch of those Spanish fellows in the Wild West show. Darn good cowboys. And Agatha's married to a Spaniard."

"What do you have against her daughter?"

"Do you know what Dulce means in Spanish?"

Amelia shook her head.

"It means 'sweet.' That girl is about as sweet as a lemon before it turns yellow."

Soon after Agatha disappeared into the house, Boone came out looking unhappy. "Why don't you go get Miss Wellesley's bags," he said to Carson, then turned to Amelia. "I hear your living arrangements have been resolved."

"At least until the wedding," Amelia said brightly.

Boone gave Carson a quick look, which Amelia saw but couldn't quite interpret. "Right. Let me show you to your room. It's not much, but it'll have to do given the alternatives."

Amelia began to follow Boone, then turned to Carson.

"Didn't you think about this at all when you sent for me?"

"I just figured it'd work itself out," he said, grinning.

For some reason that grin, that used to make her heart melt, was slightly grating. It was almost as if Carson thought he could grin everything away. If he murdered a man in cold blood, no doubt Carson would truly believe he could wink and smile at the jury and get off scot-free.

Boone led her into a cool hallway that seemed almost dark compared to the brightness outside. "The garden is lovely," Amelia said.

"It's a nice bit of color."

They passed a door with frosted glass and the word "Office" stenciled in black on it. In the corner, in much smaller letters, were the words: Boone Kitteridge, M.D.

Amelia stopped dead.

"Mr. Kitteridge."

"Yes, miss."

"What is this here?" she asked, pointing to the door.

"My office," he said, as if stating the obvious. Boone Kitteridge, unlike his brother, who could talk the paint off a wall, was a man of few words.

"Are you a medical doctor?"

He continued down the hallway. "I am."

Carson's lies about his older brother loomed even larger. He'd had her completely convinced that his brother was a simpleton who needed him. It was the reason, he'd repeated over and over, for his need to return home before they married. He could not wait, he'd said, because his brother needed him to help run their fictional ranch. His *dimwitted* brother.

"You went to university?" she asked.

"Tulane in New Orleans."

Amelia stalked after Boone, feeling her anger and bewilderment toward Carson grow. Had everything been a lie? She knew many of the stories he'd told had been embellishments, or even downright fabrications. It had been part of his charm. But to lie about the most basic things, like what his town looked like, that his brother was slow, that he owned a ranch. Those lies seemed so unnecessary, and somehow cruel.

The lies were piling up so high it was beginning to get difficult to wade through them all. He told her that he loved her, but did he? He told her that he'd sent for her, but had he?

With her throat closing up from unshed tears, she found herself in a sunny, whitewashed room with a simple but clean bed in one corner and a chest of drawers in another. It was far smaller and far simpler than the meanest servant's quarters back home in Meremont.

"The toilet's down the hall. Second door. It's the only one in Small Fork," he said, with a hint of pride.

When she didn't react, he said, "I suppose you're used to such things."

"What? Oh, the toilet," she said absently, staring at the lacy curtain that fluttered limply in the arched window, as if it were unused to catching a breeze. "Yes. We have several. I . . ."

"You all right, miss?" Boone asked, taking a step toward her.

"Thank you, Mr. Kitteridge, I'm perfectly well," she said, even though she felt completely horrid. "Or should I call you Doctor Kitteridge?"

"That's not necessary," he said, sounding almost

embarrassed by the title. "I'd just as soon you call me Boone."

Suddenly, Amelia felt light-headed, from the heat, the stress, the lack of food. "Boone," she said calmly. "I do believe I'm going to faint."

Boone immediately led her to the bed. She was deathly pale, her skin bathed with sweat.

"Agatha, I need a cool cloth," he shouted, grabbing one wrist and holding it to feel her rapid pulse. "Are you wearing a corset, Miss Wellesley?"

"Yes," she said.

"Well, I suggest you remove it. Or at least loosen it."

She looked up at him and he felt the blue of her eyes as an almost tangible blow. "But, Boone," she said, making the smallest attempt at a smile. "I hardly know you."

And then she fainted dead away.

Boone watched her eyes roll back into her head and caught her before she tumbled forward to the floor. He laid her back and immediately began undoing the tiny buttons that started at her throat and moved down to just below her waist. When Agatha entered the room with the cloth, he laid it on the girl's head and squeezed so that the cool water soaked into her hair.

"Agatha, could you please explain to me why women need to wear these things?" he asked as he began unlacing the offending garment.

"I don't. And Dulce wouldn't be caught dead in one."

Boone was quite aware that Dulce didn't wear a corset. In fact, nearly every man in Small Fork, with the exception of old Blind Pete, knew Dulce didn't wear much of anything to cover up her body.

Within moments of his beginning to unlace her corset, those blue eyes opened and gazed at him with a certain amount of pique.

"You fainted," Boone said. For some reason he found it necessary to explain why he was unlacing her. The girl made him extremely uncomfortable, and he had to fight to maintain his impassionate doctor's demeanor, though for the life of him he didn't know why it was such a struggle. Hell, of course he knew why. Lying before him in a state of half dress was perhaps the most beautiful bit of femininity he'd ever seen. And she was smiling at him.

"I fainted. And so you took advantage of that moment to undress me?"

Boone almost smiled. Almost. "The reason you fainted, I suspect, is a combination of the heat and this corset."

"I've been wearing corsets since I was sixteen years old and I've never fainted before. It is this heat. I daresay I've never felt anything like it in my life."

"Where is she *from?*" Agatha asked.

"I'm from Hollings, England. It's near the sea. The wonderfully cool, refreshing sea," she said darkly.

"Fancy talk," Agatha muttered, but with absolutely no malice. It was as if everything that came out of Miss Wellesley's mouth was a combination of amusing and amazing.

Amelia pushed Boone's hands away. "I'm quite fine now," she said, and sat up, only to instantly grab at her head, which no doubt felt as if it were about to fall off her slender shoulders.

Agatha disappeared and reappeared in less than

a minute with a glass of water in her hands. "Drink this. And when was the last time you ate? Honestly, Boone, a good breeze could blow this one over."

Boone watched as she reached for the glass with a shaking hand.

"I don't understand it. You're going to be thinking I'm some sort of pampered weakling. Honestly, I've never been fragile. My brother would joke how I should have been a boy because I like to climb trees."

It suddenly dawned on Boone just why a young girl would travel from England to Small Fork, Texas, in pursuit of his brother. He didn't know how he could have been so stupid. No woman in her right mind would leave her home to chase Carson, especially not a lady from England who obviously would have no trouble finding a husband. Unless, of course, she'd done something unforgivable. Unless, she was running away.

"Agatha, would you excuse us please?" Boone said, and watched as Agatha's eyes widened.

"You think?"

Boone shook his head to silence the woman. Clearly Agatha had come to the same conclusion as he, at about the same time.

Lady Amelia Hollings was obviously pregnant, and it was just as obvious, given that she hadn't seen Carson in seven months, that it wasn't his brother's child.

# Chapter 3

Amelia watched, looking slightly bemused as the older woman left the room.

"I'm dying," she said dramatically, making fun.

"You're pregnant."

Of all the reactions he'd thought she'd give him—guilt, shame, defiance—he had least expected her to begin laughing.

"I'm what?" she asked between perfectly unladylike guffaws.

"Is it possible?" he asked, for some reason praying it was not so.

"Are you telling me that the only reason for a woman to faint is because she is pregnant? What sort of doctor are you?" she said, giggling. "Unless my name is Mary and my husband is Joseph, I do believe I am not with child."

Boone felt his cheeks flush. "It seemed likely, given you came all the way from England chasing after my brother."

Now it was Amelia's turn to flush. "I was not 'chasing after' your brother. He is my fiancé and we planned for me to come to Texas. Next time you make such a prognosis, Doctor, perhaps you should get more information. That sort of erroneous diagnosis could ruin a girl. Even the hint of such a thing. But perhaps Texas is so far removed from polite society, you were unaware of that."

"It seems to me that if Carson had a fiancée, he might have mentioned it to me," Boone said, feeling his temper inexplicably rise. He rarely showed his anger and he disliked people intensely who did. Taking a calming breath, he stood.

"I did mention her," Carson said, smiling from the doorway.

Carson had mentioned many women he'd met in England, Boone knew. It was that he'd failed to mention he had a fiancée.

"Now what are you two fightin' about?" Carson asked. "You look like a couple of cats vyin' for the same mouse." Boone and Amelia both glared darkly at Carson.

"Your brother insulted me," Amelia said, lifting her chin. Carson gave Boone a sharp look, and Amelia hastened to add, "Well, not in a calculated way."

"She fainted, and I thought she might be pregnant," Boone admitted.

Carson's eyes widened, and he let out a whistle. "If there's one thing Amelia aims to protect, it's her virtue."

"As it should be," Amelia said.

"She *did* faint."

"It's hot here," she said. "Neither of you seem to notice. In fact, other than that mangy dog in front of your store, no one seems to notice."

"It's not hot," the men said in unison.

"And the dog's not mangy. He's just old," Boone said.

Amelia picked up the wet cloth and pressed it against her cheek. She looked like she was about to cry, and Boone wouldn't have blamed her if she did. He couldn't imagine traveling all that way, expecting a happy fiancé and a prosperous ranch, and finding his brother instead.

"You should lie here and rest," Boone said. "You're not used to the heat. It gets cool at night, don't worry."

"Cool?" Amelia asked, with rather a pathetic amount of hope.

"Temperatures can drop to the sixties."

"That sounds purely delightful," she said, looking at Carson with such love it made Boone want to leave the room.

He did, followed by Carson, and went down the hall to the store. He'd always planned to have Carson help out and eventually run the store, but his younger brother had never shown any interest in doing so. Some days Boone was so busy with his practice and running the emporium, it was near impossible. If it wasn't for Agatha, he wouldn't have been able to manage. When the ranches were getting ready to drive the cattle to Abilene, they went through Small Fork and both his mercantile and doctor's office were busy. But all the ranches had already begun their drives, leaving Small Fork sedate and quiet for a time.

When they reached the relative privacy of the store, Carson let out a foul curse. "What the hell am

I gonna do?" he said, looking to Boone for answers as he always had.

"The way I see it, you either marry her or you don't."

Carson gave him a dark look, but Boone had little patience for his brother's dilemma. It was just one in a long line of dilemmas Carson had gotten himself into, and this one, he decided, his little brother was just going to have to solve by himself.

"It's not my fault she came," Carson said, sounding like a spoiled six-year-old. "She came on her own. We agreed that I would send for her. I figured after a while, she'd meet someone else and move on. Hell, I know her brother didn't want her to come."

"The thing is, Carson," Boone said with forced patience, "the girl is here and it looks to me like she's still expecting to walk down the aisle with you. You've got to tell her the truth."

Carson shook himself as if Miss Wellesley was on his back, clinging, while muttering, "Damn, damn, damn," over and over. He stopped finally and looked at Boone with an almost tortured expression in his eyes. If Boone didn't know better, he'd say that Carson *was* actually tortured by the circumstances.

"She told me she loved me," he said, as if that were the worst possible thing to hear from a woman's lips. For Carson, it probably was.

"And how do you feel about her?"

"She makes me horny," he said hopefully.

Boone let out a low chuckle.

"Why in hell did she come?" Carson asked again,

as if this time he was hoping the answer would be different.

"You've got to deal with this," Boone said, a clear warning in his voice.

"Don't worry," he said. "I will."

When Amelia woke up, it was to a world gone soft and pinkish yellow. Her room glowed in the early evening light, and she smiled because she hadn't seen anything so pretty in a long time. Best of all, it was no longer hot, but pleasantly warm. She felt amazingly rested and content, considering how miserable she'd been just a few hours ago. Smiling, she stretched luxuriously.

"You're as pale as a fish belly."

Amelia let out a small screech to hear the strange female voice in her room.

"I'm Dulce Sullivan."

Amelia found a dark-haired, dark-eyed woman staring at her. Her skin was the color of tea with a bit of cream.

"I'm supposed to make sure the men don't get beneath all those skirts," she said, nodding to her dress, which had become a frothing mess in her sleep. Or perhaps in her faint.

"I'm pleased to make your acquaintance, Mrs. Sullivan. You may call Miss Wellesley."

Dulce stared for two beats, then burst out laughing. "My mother was right," she said.

"Right?"

"You are the strangest-talking woman I've ever heard in my entire life."

"Yes, well, strange is in the ears of the hearer,"

Amelia grumbled. That only made Dulce laugh even harder.

"I'm sorry, I'll get used to you eventually." The woman hardly looked sorry at all. She appeared rather pleased with herself. "For as long as you're here."

She said this last with forced emphasis, as if trying to tell Amelia something without saying it aloud. Dulce had a way of looking at her that made her distinctly self-conscious, with a hostile undertone, perhaps. "I plan to be here for the rest of my life," she said.

"That right? I just don't see it. Fainting types don't last long out here."

Amelia sat up and straightened her skirt and her spine. She supposed she did look like a "fainting" type. Everyone, even her brother, had underestimated how tough she was, and part of that was her appearance. She always had been pale, and having golden blond hair didn't help. She was petite and thin and sweet looking, which was why whenever she asserted herself, everyone appeared slightly shocked.

"Mrs. Sullivan. I have traveled across an ocean, then traveled by myself across this vast country. I would hardly say that is the action of a weak woman."

Dulce stared at her and Amelia thought she'd gotten through to her when the girl started laughing again. "Just can't take a word out of your mouth seriously. Just can't."

Amelia let out a sigh and stood, grateful that the room didn't spin around her. "If you are going to laugh each time I speak, Mrs. Sullivan, I'm afraid this arrangement will not be acceptable."

Now that shut the girl up. "First off, call me Dulce. What exactly am I supposed to do? My mother said you just needed a female about to keep the men away."

"Not men, man. Carson is my fiancé and there are times when, well, he doesn't act the proper gentleman." Amelia could feel her cheeks flush and was so mortified, she failed to see Dulce's dark look. "But that is not the only reason you are here. I also need a maid."

"A maid? My mother does maid stuff."

"No, a personal maid. You will do my hair, help me change. Take care of my clothing. Make certain it is fresh and the wrinkles removed." Amelia shrugged. "I've been making do, but most of my gowns are simply impossible to put on by myself, never mind my good corset, which laces in the back."

Dulce shook her head, her eyes incredulous. "You want me to dress you?"

"Well, yes. To assist me," she said, feeling somehow ridiculous for wanting such a basic thing. "Look at this dress," she said, opening her trunk and taking it out. It was a lovely gown, made for her London Season by one of the best dressmakers in town. She held up the deep blue silk gown, and turned it round to show Dulce the intricate back held together by tiny buttons. "I could never get this on or off without assistance."

"We don't have fancy dances around here where you could even wear such a thing," Dulce said, eyeing the gown as if it were made of rat fur instead of the finest washed silk. Amelia could already see that Dulce didn't put much thought into her own wardrobe. She wore a loose blousy top and a plain brown skirt, but she looked hardly ordinary. There was something wild about Dulce, some underlying smoldering heat that was difficult to pinpoint. She had the look of what her brother would have called a "tart."

"Oh," Amelia said, looking down at the gown, which was one of her favorites. "Practically the only dress I have that doesn't button in the back, besides the few I've been wearing, is my riding habit."

"You have a special dress for riding a horse?"

Amelia dug through her things to find her favorite article of clothing, her dark green wool riding habit. She loved its smart looking jacket, with its wide shawl collar and sleeves that puffed near the shoulder and narrowed on her wrist. She wore the cutest little top hat with it and felt so jaunty and unconventional, and she'd pictured herself many times riding beside Carson in his fancy cowboy gear.

"Of course. Isn't it lovely?" she asked, holding it up for the skeptical Dulce to see. "I'm not very good at riding, but I've been practicing so that I might be able to keep up with Mr. Kitteridge."

"Waste of cloth if you ask me."

"I didn't," Amelia said, with a flash of anger showing in her eyes. "If you could hang up all my dresses and take care of my things, that would be lovely." She was done trying to make polite conversation with this difficult woman.

"What are *you* going to be doing?" Dulce asked, completely taking Amelia aback. Clearly this girl had never before been hired as a servant—and

Amelia had never before been confronted with such hostility from an employee.

"I'm going to be doing whatever I please," she said, and had the satisfaction of seeing Dulce frown fiercely. Amelia was normally an exceedingly polite young woman, but she'd had quite enough of Dulce's criticism and hostility.

She walked from the room, trying to look like a queen, but the anger flushing her cheeks ruined the effect entirely, she realized. She didn't know why the girl rubbed her the wrong way, but she did. Perhaps she should try to be more patient with her—and act slightly less rigid. It was clear that the behavior of servants was not the same here in this land.

As she walked down the hall, she realized she was still wearing the same dress she'd had on all day. It was a wrinkled mess, with a fringe of dust along the edge of the skirt. Amelia frowned, knowing she couldn't return to her room now and ask Dulce to help her dress for dinner.

The apartment part of the building was simply a long hallway that stretched back toward the courtyard from the mercantile. On either side of the hall was a series of doors that led no doubt to other bedrooms. When she found herself at the back entry to the store without having encountered another soul or even another room, Amelia stopped, turned, and looked back, thinking she'd somehow missed something. There was nothing to do but begin opening doors and pray she did not walk into someone's bedroom.

When she opened the first door nearest the garden, she smiled. It was the kitchen and it was completely empty. Her stomach rumbled as she looked around for someone preparing food. But no, she was completely alone.

Amelia had not grown up in a wealthy home, but she'd always had a few servants running about: a maid, a cook, and a housekeeper. Her family had been poor compared to the way her friends had lived because her father had been a second son. Her brother had inherited the earldom only after their childless uncle had died.

Still, Amelia was not used to fending for herself. Stealing pastries from Cook's tray was her only experience foraging for food. She stepped into the room and began looking into cupboards.

"You won't find anything," Dulce said cheerfully from the door. "At least nothing fancy."

"Do you know what time they dine?" Amelia asked, ignoring the way the other girl was attempting, rather poorly, not to smile.

"I have no idea when they *dine*," she said, putting stress on the last word as if she somehow found it offensive. "But I do know if they did, they would have done it already. It's nearly eight o'clock."

Amelia stared at the empty kitchen with a certain amount of dismay. Eight o'clock was when she usually dined at home, and often later if they were eating out at another estate.

"Where is everyone? Where are Carson and Boone?"

Dulce shrugged. "I'm going to bed. You're all unpacked. And if you hear screaming, don't worry, it's just Boone."

She said the words with a certain amount of glee, as if she were trying to frighten Amelia. Still, Amelia couldn't resist asking, "Why would he scream?"

"The devil visits him at night," Dulce said, a wicked gleam in her eye. Then she shrugged, as if knowing she wasn't frightening her listener. "He has nightmares. Wakes Carson up near every night when he's here."

"I'm certain I won't be disturbed. Good night." Amelia didn't think it was possible that the girl had managed to hang and fold everything neatly, but she didn't say anything. Suddenly, Amelia felt a fierce longing for home, for the polished marble floors, the thick velvet drapes, the smell of flowers blooming madly outside her window. She missed the bustle and politeness of efficient servants, her brother's friendly banter, the laughter and general noise of her little cousins.

Amelia had spent much of her childhood utterly alone. Her older sister had died when she was eight, her parents when she was twelve. Her brother, Edward, had gone into the military because there was no other way to respectably make a living. Of course, their uncle, the earl, had been kept oblivious to any of their financial worries, her brother's pride knowing no limits.

But Amelia hadn't minded being part of the poor gentry. They'd had enough income from their rather sad estate to support a small staff and the upkeep of their home. She'd never felt poor or deprived. But, Lord, she had felt lonely. Her brother came home when he could, but his visits seemed few and far between. She grew up in a household of elderly servants who hadn't a clue how to make a young girl happy.

When her brother inherited not only the earldom but also his stepaunt's six children, Amelia

had been ecstatic. Finally, she had a family, someone to talk to. She wished more times than she
could remember that everything could stay the
same, that she would remain a young girl surrounded by children and an adoring stepaunt.
She'd never been happier in her life—until she'd
met Carson.

It had been perfect. Her brother was getting married, her stepaunt and her cousins were moving
into their own lovely little estate, and she was going
to Texas to start her own life, her own family. Because more than anything in the world, Amelia
didn't want to be left alone, an afterthought, the
extra wheel that really didn't belong.

She swallowed down the burning in her throat,
squeezing her fists in disgust that she had allowed
herself to fall into self-pity. It was just . . .

Nothing was the way it was supposed to be.

Taking a bracing breath, Amelia began opening
cupboards, finding dishes and pots and pans but
nothing edible. Finally, she found the pantry and
stood staring rather forlornly at three eggs, a sack
of flour, a sack of cornmeal, a few cans of corn,
canned peaches, and what appeared to be pears.
Amelia poked her finger at some sort of salted
meat, and frowned. Nothing looked even remotely
palatable, except perhaps the eggs. The icebox was
empty, and Amelia suspected it hadn't held ice in
quite a while, for the drip tray was dry as a bone.
Surely even a place as remote as Small Fork had ice
shipped in regularly.

"I'm afraid you won't find much to eat."

Amelia turned to find Boone standing at
the entrance to the kitchen. His hair was wet and

slicked back but already starting to curl, and his cheeks were ruddy as if he'd been buffeted by a strong wind. The Kitteridge men were ungodly handsome, but unlike Carson, Boone seemed to be completely unaware of God's gifts.

"Are you feeling better?" he asked, giving her an intense, sweeping look that was slightly unsettling. She was suddenly acutely aware that her hair was down, her dress a wrinkled mess, and her feet shoeless. The tile had felt so blessedly cool, she hadn't wanted to put on her shoes.

"Much better. But I am hungry. Starving, actually." She gave him an embarrassed smile. "I really don't know how to cook anything." She glanced doubtfully at the stove, an ancient thing that looked like it had been in use for one hundred years. The only thing she knew for certain was that she needed to put wood in it to start a fire.

"I thought Carson was . . ." He stopped and looked down at the floor, almost as if he were angry. "I guess Carson didn't want to wake you. He and I usually eat at the hotel nights I don't cook. Agatha leaves at four to help her own family."

"You don't know where Carson is?"

"No, miss. But I'll tell you what. I'll run over to the hotel and get you something and bring it on back here. This time of night there aren't too many ladies hanging around the saloon, so it's best you wait here."

Amelia had the terrible feeling that Boone was covering up for Carson, that her fiancé had forgotten her. Or worse, was avoiding her. "I'll just go out to the garden, then."

"Okay, but watch out for rattlers. They don't usually come out this time of night, but it was warm today."

"Rattlers?"

"Snakes."

The only snake Amelia had ever seen was a harmless infant grass snake, and she'd thought it rather charming. "Oh, I'm not afraid of snakes unless they bite."

"This one bites and can kill you if it gets you good."

Amelia smiled politely. "I'll just wait here, then, shall I?"

Boone nodded then headed for the door, but before he left, he poked his head back into the room. "They come indoors, too."

Amelia looked up, surprised, then narrowed her eyes. He was teasing her. At least she thought he was, because he certainly wasn't smiling. "You are joking," she said with false bravado.

"Probably." And then he was gone.


Boone stepped out of his home and stopped dead. He could see a man with a long blond ponytail leaning against the saloon's wall, his arms around a woman, obviously kissing her. He didn't know his blood could boil any hotter, but there it was, boiling madly, his temper rising so fast he shook with it.

Boone spun around to make certain his brother's fiancée hadn't followed him out, then strode across the dusty street, all the while telling himself to calm down. It was fierce, this temper, and one he frankly feared. Ask any man or woman in Small Fork, and they'd tell you Boone Kitteridge didn't have an angry bone in his body. He never raised his voice, never mind his fist.

But they didn't know what was happening beneath the surface, how close that surging heat was to exploding, how many times he'd thought about knocking the lights out of someone. Boone, himself, didn't know how he tamped it down, but he did. He didn't want to be like his father; he didn't ever want to lose control and hurt someone. Even if they deserved it.

And right about now, his brother definitely deserved it.

"Evenin', Geraldine."

The woman pulled slowly away from his brother's kiss and gave Boone a drowsy smile. "Well, hey there, Boone."

Then Boone turned to Carson, his gray eyes shooting bullets, though his little brother was completely unaware of it. "You think this is a good idea, with your fiancée right across the street?"

"She's not really my fiancée," he said, smiling down at the woman still in his arms. Carson was drunk, as usual. The two of them swayed together, clearly having shared a bit too much whiskey.

"She damn well is your fiancée, and you better get your ass over there. She's hungry and it's clear to me, if not to you, that she's feeling a bit lost about now. She doesn't even know how to start a fire in a stove. She's hungry and I was heading over here to get her something to eat. Maybe you ought to bring it to her instead."

Carson looked ill at the thought, and Geraldine tightened her hold on him.

"He ain't goin' anywhere, are you, love?" Geraldine asked, then planted a sloppy kiss on his mouth. Before Boone's disgusted gaze, the two deepened their kiss and he could feel the anger coming back in force. He could feel his hand clench, and took a deep breath to stop the force of his rage.

"You beat all, you know that, Carson?"

Carson tore his mouth away from the whore and looked at his brother, really looked at him, his eyes filled with fear and self-loathing that was almost tangible. "I know, Boone. Could you just handle her this one night?"

"He can't handle any woman, you know that," Geraldine said, giggling drunkenly, and Boone felt a surprising rush of humiliation.

Carson pushed her rather ungently out of his arms. "You go back in, Gerri. I'll be there in a minute." Then he slapped her on the derriere to temper his words, causing the woman to giggle again as she walked unsteadily down the boardwalk toward the saloon entrance. He pulled off his hat and scratched his head before turning back to Boone. "I'll take care of things in the morning."

"What are you going to tell her?"

"I don't know," he said, slapping the dirty Stetson back on and grinning. "I'll figure it out tonight."

Boone let Carson go, then ordered up some food for Amelia—a thick beef stew, which was the only bit of food the kitchen had left at this late hour. When he returned to the house, Amelia was sitting at the kitchen table in the dark. Only her dim outline was visible in the day's dying light, wisps of her blond hair seeming to softly glow, making her ethereal. Having someone like her in his home did not seem real. She looked like a little girl waiting for her supper, and his anger toward his brother grew.

"I didn't know where the matches were and by the time I realized I should light a lamp, it was too dark to look for them," she said softly, with apology in her voice.

Without a word, Boone reached for the matches by the stove, then lit a small lamp on the kitchen table. "We have gas lighting at home," Amelia said, staring at the lamp, her blue eyes impossibly vivid in her pale face. "And my brother was talking about getting electrification. Can you imagine?"

"I think it'll be a while before we get electricity out here," Boone said, sitting down at the table across from her. Compared to her soft lilt, his voice sounded harsh, the way blaring trumpets sound after a flute solo. "You'd better eat before it gets cold."

Amelia looked down at the stew and smiled. It looked wonderfully normal. Taking a spoon she dug in, and closed her eyes at the wonderful flavors that flooded her mouth. "It's good," she said, smiling. "I don't know if it's the best stew I've ever had, or if I've never been so completely starving before." She expected Boone to smile, but he just stared at her as if she were a foreign creature sitting at his table.

It was hard to believe he was Carson's brother. They seemed so opposite. Carson was full of charm and smiles, Boone so serious. She was quite certain she hadn't seen a smile from him since her arrival. Still, she had to admit he had a quiet appeal. If she wasn't in love with Carson, she would probably better appreciate Boone's dark beauty. His hair was the color of rich chocolate and cut rather short, unlike Carson with his wild mane of blond waves. Boone's eyes were deep gray and fringed with long, dark lashes, while Carson's were blue with reddish gold lashes. And Carson had that wonderfully rich mustache, while Boone was clean-shaven.

Amelia knew Boone was the older brother, but he looked ten years younger than Carson. Yes, it was hard to believe her untamed, strong cowboy was brother to this neat and solemn man sitting across from her.

"Did you see Carson?" she asked before taking another mouthful. It really was the most wonderful stew.

Boone looked down at his steepled hands as if he'd suddenly become aware he'd been staring. "No."

"I'll have to tell him he's been exceedingly impolite disappearing like this," she said lightly. "I feel rather abandoned." Amelia looked up and found Boone staring at her again. It was quite disconcerting, actually.

"Do I have something on my face?"

Boone looked slightly startled. "No."

"Then why are you staring at me like that?"

Boone opened his mouth as if to deny he'd been staring, but shut it and let out a short, impatient breath. "I just can't figure out what you're doing here."

Amelia decided to ignore that rude comment. "I'm eating," Amelia said, being purposefully difficult.

"I mean," Boone said with forced calm, "what in God's name made you think it would be a good idea to marry my brother?"

Amelia hardly thought Boone was being very brotherly at the moment. "Your brother is charming and handsome and intelligent. Qualities that were apparently given out sparingly in the Kitteridge family." She lifted her chin smugly. "And he loves me."

Boone had been looking at her with an expression one could only describe as complete bafflement, but at the last, he lowered his gaze. "That's just plain stupid," he said finally and without a bit of meanness. It was as if he were calmly informing her that she was of deficient intelligence, a gentle diagnosis from a caring doctor.

"I beg your pardon?"

"I don't mean to sound harsh, but you came halfway across the world for my brother. I just don't think a woman of high intelligence would do such a thing."

Amelia felt as if he'd just slapped her—that's how stunned she was by his cavalier words. What hurt the most was that she knew, deep down inside, coming to Texas was probably the most foolish, ill-conceived, impulsive act anyone of her acquaintance had ever done. By far. But she wasn't going to let the man sitting across from her know that. She was about to set him straight when she burst into completely unexpected tears.

"You're right," she said, feeling the strain of the last weeks hit her like a tidal wave. He pressed a handkerchief into her hand and said nothing as she cried copious tears. "It's clear that Carson wasn't expecting me. I know that. I'm *not* stupid. Nor blind. And it's just as clear he wishes I hadn't come. He was so different back in England. Like a different man altogether. When he looked at me then, it was like I was the most important thing in the world to him. I don't understand it. I don't think . . ." She let out another sob. "I don't think he . . . he . . . loves me at all."

"I wouldn't say that," Boone said. And Amelia looked up at him with ridiculous hope in her eyes. "He's a man who likes his freedom. I think he likes you too much, and it scares him a little."

"Then why did he ask me to marry him? Why did he formally ask my brother for my hand? It was in the *Times*," she said, as if that would prove to the world that Carson did, indeed, love her. Oh, how she wished Carson was here reassuring her, instead of this cold man in front of her.

As Amelia watched, Boone's cheeks turned ruddy and he looked down at his hands again.

"Was it for the money?" she asked, slightly horrified by that thought. But the man across from her just gave her a confused look. "If not the money, then what? He begged me to . . ." She stopped. Carson hadn't begged her to marry him, he'd begged her to make love to him. All those nights he'd kissed her and touched her and she'd push him away when he went too far, telling him over and over she would not do *that* until she wore his ring. She'd very nearly succumbed more than once, because, Lord, he could be so very persuasive with those hands and that mouth.

Amelia slumped back in her chair and stared at Boone until she saw the truth in his face. "For *that*?"

"I couldn't say."

"But surely you suspect?"

Boone shook his head once, almost as if avoiding a blow. "I don't know what goes on in that boy's head. I never have. I think you need to have a serious talk with him. Tomorrow."

Amelia nodded and moved a piece of carrot around the bowl with her spoon, just to give herself something to do other than cry. "Why would he do that? It can't be true. You don't know what you're talking about," Amelia said, her anger starting to grow. "What man would get formally engaged just for the pleasure of making love to a woman?"

Boone gave her a strangely intense look, as if he could see right through her. "A man would," he said softly.

Amelia shook her head. "No. It wasn't like that. And when I see Carson, he'll tell me. I'm tired and weepy and for some reason you're being cruel to someone you don't know. I don't even think you know your brother, either. I know him," she said, holding her hands against her heart as fresh tears fell.

"You're probably right," he said without meeting her angry gaze.

"I know I am." And at that moment Amelia was completely sure of herself; all the doubts she had about Carson swept away. Carson had been happy to see her, had held her and made her feel loved. No man could touch her and kiss her the way he had unless he loved her. Yes, he should be here with her now instead of his rude brother, but he was probably doing something important, something for her, no doubt. Carson was the most considerate, kind, exciting man she had ever met, and his brother was simply being contrary. And if Carson lied about certain things, it was understandable. He loved her so much, he wanted her to love him back, and probably lied about the big ranch because he knew her brother would never have agreed to their marriage otherwise.

Amelia gave an inner grimace at that thought. Edward would be livid to know his little sister had traveled all this way only to be put in the tiny back room of a shop. She prayed her brother never found out that Carson had lied so outrageously. It had been difficult enough to get Edward to agree to allow her to marry a commoner, never mind a man who didn't appear to have a pence to his name.

Her brother had just married an American girl, so he'd been more lenient with her than he might have been otherwise. Edward was many things, but he certainly wasn't a hypocrite. She'd loved him for that, for his willingness to let her follow her heart, even though it meant following it all the way to Texas. She just prayed her brother never found out that the letter she'd claimed had been from Carson sending for her had been nothing but a blank piece of paper.

"You know how to work the pump?" Boone asked, breaking into her thoughts.

"The pump?"

Boone motioned to a water pump on the large kitchen sink. "Yes, of course," Amelia said. She didn't point out that they'd had hot and cold running water from faucets in her home, and that the only pump she'd ever used had been in their gardens.

When she didn't immediately move, Boone nodded toward her bowl. "I've got to return that tonight or George will have a fit."

"Oh," she said, staring down at the bowl. "You want me to clean it."

"If you could."

"Oh." Amelia would never admit that she had never washed a dish in her life. She went to the sink and rinsed the bowl, wiping it clean with a cloth that hung from a hook above the sink. She began to giggle and turned to Boone, who stared at her as if she'd gone mad.

"That was the first time I've ever cleaned a bowl," she said. "And I do believe I've done an outstanding job of it." She held up the clean bowl for his inspection.

Boone just shook his head. "Lady, you are in a world of trouble." He took the bowl and left the kitchen, leaving Amelia behind, giggling and thinking she had, indeed, gone quite mad.

With a full stomach, Amelia made her way down the darkened hallway to her room. Back home, she'd probably just be getting ready to go out for the evening, or snuggled by a fire reading a book. But she was dreadfully tired, and since there was no one to talk to and no fire to snuggle by, she lay down gratefully on her bed, thinking about the next day and Carson. Things would seem better in the morning. Everything would work out just fine, she knew it would. Carson would hold her, tell her not to worry, and they'd talk about the wedding and the family they'd have together. She fell asleep with a smile on her lips, picturing herself standing before a tiny rose-covered cottage with Carson by her side.

Amelia was in the middle of a wonderful dream. She was at a ball back home dancing to her favorite waltz, with Carson looking down at her the way he used to. He was beautiful, his bright blue eyes sparkling, his hair long and wavy and glossy, his beard trimmed and dashing. Every eye was on them, every woman in the ballroom gazing at them with a combination of envy and appreciation. He wore all white, his silver buttons glinting in the gaslight, his arms strong as he swirled her around the ballroom.

But for some reason, he was starting to shake her shoulder as they danced, and she scowled at him.

"Stop that," she muttered.

"But darlin', you have to wake up."

Amelia opened her eyes and saw Carson, not the hero of her dreams but the unkempt, wild-looking man she'd been with that afternoon, and she tamped down her disappointment. Carson drew her into his arms and she was enveloped in an almost nauseating smell of smoke, cheap perfume, and liquor.

"Is something wrong, Carson?"

He pushed her back, his large hands on her shoulders, and for some reason he seemed like a complete stranger, not her beloved, not the man who used to pull her into the alcoves of her home and kiss her until her knees were weak.

"I have to go. I didn't want to leave without saying good-bye."

A waft of boozy breath enveloped her.

"You're drunk."

"Not drunk enough," he said, and even in the moonlight she could see the flash of his brilliant smile. At least that hadn't changed.

"I don't understand. I just got here. Where are you going?"

"Why do you have to do that?" he said, sounding almost angry. "Why do you have to look so pretty? Why do you have to be so goddamn *nice?*"

"I'm sorry."

He let out a curse. "Don't you realize how rotten I am yet?"

She shook her head. "I don't know, Carson. All I know is who you were in England. And you were wonderful there."

"I was a complete jackass. Hell, Amelia, you're making this so hard. You're making me not want to leave."

The truth was finally dawning on her, and she felt her insides clench sickeningly. "You're not coming back?"

"I . . ."

"Oh, God, I'm such an idiot," she said, horrified by the truth that had been there all along, if she'd only been wise enough to listen to the reasonable part of her brain, rather than her heart.

"I'm comin' back, darlin'. Don't cry. Please. I'm comin' back."

Hope surged, but immediately left her when she saw the look on his face. He was lying, just as he had lied so many times before. But this time he didn't even bother to try to hide it. Amelia may have been naïve, may have even believed that Carson loved her, but she was not a complete fool.

"Don't lie to me," she said. "Please, Carson. If you don't mean to come back, don't lie."

"I don't know what I'm going to do," he said, sounding tired. Then he flashed her a grin that tore at her already beaten heart. "I might just stay. You never know."

But the next morning, Carson was gone.

# Chapter 4

"Hey, your highness, looks like your prince has flown the coop," Dulce said, nudging Amelia on the shoulder.

It took a few seconds to clear the fog from her brain, for she'd been deeply asleep and having a wonderful dream in which she'd been home at Meremont playing tag with her cousins on their beautiful green lawn. They'd all been barefoot, and the grass had felt so cool and soft between her toes.

"Go away," she muttered, trying in vain to go back to that happy dream.

"Didn't you hear me? Carson's gone. Packed up and left."

Amelia opened her eyes to see Dulce smiling down at her. "Guess you ain't getting married after all."

Finally, what Dulce was saying got through the fog. "Carson's gone?" Of course he was.

"Well, his duffel's gone, his horse is gone, and he grabbed all the food he could carry. Plus he took all the money out of the till. Boone's crazy mad." This all seemed to delight Dulce, who appeared to be on the verge of outright laughter.

Amelia threw off the covers. "My blue day dress, if you please."

Dulce rolled her eyes and sauntered over to the wardrobe where Amelia's gowns had been crammed in haphazardly. "This one?" she asked, pulling out a ball gown.

Amelia quickly searched and pulled out her dress, one of her favorite day dresses made of light blue wool. It had the most lovely sleeves that puffed out beautifully at her upper arms but hugged her forearms from her elbow to wrist. The light wool was intricately embroidered with flowers that were just slightly darker than the full skirt. It was a beautiful dress, one she'd pictured wearing with Carson strolling down the main street of Small Fork. She tossed the dress on her bed. "Where are my unmentionables?"

Dulce nodded toward a chest of drawers. "Top drawer."

Within minutes, Amelia was pulling on the dress, and waiting with what she thought was incredible patience for Dulce to button her up. It seemed as if the woman had never buttoned a button before, so slow was she proceeding. When she was finished, Amelia said, "Where is Dr. Kitteridge?"

"Who?"

She gave the obstinate woman a tight smile. "Boone."

Dulce smiled, and Amelia knew her suspicions were correct; the woman was delighting in antagonizing her.

"Can't say."

But when Amelia's eyes welled with tears, the woman's face softened almost imperceptibly. "Probably out front in the store."

"Thank you." Amelia dashed away the tears and hurried toward the store, praying Dulce was lying about Carson disappearing. It couldn't be true. Couldn't. He'd formally proposed. He'd asked her brother's permission. *Please, please be here. Let this all be a bad dream. Please.*

But the minute she walked through the shop's back door and Boone looked up to see her, she knew. "He's gone," she said, her voice dead.

Boone gave her a long stare, then simply nodded.

Amelia slumped against the wall, and Boone took a step toward her as if fearing she was going to faint. She held up a hand to stop him. "I'm fine," she lied. She closed her eyes, not wanting to see the pity in his face. She didn't even feel surprised, really. It was more a sense of the inevitable, as if she'd known all along that her dreams would never come true.

How many times had she done this to herself, created a fantasy life that could never match reality? She'd spent her childhood, alone in a dreary manor, dreaming of a family that, one by one, had died and left her. Why, after a lifetime of failed dreams, should she start believing they'd come true now?

Finally, she said, her eyes still closed, "Did he leave a note?"

"Not that I saw."

"Then how do you know he's gone? He could be just . . ." She tried to think of a scenario that would justify a man not being around for his fiancée who'd just traveled halfway across the world to see him, and could not. "I can't believe it." But she could. She did.

Amelia pushed herself away from the wall and walked to the counter, where Boone stood looking at her like she was some abandoned orphan, which was exactly what she was. She hugged her arms around herself, feeling completely lost and more frightened than she'd been in a long time. Not since she'd awoken from being so very sick, only to find that her mother and father were both dead, had she felt this completely bereft. "Did he really take your money?"

"He sure did."

"I'm so sorry. None of this would have happened if I hadn't . . ." She stopped because her throat closed up and she didn't want to cry in front of this man again. She'd already done that once, which was unforgivable and completely ill-mannered. Instead, she forced a smile. "I'll go home, then. It will be as if I was never here. I'll just pack my things and be gone as soon as the train comes by. When is it next due?"

"Two days."

She'd had no idea the train didn't come by daily. The thought of staying in his place for even that long was almost beyond bearing. She wished she could blink her eyes and be home at Meremont with her brother, and everything could go back the way it had been before she'd turned into such a foolish, ridiculous child. "Can you put up with me for two days, or would you like me to go to the hotel?" she asked pleasantly, ignoring the fact that her voice was shaking, that her entire body was shaking.

"You can stay here," Boone said, almost angrily. Amelia was perceptive enough to know he was angry with his brother and not her.

"Well, then. It was a lovely visit and I'll try to keep out of your way for the next two days."

The two were distracted when the bell above the shop's door jingled loudly and a woman came in. It was difficult not to stare at her, and Amelia used all her proper upbringing not to. The woman darted in, as if she were being chased. She wore a large, floppy straw hat and had a colorful bandana over most of her face. What Amelia could see of it was pockmarked and scarred, and it was clear that something, not disease, had marred her terribly. She looked at Boone to gauge his reaction, and was completely stunned. He was smiling.

And God, he was beautiful when he smiled.

"Julia. Good morning."

The woman mumbled a greeting, her head down as if she realized they were not alone.

"Julia, this is Lady Amelia, all the way from England," Boone said, sounding strange. He was looking at Amelia, silently telling her to be kind. How annoying.

Amelia gave him a look, then held out her hand. "Pleased to meet you, Miss Julia. I met Dr. Kitteridge's brother, Carson, in England when he was with the Wild West show, and as I was in the area, I thought I'd give him a visit."

The woman shook her hand and Amelia was struck by how beautiful it was, strong and sure and gentle.

"Do you live here in town?"

The woman darted a look at Boone, and a silent message was passed between them before she nodded. Then she handed over a list of items she needed, which Boone carefully catalogued in a ledger.

"Miss Wellesley, would you mind handing me one of those sacks of salt there behind you?"

"Not at all," Amelia said, glad to be given something to do. The two of them went about filling the order, and Amelia was highly amused when Boone followed behind her, straightening out jars and bottles that she'd knocked askew.

Just for fun, she moved a jar of peaches the tiniest bit, then laughed aloud when Boone put it back.

"I hardly see how that makes a difference," she said.

"I like things the way I like them."

To her surprise, Julia waggled a finger at her and Amelia laughed again. "I'm sorely tempted to rearrange the entire store."

"Not if you value your pretty behind," Boone said darkly.

Julia giggled and Amelia was delighted, because it was so unlike Boone to say such a thing—at least she thought it was. It was the first time Boone had even remotely seemed like Carson.

Once the woman's order was filled, Boone added up the items in his ledger and efficiently packed them all in an old potato sack.

"Miss Wellesley, I wonder if you could watch the store for a moment." Without waiting for an answer, Boone held out his hand for Julia to precede him to the back of the store, and presumably to his office.

"No, actually, I'm quite busy," Amelia said to the empty room, then resigned herself to standing behind the counter and praying no one entered because she still felt as if she might burst into tears at any moment. She gazed down at the ledger, smiling because it reminded her of Edward, who spent so many hours perusing similar ledgers. Except this one was distinctly different. It was simply a list of charges that went on for pages and pages. Charges that never appeared to be paid. She flipped through and found other similar accountings, but those had columns indicating the balances had been paid.

Boone had apparently been giving this woman free food and sundries for years, each date carefully filled in, each item marked, but none ever paid for. She shook her head, wondering why he'd be so meticulous in writing down all the groceries, when he must know she would never pay for them.

Unless he was simply being exceedingly kind by not only giving her the items, but also saving her pride, assuming that some day, she'd pay for them.

"You're to put on that salve daily, Julia. I mean it," he was saying as the two entered the store again. Amelia quickly closed the book, feeling slightly guilty that she'd been so nosy.

Julia said, "Yes, sir," and then she saluted. As she walked to the counter, she let her finger trail along the curve of a pretty little vase, then gathered up her order.

"Thank you," she said.

"It was a pleasure meeting you," Amelia said. "I

am leaving on the next train, but I hope to see you before I go."

The woman stared at her, and for the first time Amelia saw that she'd once been quite pretty. Her face had a lovely structure and the one eye that she could see was the most striking shade of green. Then she turned and left without saying another word.

When she was gone, Amelia turned to Boone. "What happened to her?"

"Her husband didn't care for the way she made cornbread," he said briskly.

"Cornbread?"

He stared at the door where Julia had just departed. "He was a drunk and shot her in the face because she burned the bottom of the cornbread."

"My God."

"And now people treat her like *she's* the animal," he said softly, but with an anger that fairly seethed around him.

"What happened to her husband?"

"I guess he thought he'd live a lot longer if he wasn't around these parts," Boone said.

Amelia hugged her arms around herself again, this time her own troubles momentarily forgotten. Boone had more than hinted he would have killed the man had he stuck around, and she found herself glad of it.

"Was she lovely?"

"She was."

Just then Agatha burst into the store from the back room. "Sorry I'm late. Goddamn no-good husband can't do nothin' for himself. Lazy bastard. I'm surprised I don't have to wipe his . . ." She stopped dead when she saw Amelia. "Oh. Miss Wellesley," she said, suddenly sounding sweet. "I didn't see you there. How are you this morning?"

Amelia hid a smile. "Very well, thank you. Dulce has been a wonderful help to me."

Her eyebrows lifted. "Really?"

She heard something behind her that might have been Boone's attempt at a laugh. It sounded more like a man choking.

"Unfortunately, I'm going to be leaving Small Fork shortly, so I won't need her services as long as I thought. I do apologize." Amelia was amazed that she could sound so normal when her heart had just been broken and her throat burned from unshed tears.

It took the sharp Agatha perhaps two seconds before she realized what Amelia was truly saying. "That no good . . . Carson skipped town, didn't he?" she asked, her hands fisted and planted firmly on her hips. Amelia was warmed by her show of female loyalty.

"I'm afraid he did," Amelia said, trying not to let her voice crack, for her emotions were still near the surface, despite her valiant effort to maintain her dignity. But Agatha was much too perceptive.

"Oh, my poor dearie," she said, then walked over to Amelia and pulled her head rather forcefully down onto her large bosom for some motherly comfort. "I can't say I'm surprised. It's not the first time he's done something like that. He's broken more women's hearts in these parts than I can count, including my poor Dulce before she married Mr. Sullivan."

Amelia pulled back, stunned.

"Oh, yes, Carson was my baby's first love. Head over heels she was. He's got a way about him. That Kitteridge charm can make smart women do stupid things." She turned to Boone. "Not you, Boone."

"The charm somehow bypassed me," he said sardonically.

"Carson got it in spades, poor Dulce. All he wanted . . . Well, let's just say he wanted something he shouldn't have had."

Boone stepped in, taking Amelia's arm and leading her toward the back entrance. "Thank you, Agatha. If you could watch the store for a few minutes."

Just as they were walking through the door, the bell rang, marking the entrance of another customer, which Agatha met with a frown. Clearly, she was not done espousing the dubious charms of the Kitteridge men.

Boone immediately led Amelia to his office, where she could find some privacy and no doubt cry her eyes out. Not that he was going to stick around to watch the waterworks, but he felt he ought to do something.

Last night as she sat across from him looking so pathetically sad, he'd been sorely tempted to hold and comfort her. But as he'd never done such a thing before, he was unsure how to do it, and just as uncertain whether or not she'd welcome a stranger's embrace. And the thought did occur to him that he might have enjoyed it a bit too much for such a gesture to be considered altruistic. She was still his brother's fiancée after all.

He didn't know how his brother could walk away

from her. Boone might not have known many women in his life, but he'd seen his fair share, and he could honestly say he'd never beheld a girl quite as lovely as Amelia. Even with her nose red from her efforts not to cry, she was the prettiest thing he'd ever laid eyes on.

Clearly, though, she wasn't the brightest candle in the window, not if she fell for Carson's load of malarkey. He couldn't truly blame her. His little brother had a gift, though Boone was damned if he could understand it. Carson was hardly clean, he had hair past his shoulders and a ridiculous mustache, and yet women turned their heads and blushed when he walked into a room.

He led Amelia to the small waiting room and sat her down. "You may begin crying as soon as I leave," he said matter-of-factly.

She looked at him as if he were mad. "I'm not going to cry."

"You sure looked like you were going to back in the store," he pointed out.

"That may very well be, but I certainly have no intention of crying now. I'm going to pack my bags, see to my funds, and . . . and . . . wait. But I'm not going to cry."

As Boone watched, her eyes filled with tears and he felt about as helpless as a kitten facing a mountain lion. "I've got to get back to the store," he said, handing her his last clean handkerchief.

She simply nodded and pushed the cloth against her already red nose. How she could make crying look lovely he didn't know, but the urge to draw her into his arms was nearly overwhelming. The strange thing was, he'd seen women suffering far more than Amelia, and the urge to comfort them had never hit him before. He'd always maintained a professional attitude. But this woman needed only to shed a couple of foolish tears for his recalcitrant brother, and he wanted nothing but to heave her against him and draw out all her pain. Of course, he never would.

Instead, he patted her on the shoulder, the same way he patted his dog's head, stopping cold when she reached out and clutched his hand, pressing it against her shoulder in an almost desperate gesture. He could feel her body shuddering as she tried to control herself, and he let her hold his hand as he stood there, awkwardly wishing he had the courage to hold her.

She let go abruptly, as if sensing his discomfort, and turned away slightly, her back bending as if she were trying to hold herself together.

"I have to get back to the store," he repeated stupidly. And then he walked out of his office, his face set so that no one, not even Agatha, who knew him so well, would recognize the murderous rage he now felt for his brother. If Carson were to stick his smiling face within punching distance, he'd knock his head off.

"She all right? It took my Dulce quite a while to get over that heartbreak," Agatha said. "And they never got close to talking about marriage." She tsked and shook her head. "Can't understand why that fool girl would travel all the way from England."

"Apparently, they were actually engaged. Carson even asked her brother's permission, and the announcement appeared in the newspapers there."

As he said the words, he realized he likely had been unfair to the girl. Carson had proposed, had asked her brother for permission. What girl wouldn't have thought they were going to get married after all that? It just made what his brother had done even worse. "He spun tales so rich this time that I think he half-believed them himself."

When Carson had returned from England, it had been as if he were returning a hero. Always self-assured, Carson had been brimming with confidence after his days as the star of the Real Wild West Show. He'd had tales of balls and ladies, and being welcomed into some of the most exclusive men's clubs in London. He'd had flyers and posters featuring him in all his glory, wearing a ridiculous white costume. And for the first time in his life, he'd had a bit of money.

But all that was gone now. The money, the bravado, leaving behind a man who was slowly realizing he could no longer pretend his life was better than it was.

Agatha snorted. "If he asked her to marry him, then he should have done the right thing and married the poor thing."

"She's better off with a broken heart than married to my brother," Boone said with painful honesty. Carson might not have been as mean as his father, but they were too much alike in other ways. And Lord knew his father had been just about the worst husband a woman could find. But he'd been damned charming on those rare occasions when he wasn't roaring drunk.

"She's leaving on Friday's train?"

"I don't think that's soon enough for her."

"No doubt she's feeling a bit foolish as well as brokenhearted, poor thing. Can you imagine traveling halfway across the world for someone?"

"I can't imagine crossing the street," Boone said, making a rare joke.

Agatha laughed. "Someday you will. Mark my words. Though probably not in these parts. Other than my Dulce, there aren't many respectable women." She eyed him carefully. "What about that Stella?"

"Stella?" he asked. "She's fifteen."

"She's eighteen. About the same age as that girl back there," she said, jerking her head in the general direction of his office.

"Eighteen? Stella looks twelve."

Agatha smiled. "When was the last time you saw her?"

"Probably when she was twelve."

"You'd better believe Stella Henderson don't look twelve anymore." Agatha got a speculative look on her wrinkled face.

"I'm sure Stella has her sights held a bit higher than me, Agatha. Or her parents do."

Agatha sniffed. "You're right. You could do far better than to end up with in-laws like the Hendersons."

"I think I can do far better staying a bachelor," Boone said truthfully. He didn't want a wife and kids and all that worry. He liked his life the way it was, taking care of the store and the few patients that came his way. The last thing on his mind was getting married.

\* \* \*

Amelia stared at her trunk as if staring at it would change the fact that her emergency money, the money she needed to return home, was not there. No one knew about the secret compartment except her. And her maid.

She let out a groan and buried her head in her shaking hands as she kneeled by the empty trunk. It all made sense now, her maid's tears, those strange looks she kept giving her new love, the way she'd practically run off the ship and disappeared into the crowded New York City wharf. At the time, Amelia had been so happy for her maid, she'd simply assumed the girl wanted to hurry up and get married. If she wasn't the most gullible woman, she didn't know who was. She wondered if anyone she knew was what they seemed. Her maid, and now Carson, had betrayed her in ways that just a few weeks ago she could never have imagined.

"He ain't worth your tears," Dulce said, standing at the entrance to her room, looking on with pure disgust at her display of despair.

Too overcome by the desperation of her predicament, Amelia could only shake her head. She couldn't leave. She was stuck here in this hellish place. Stuck until her brother sent money—her brother who was on his honeymoon somewhere in Europe. She didn't even know where to reach him. Lord only knew how long it would take for him to get the funds. She knew no one in this country, not a soul.

"Oh, God," she moaned.

"Should I get Boone?" Dulce asked, sounding bored.

Amelia could only nod and let out another

groan. She heard him come into her room and tried to get control of herself.

"Dulce said you wanted to see me," he said so gently Amelia nearly launched herself into his arms in gratitude. But Boone had a way about him that told her he would not welcome her with open arms. At that moment she just needed someone, anyone, to hold her and tell her everything was going to be all right—even though she knew in her heart that nothing ever would.

"M-my m-money," she managed to get out. "It's gone."

"What money?"

"The money I was going to use to go home with. It's gone. And now I'm stuck here, in this godforsaken place," she wailed.

"Slow down," Boone said, helping her to stand. "What money? Where was it?"

"It was in my trunk in a secret compartment. No one knew where it was except me and my maid," she said bitterly. "She must have taken it. I can't believe it. She was my friend. And now I'm stuck here *forever.*"

She could tell Boone thought her histrionics were slightly amusing, for he looked as if he were fighting a smile. This dour man whom she'd only seen smile once, was now fighting a smile when faced with her abject misery. The cad.

"How much was it?"

"Five hundred pounds sterling."

Boone let out a slow whistle. That was more than two thousand American dollars.

"It was my brother's wedding gift," she muttered. "It was a bit of a nest egg, to help us out. Just in case."

The full extent of all she had lost was starting to hit her. She was reeling from it. How dare her maid steal from her? And how dare Carson lie and lie and then disappear as if she'd meant nothing more to him than a flirtation? He'd said he loved her. He'd asked her brother for her hand. She felt her fist clench, and she glared up at Boone as if he were to blame for all her troubles.

"Where is he?" she demanded.

"Who?"

"That dastardly fiend you call your brother. Where it he? I know you know."

Boone looked momentarily confused. "He didn't steal your money. He may be low, but he's not *that* low."

"I know he didn't steal my money, he stole yours. But I want to know where he is so I can . . . I can . . ."

"You can what?"

"I don't know," she said, growing frustrated. "I want to hurt him. I want to scream at him. I want him to know what he's done to me. How dare he run away like a frightened rabbit. Where is he? Where is he? Where is he?" she shouted over and over, then took her fists and aimed them toward his chest. He gripped her wrists in an iron grasp before she could make contact, immediately stopping her tirade.

"Don't. Hit. Me." He said the words succinctly, low and harsh.

Amelia was breathing hard and staring at his large hands gripping her slim wrists. "I wasn't trying to hurt you," she said, and he immediately dropped her hands and stepped away. She gazed up at him, her anger quickly replaced by confusion.

"I just want you to tell me where he is." She looked up at him but he wouldn't meet her gaze, and it was only then that she realized how very angry he was, how tense was his body, how he held his arms rigid by his sides. "I'm sorry. You are not to blame. You do not deserve my anger. Unless you know where he is. Then I must warn you I might very well get angry with you." She watched carefully as he visibly relaxed, as a sheepish look replaced his anger.

He shook his head. "I don't know where my brother is. And if I did, I'd drag him back here and tie him up while I fetched the preacher."

"I wouldn't marry him now if he were the last man on earth," Amelia said, crossing her arms.

He let out a grunt as if he didn't believe her.

"You don't think I mean it?" she demanded.

"I think my brother could come back this minute, hat in hand, beg your forgiveness, and that would be that."

Amelia's nostrils flared. "You don't know me well enough to predict my actions."

"I know you came here all the way from England to marry a man who forgot you existed the minute he stepped on American soil."

Amelia could not believe how insufferable this man was. He might look like an angel with his curling brown hair and freshly shaved face, but he surely was the most disagreeable man she'd ever met. "There is no need to be cruel," she said, hoping to make him feel a bit of shame for causing her to feel even more foolish.

Boone shrugged. "Just stating the facts as I see them."

"You are the rudest, most despicable man I have

ever had the misfortune of meeting. It is eminently clear to me that you have never had the occasion to move in polite society. Obviously you have no idea how to comport yourself with a lady." My, it felt good to give this man a thorough tongue-lashing.

He clenched his jaw and for a moment Amelia thought she'd made him angry. A closer look, though, showed that he was really trying to stop laughing. Those cold slate eyes were twinkling. Twinkling! And that really incensed her.

"You, sir, are a misogynist."

"I like women just fine," he said, letting out a low chuckle. "That is, women who use their brains and not . . . other parts."

Amelia gasped and turned beet red. "How dare you!"

Boone looked momentarily confused, and then it was his turn to blush. "Oh, Lord, I meant your heart. Women who think with their hearts instead of their brains are doomed to heartbreak. And my brother has a way of making seemingly intelligent women do the dumbest things." Boone had been trying to soothe her ire, but apparently this was one woman who could not be soothed with calm reason.

"Do you not think for a moment that I don't know just how stupid I was to travel here? Do you think I need it pointed out on an hourly basis? Perhaps you should borrow some of your brother's charm because you, sir, certainly need a large dose of it. I'd rather be charmed to death than bored to death." Amelia smiled smugly, obviously proud that she'd come up with a suitable insult for him. But if she thought to hurt him, she was going to be sorely disappointed. He threw back his head and laughed.

"Bored to death," he repeated, as if she'd made the funniest of jokes. "You are something else, Miss Amelia. I haven't had this much fun in years."

"So happy to have been of help," she grumbled.

He gave her a lopsided smile, because he knew full well how horrid he'd been. "I'll keep my ears open for news about Carson. If he's nearby, I'll go get him, and then the two of you can sort out what you're going to do."

"Is murder an option?" she asked darkly.

"Unfortunately, no," he replied goodnaturedly. "I'd give you a loan but my charming brother ran away with nearly everything I had. And that wasn't much. I could probably get you as far as St. Louis."

"Where's that?" Amelia asked, hopefully.

"About nine hundred miles west of New York City."

"Oh." It seemed as if, right before his eyes, some of her bravado left her, for she sat down on the bed as if she could no longer bear the weight of all that had happened to her.

Boone wished he could help her, he really did. Because the last thing he needed around him was a woman like Amelia, a spoiled rich thing who probably hadn't suffered a day in her life. No one with hands that soft and skin that pale had ever worked for anything.

Other than Agatha, who was about as tough a woman as he'd ever met, his experience with women was limited to his practice. He'd never had a sweetheart, never lain between a woman's legs, never kissed a girl on her lips. With that thought, his eyes drifted to her soft, well-formed lips and he felt a flood of lust so strong he turned away abruptly. He'd gone twenty-eight years without a woman and had thought, perhaps, he'd go another twenty-eight years. The one time he'd tried, with the whore Geraldine, he'd been so nervous, his body had failed him miserably. She'd laughed, not in a cruel way, but because she thought it was cute that a twenty-year-old was shaking like a leaf, staring at his uncooperative male part in horror. She'd told him he could try again another day, but the thought of lying between her legs where dozens of other men had been, including his own sixteen-year-old brother, made him slightly nauseous. And that made him think there was something wrong with him, for wouldn't a man, a real man, want to bed a woman, any woman?

And here he was, eight years later, lusting after another of his brother's conquests.

"Boone?"

He let out a sigh and turned back to her, trying to resist drowning in those eyes of hers. Truly, he had never seen anything quite so pretty as those eyes, even red-rimmed and slightly swollen from her tears. She'd only been in his house one day and already he was feeling himself drawn to her, like a helpless animal pulled down by quicksand. Now she was going to be stuck here for weeks. If he had the money to give her, he would have gladly done so. But with most of the people in this little town far poorer than he, he accepted barters rather than cash most of the time. "Everything will work out," he said, and was surprised when she smiled at him.

"No, it won't. But thank you for saying that. Is there a telegraph office in town?"

Boone shook his head. "The closest one's in Abilene."

The poor girl looked like she couldn't take one more bit of bad news. "Where is that?"

"About three hours east of here on the T&P," Boone said. "That's if the train's in the mood to go fast."

"That's not so bad," she said, but he could tell she was slightly dismayed that it was so far. "Is it cooler there?"

Boone chuckled. "Not that you'd notice. Maybe you should start wearing your summer frocks."

Amelia looked down at the pretty blue dress she was wearing. "This is a summer dress," she said.

To Boone, it looked mighty uncomfortable, with a lacy collar that covered her neck completely and sleeves that ballooned out on her upper arms, but fit tightly down to the delicate bones at her wrist. It seemed silly and completely impractical.

"Perhaps you are right. This was made for English summers, not summers spent in tropical heat. In Hollings in the summer, even in July and August, the temperature rarely gets past eighty degrees. And when it does, it feels as if it's sweltering."

"It hasn't gotten hot since you've been here," Boone said, just to see what she'd do. Someone watching might have thought that Boone Kitteridge was flirting, but since he'd never flirted with a girl in his life, Boone would have denied such a ludicrous notion.

"I pray you are joking," she said darkly. "If I'm to be here for weeks, I should have some dresses made from a lighter material. Perhaps muslin. That's what all the women in India wear, I've heard."

"I've got some material in the back of the store. Most women 'round here go to Fort Worth if they want something fancier."

Suddenly, Amelia felt overwhelmed. Just talking about dresses was too much. And, she realized, this tiny town no doubt did not have a seamstress, and she would be expected to make the bloody thing herself. How she hated Small Fork. And herself. And her bloody, bloody foolish heart. "I wish I could blink my eyes and be home. I wish I could go back in time and give myself a good lecture on all the reasons I should not come here."

"Sometimes the best thing to do is look forward, not back."

Amelia shook her head. "But I don't like what's ahead. I don't want to go there." She pressed her fingers against her mouth, as if she could stop the rampaging thoughts in her head. What she really wanted was her silly dreams to come true. Why couldn't they, just once? Why couldn't she have her happy ending? Amelia knew she was not a sensible girl, just as she knew her silly daydreams were never going to come true. So she took a deep breath and searched for that sensible girl she knew was some-where inside her. That girl knew reality, knew her mother and father and sister were dead, knew she was never going to be a family with them again, knew she was never, ever going to live on a ranch with Carson and raise their children together. She knew all this. She did. But it was so, so wonderful sometimes to just pretend that none of the bad things that had happened to her over the years were real.

Amelia gave herself a bit of a shake, then took a deep breath. "I shall cross that bridge when I come to it," she announced stalwartly. "There is nothing to do about what I've already done. You are right. I can only move forward and forget all this ever happened." She clenched her fists to give herself the resolve to listen to those words of wisdom. "When are you leaving for Abilene?" she asked.

"When am *I* leaving for Abilene?"

"Surely you didn't think I would travel there myself," Amelia said, completely dumbfounded by his reaction.

"You came here by yourself," he pointed out with infuriating logic.

Amelia could feel her eyes start to burn with tears. God help her but she'd never been this weepy in her entire life, and she refused to give in to it.

"Hell, if you're going to start that crying again, I'll go."

Amelia lifted her chin. "I was not going to start crying and I would never use tears to manipulate a man," she said with a certain amount of guilt. She was fairly sure she might have used tears more than once in her life to get her way with her brother. But she was not doing that now. She despised these particular tears.

Boone narrowed his eyes at her. "I may be just a country doctor, but those sure look like tears to me," he said.

Amelia smiled, unable to keep her ire up. "Perhaps a smidgeon of a tear. But I am not crying. And

I would very much appreciate it if you could go to Abilene for me."

Boone grunted what Amelia thought was consent. "I have some business there anyway," he said.

Just then a small furry animal seemed to appear out of nowhere, and jumped on Amelia's lap. She let out a screech before realizing it was just a little black-and-white cat. "Oh, what a pretty kitty," she said, then let out a small cry when she saw it was missing one eye. "Poor thing."

"That's Blink," Boone said.

Amelia laughed. "What a positively terrible name for such a pretty girl." The cat was kneading her lap rather painfully at the moment, but Amelia didn't care.

"Boy."

"Even so. Poor thing."

"You probably won't like what I named my dog, then."

"The old dog out front?"

"Three Legs."

Amelia's mouth gaped open, but she let out a laugh. "I didn't notice that particular affliction."

"That's because most of the time he's too lazy to get up. But he gets around just fine if he puts his mind to it."

Amelia smiled as something immense dawned on her. "You save things," she said, as if making a great discovery.

"I am a doctor," he stated.

"No. That's not what I mean. I mean, you can't help yourself. Julia, the cat, the dog. Me. You, Dr. Kitteridge, as disagreeable as you are, are rather nice."

"I never said I wasn't."

"But you've been acting absolutely horrid to me this entire time, and you're not horrid at all, are you?"

"I can be if you want."

Amelia gave him a look of pure exasperation. "You never had any intention of making me go to Abilene by myself, did you? Be honest."

"Probably not," he said, as if admitting a great flaw.

Amelia felt a great sense of relief for some strange reason. A bit of the tension that had made the base of her head ache for days was slightly relieved. She put the cat aside, stood, and gave his cheek a quick kiss.

"Thank you," she said, then turned back to the cat, not noticing that Boone's entire body turned rigid, his face to stone, as if she'd struck him, not kissed him.

Boone mumbled something and left the room before he made a complete idiot of himself. It had been the most innocent of all kisses, but seeing that it was his first, it pierced his heart in such an unexpected way, it nearly drove him to his knees.

# Chapter 5

Boone had learned at an early age that something was inherently wrong with him.

He was four years old when his mother died giving birth to the blond-haired, blue-eyed angel that turned out to be Carson. His little brother was the spitting image of his father, and as soon as he could, John Kitteridge would carry his little son about proudly, showing off Carson while Boone walked behind.

Boone couldn't remember his father grieving for his dead wife, so Boone did that for him. Boone's only real memory of his mother was simply a feeling that he missed her desperately. He couldn't remember her face, her smell, the color of her hair. He couldn't remember, no matter how hard he tried, whether she'd tucked him into bed or given him a good-night kiss. He only knew that as a little boy, his life changed the instant his mother died and his brother was born.

It didn't matter, even all these years later, how many times he told himself that his father had been a cruel drunk. The seeds of doubt planted by John Kitteridge lived still. Because his childhood had been long years of living in hell, of desperately protecting his little brother, of beatings that left him bloody and words that left him raw.

He knew everyone felt sorry for him. But because there was something missing in him, no one did a thing. Carson was so loving, so handsome, so full of little-boy mischievousness, how could it be that the father was only good to one child? It must be that Boone deserved it. He must be doing something to get that whupping. You'd think the kid would learn.

The thing was, it didn't matter what Boone did—he still got blamed and beaten. He wasn't sure if he was the dumbest kid or the bravest, but he even took the blame when Carson did something. As if his father would ever lay a hand on his little brother. When Carson got older, he reveled in his father's attention and joined in on the belittling, sneering when his father sneered, laughing when his father did. But Boone knew, even then, that it wasn't his little brother's fault. How many times did he lie in bed and wonder what was wrong with him, that his father hated him so.

Boone's life changed when he was ten years old, the day Roy Johnson, the original owner of Small Fork's only mercantile, gave him a job. Even then Boone suspected the man felt sorry for him, but he didn't care. He had a job and money to buy food for Carson when his father spent it all on booze. Roy, a gruff man whose own wife had died years before, gave Boone the only kindness he'd ever had.

Boone worked at the store every day but Sunday and, more often than not, showed up at the store Monday morning with new bruises that Roy would examine and scowl at.

One day, after a particularly bad beating, Boone didn't go to the store. His face was swollen and one eye was open just a slit, and he couldn't bear the thought of Roy looking at him and feeling sorry for him. He hid in their shack-of-a-house, trying to quietly clean up the mess his father had made. His father was snoring off a drunk in another room and if you woke him up, it was purely the scariest thing on earth. But if he woke up to this mess, it would be worse. So Boone tiptoed about, picking up the pieces of crockery and dried-up food scattered about their tiny front room, praying his father wouldn't wake up.

The snoring stopped and Boone froze, his hand clutching the skin of a baked potato. He began to shake fiercely, his eyes pinned on the bedroom door, his ears straining to hear whether his father was getting up. When he heard the telltale creak of the bed and his father's groan, he nearly peed his pants. He couldn't get hit again. His face still hurt so much. He couldn't take it, not one more time. He just couldn't.

That's when Roy knocked on the door, and Boone nearly jumped a foot off the floor.

"Boone, you in there?"

Boone went to the door, torn between letting Roy in to see him, and keeping him out for fear his father would do something horrible to Roy. He opened the door a crack.

"I'm not feeling too good today, Mr. Johnson," he'd said.

Roy pushed open the door and Boone would never forget the expression on his face when he took a look at him. He seemed torn between murderous rage and terrible grief. "Let me in, Boone. This has got to stop."

Panic such as Boone had never known flooded him. "I'm okay, Mr. Johnson. I'll just finish cleaning up here and be right . . ."

"What the hell are you doing here, Johnson?" his father boomed from his bedroom door.

Boone would never forget what happened next. Roy gently took Boone's arm and pulled him back so that he was behind his boss. Protected. "Boone, you go on down to the store now. I'll be right there. Go on, now." And Boone ran as fast as he could to the store, and waited, shaking like a leaf, more frightened than he'd ever been in his life. He just knew it would be his father walking through that door to bring him home. He just knew it.

But it was Roy, looking grim, with not a scratch on him except for his knuckles.

"You're living with me now, Boone."

"I can't," he'd said, even as hope surged through his veins.

"You sure can. Your father agreed." He smiled then, a strange smile that Boone didn't really understand until later, when everyone was talking about how mild-mannered Roy Johnson beat the living hell out of John Kitteridge.

"I can't leave Carson."

Roy hunkered down and placed two gentle hands on Boone's skinny little shoulders. Boone still remembered thinking that it was the closest thing to an embrace he'd ever felt. "I'll tell you what. If Carson shows up with bruises just once, he can live here, too."

"But Carson can't take care of himself. I do it," Boone said, tears streaming down his battered face.

"I don't think your daddy will let me take Carson," Roy had said sadly. And Boone knew then, without one doubt, that his father didn't love him and probably never had.

Boone lived with Roy until he went off to college and medical school. For a time, Carson became a stranger and Boone couldn't help wondering what his father had told him about what had happened. But when their father died, Carson was back, needing him. As always. By then, Boone was a grown man in college. Boone traveled home from Louisiana every chance he got, and when Roy died three years ago, he left everything to Boone.

All those memories came surging back, just because a sweet-looking woman had kissed his cheek.

Two days later, Amelia was standing behind the counter at the Kitteridge Mercantile, neatly cataloguing purchases and waiting on the curious customers who came in a constant stream. It seemed as if nearly every resident of Small Fork strolled into the little store with some excuse or another to see just what an English lady looked and sounded like.

Amelia was used to small towns, for Hollings was the quintessential small English village, a place where everyone knew every else's business, and so she took their curiosity in stride. In fact, she was surprised it had taken the townsfolk so long to try to get a glimpse of her.

Boone had shown her how to mark sales in his ledger, for he didn't have a cash register in the store. Apparently, she was to earn her keep until her brother's money arrived. It was the least she could do for the man who was taking what would be a four-day trip just to send a telegraph for her. Because the train only ran twice a week, Boone would be stuck in Abilene until Tuesday, and someone had to help out Agatha at the store.

"Mama said you was a princess," a dusty little boy said. It seemed as if everyone in town was covered with a fine layer of dust, but perhaps it was just Amelia's imagination.

"I'm not a princess," she replied, probably sounding very much like a princess to the little boy. "I'm a lady. Lady Amelia Wellesley of Hollings, England."

"My *mama's* a lady," the boy said, full of skepticism.

Amelia smiled. "In my case, it's just a silly fancy title. You may call me Miss Amelia if you'd like."

The boy grinned and Amelia grinned back. He was the only child she'd seen since arriving in Small Fork, and seeing him made her miss her little cousins fiercely. They'd been such a rowdy bunch, and Amelia had to admit she missed the chaos and noise of the four boisterous children who still lived at home.

The boy handed over a penny and Amelia filled a little bag with lemon drops, and stuck a piece of licorice in for good measure. "Thanks, Miss Amelia," he said, as if she'd handed him a shiny new toy.

Perhaps she'd given him too much. She had no idea what a penny's worth of candy was in the states.

"Mama, she gave me a free piece of licorice," the boy said. His mother, who was cradling a baby in her arms, smiled shyly at Amelia.

"Hello, I'm Amelia Wellesley."

"Paula Brentwood. I didn't really say you were a princess. I said you looked like one."

"Thank you." Amelia smiled, but she felt rather self-conscious about her fancy dresses. She'd left behind all her plain day dresses, the ones she wore when she planned to walk to the beach or play with the children outdoors. She'd only brought her finest dresses, thinking she wanted to look beautiful for Carson. It was one more thing to feel humiliated about.

No one had mentioned Carson, or whether or not she was staying. For the most part, they came into the store, made a small purchase, then walked out, saying nothing more than hello. One thing she did notice was that either the men of Small Fork were the ones who did all the shopping, or there was a dearth of women. So far, she'd only met four, including Julia.

"Are you here long?" Paula asked, and it seemed that all the remaining customers stopped what they were doing and leaned her way to hear her answer.

"Perhaps a few weeks," she said vaguely, for she truly did not know how long it would take her brother to receive the telegram, and then send the money. The telegram might not reach her brother for weeks. "Then I'll be going home to England." Having heard that bit of gossip, everyone in the store moved on, leaving the two women alone.

"Oh," Paula said, sounding disappointed. "I was hoping for another woman around here."

"I'm sorry. I'll be going home soon. Though it's quite lovely here."

Paula, who wore a rather smart looking shirtwaist and skirt, looked at her as if she were daft. "I'm from Fort Worth," she said, as if that explained everything. Actually, it did. Fort Worth was a grand metropolis compared to Small Fork. "My husband's the banker here. And it's a fine town, really. But . . ."

"A bit lonely."

Paula nodded, any shyness long gone. Her son, who had grown bored with the women's conversation, had wandered off outside to pet Three Legs. "My parents and brothers and sisters are all in Fort Worth. We had electricity, a telephone, central plumbing, and all manner of things I used to take for granted. Why, it's as if I've gone back in time."

Amelia giggled. "I do feel the same way. I would love a long, hot bath."

"Oh, yes," Paula said, closing her eyes as if to picture such luxury. "Jason, that's my husband, promises we won't be staying forever. We've only been here six months. But what if we do stay forever? There's no school, and not enough children to start one. And no church!"

"I suppose you'll make the best of it," Amelia said doubtfully.

Paula looked as if she was going to say something, but changed her mind. "Well, I'm certain I'll see you again before you leave. Perhaps you can visit some time. We're the house next to the bank."

"That sounds lovely," Amelia said. No doubt Paula was brimming with curiosity about Carson, but Amelia was not going to enlighten her or anyone else in Small Fork. It was far too humiliating. Let them think what they wanted. In a few weeks she'd be gone and forgotten, a small oddity that made life exciting for a few days.

Amelia knew only one thing: once she got back to England, she was never leaving again. She could close her eyes and picture herself walking along the shore, a brisk wind from the Irish Sea buffeting her face. One day, she'd meet an appropriate man at a ball or dinner, and she'd marry and have lovely English babies with rosy cheeks. She'd look back on her trip to America as an adventure, a slight detour away from what her life should have been.

Thank God, she'd be on her way home soon. It simply could not happen soon enough.

*Somewhere in the Atlantic*

Maggie Wellesley, the new Countess of Hollings, looked over at her husband and frowned. Poor Edward was putting himself through hell, blaming himself for allowing his little sister to go chasing after that ridiculous Carson Kitteridge.

To be truthful, they had done their best to dissuade Amelia from her attraction to the American cowboy, but their efforts had been fruitless. Amelia had been *in love,* and nothing short of tying her up would have stopped her from chasing after her beloved. They'd both agreed that the best course of action was to let the infatuation take its natural course. They'd thought that meant Amelia would come to her senses and realize just how foolish it would be to marry a man she hardly knew. And they'd counted on Carson Kitteridge disappearing forever and never sending for Amelia.

On that count, they'd been correct. For Kitteridge, that scoundrel, hadn't sent for Amelia at all. And the poor girl, completely in the throes of her first love, had fabricated a letter from Carson. It nearly broke Maggie's heart to think how desperate Amelia must have been to pretend Carson had sent for her. Edward had used a word other than "desperate" to describe his little sister.

He was livid. And worried. And guilt-ridden.

When they'd realized what Amelia had done, Edward had immediately sent a telegram to Carson, but they'd never gotten an answer and had no way of knowing whether the telegram had ever reached him. The silence had only fueled Edward's feeling of utter desperation and helplessness.

"I'm all she has," he said, staring out to sea. "If something happens to her, it will be my fault. What if Small Fork doesn't even exist? What if she goes to Texas looking for a fictitious place? Anything could happen to her."

"She has Anne," Maggie said, even though at this point the fact that Amelia's maid was with her brought neither of them much comfort. At the time, it seemed perfectly safe to send off Amelia with her much older personal maid. Anne was in her early thirties, a sensible woman who seemed more like a companion than a maid to Amelia. They never would have allowed her to go if it hadn't been for Anne's calming presence.

"If it wasn't for that, I would go completely mad with worry," Edward said. "Why won't the women in my life simply stay at home sewing, or some such thing?"

"Why not simply tie us up and not allow us out at all?"

"Grand idea," he said, not seeming to detect Maggie's obvious sarcasm.

"All this worry could be for nothing. What if she finds him? What if he does love her and they are already married?" Maggie placed her hand on his, which clutched the railing in a death grip, no doubt meant to be in lieu of choking Carson Kitteridge.

"Then there is nothing for us to do but wish them well. But do you really think that is what has happened?"

Maggie pressed her lips together. "No. I don't. I think, if Small Fork does exist and Carson actually lives there, he's no doubt thinking of ways to send her back home."

"The hell he will," Edward said.

"You're not thinking of forcing him to marry her?"

"He proposed to her. He asked my permission. If he doesn't, she'll be completely ruined. Can you imagine what she could face if she returned to England after this? All hope of any kind of good marriage is gone."

"Times have changed," Maggie said. "This isn't the 1850s, after all."

"Rules for the aristocracy have not loosened to the point that a girl can go running after a fiancé in another country and think she can come home to resume her life unscathed. She told everyone she knew what she was doing. Everyone. She must have written a dozen letters before she left, gushing about her new life in Texas and urging everyone to visit her when she was settled. Good God, what a mess."

Maggie laughed. "For all we know, they could be a happily married couple by now, living in complete bliss. Like us."

"Yes," Edward said rather grumpily.

"That wasn't very convincing."

His face softened as he turned to look at his new wife. "I'm sorry. My life is bliss. Or would be if not for this mess." He kissed her softly on her lips. "What would I do without you?"

"You'd be a miserable old wretch," Maggie said sternly. "There's no sense worrying about a dozen different scenarios when we don't know what has happened. We'll find Amelia. I know we will."

"I wish I could be as certain as you are."

"I wish so, too," Maggie said, smiling up at her handsome husband. The wind had turned his cheeks ruddy, making him look younger than his twenty-seven years. "We'll be in Texas within three weeks."

"Three weeks," Edward said, as if it were a lifetime. "She damn well better be happy, or else Mr. Kitteridge is going to have a lot of explaining to do."

"She will be," Maggie said, even though she didn't believe a word of it. Carson Kitteridge was one of the most charming men she'd ever met. He could make old ladies blush and young women become fools over him. She only wished he could make Amelia happy.

# Chapter 6

At the end of the first day working in the store, Amelia was thoroughly exhausted. Her face actually hurt from smiling so much at these strangers who came to gawk at her.

"I'm heading home," Agatha called, wiping her hands on her apron. "There's some cold ham and such in the kitchen if you get hungry." Agatha looked like she was about to say something, but clearly didn't want to. Amelia was so tired, she was tempted to let the older women go home without another word.

"I know it's none of my business," Agatha started.

"I'm certain it is not," Amelia said, smiling.

"Don't you sass me," the older woman said in mock anger. "Just because you're all fancy doesn't mean you can't learn a thing or two from an old lady."

"You're hardly old."

"There you go, sassing me."

"Please go on," Amelia said, slightly exasperated.

"I know your heart's broken, but I also know that

someday you'll realize you're better off without a man like Carson in your life."

"I think I already realize it."

Agatha nodded, as if she'd managed to solve all the world's problems with a single sentence. "You're all right, then?"

"Yes. Thank you." Agatha began to leave, and suddenly Amelia didn't want to be alone. Dulce had determined that with Boone and Carson both gone, she had no need to be there, which was actually a relief to Amelia. She was unused to such hostility directed at her; it simply was completely foreign to her to have someone so obviously dislike her.

"I do have one question."

"Oh?"

"It seems so unlikely to me that Carson and Boone are brothers. They seem completely different from one another."

Agatha chuckled. "About as different as two brothers can be."

"How is that possible?"

"We weren't in these parts when they were boys, but I do know they were raised by different folks, at least part of the time. That could explain a lot."

"You seem doubtful that it does," Amelia said, slightly amused by the woman's mysterious tone.

"Sometimes people just come out bad."

Amelia stiffened. "Carson is hardly bad."

"Now, how'd you know I was talking about Carson?" she asked, cackling theatrically like an old witch. "Oh, goodness." She apparently found herself quite amusing. "Boone's just dependable and Carson, he's his daddy's boy through and through."

"What was their father like?"

"He could surely put on the charm, but he was a mean drunk. Meanest I've ever seen. Mean to everyone but Carson."

"Boone?"

"Like I said, Boone didn't live with his father. I don't know the particulars of it, but there's surely a reason for that."

Amelia bade her good night, and found herself quite alone in the store. It was closing time, so she lowered the shade and locked the door, looking about the store to make certain everything was where it ought to be. Boone was more nervous about leaving the store than leaving any possible patients. In the days she'd been in Small Fork, the only patient he'd had was Julia. It seemed strange that a town without a telegraph office or electricity would have a doctor.

She went about straightening shelves, as she had noticed that Boone liked things just so. She smiled, remembering him going around the store, moving items a tiny bit so that they were perfectly aligned. When she came to the small vase that Julia had touched, she impulsively picked it up and wrapped it in some cheesecloth. Then she took a bit of ribbon and tied it, creating a pretty little package.

All women should have pretty things, she decided.


The outside looked like a shack, a squat little building in the middle of a field. It could have been an overlarge animal pen, but it was Julia Benson's home.

The twenty-six-year-old woman had not lived there with her husband, the man who'd shot her in the face, then made her try to cook his supper until she collapsed in a bloody heap on the floor. Afterward, he'd gone to the saloon, covered in her blood, startling even the hardened men who sat there night after night drinking their cheap whiskey.

"Ain't my blood, you goddamn idiots. It's Julia's. She had an accident with my shotgun." Then he'd laughed. Carson Kitteridge hadn't been too drunk that night to realize the implications of what he'd said. Julia was hurt, pretty Julia Shaddock, that quiet little thing who used to share her sugar cookies with him when they were both just kids. He hadn't thought about her in a long while, but he knew who she was married to, and sometimes felt a twinge of sadness that she should be tied to such a terrible man. He wondered how someone so sweet and pretty could have ended up with a man so hard and cruel.

And so Carson had staggered out of the bar and gotten Boone, the one man he knew who could help Julia and protect her from a man like Sam Benson.

After Dr. Kitteridge saved her life, she moved in to her little shack and created her own world of magic and beauty. No one bothered her, except the occasional boys who threw rocks at her house. They were too afraid to get close, and so never did any real damage.

Sometimes she wished Boone Kitteridge hadn't saved her, hadn't been able to stop the blood that seeped from her skull, had let her fade away and die. More than sometimes. But he had, and she lived and lived.

It had been three years since Sam had shot her. She was still married to him, and knew that some-day he'd come back and finish her off. She hated him. She'd always hated him. But her daddy had caught him in her bed, even though she hadn't in-vited him there, and she had to get married. No one believed her when she'd said Sam had been trying to force himself on her. They believed him. And no one believed she hadn't deserved what she got. Not even her mama. She hated her, too. She hated everyone except Boone and Carson Kit-teridge.

And that day, she added Lady Amelia to her short list of people she didn't hate.


Amelia stared at Julia's home, uncertain whether she should announce her presence before knock-ing. From what Boone had told her about the woman, she knew Julia was a rather private person, almost a recluse. Suddenly, she was uncertain whether she should have come at all.

It was such a squat little structure, completely uninviting. And it looked as though a strong wind would blow it over, making it tumble like the strange bushes that sometimes rolled through town. Agatha had called them tumbleweeds, a name, Amelia thought, that was perfectly appro-priate.

She needn't have worried about knocking, for the door opened long before she reached the house.

"Lady Amelia. Is something wrong?" Julia was in

the shadows of her house and not yet visible, but for one pale hand braced against the door.

"No. I've come for a visit if that's all right. I've a present for you." Silence. "I'd like to give it to you, if you don't mind."

"You can leave it outside the door."

Amelia nearly did just that. But she'd always been a bit stubborn about such things, and instead said, "I could hardly allow you to be so rude. So if you don't mind—" And she walked toward the door with determination. Julia let out a sound, and backed away. But she'd left the door open.

Amelia braced herself for what she was certain would be a poor little place, but as soon as her eyes adjusted, her mouth opened in awe and she stared about in complete wonder. The room sparkled, rays of light bursting from tiny crystals that seemed to hang in the air like magic. Brightly colored feathers, pretty rocks, and even tiny bits of bleached bone covered nearly every surface of the home.

"It's beautiful," she breathed. "Simply exquisite." She quickly realized that the "crystals" were really nothing more than bits of broken glass suspended by delicate threads from a beamed ceiling. Still, the effect was stunning and whimsical.

"It's pretty this time of day. And in the firelight," Julia said, coming toward her as she finished tying a scarf around her face.

"I'm afraid my gift will seem rather dull now," Amelia said, laughing and handing the woman the vase.

The one room was all there was to the home. A bed covered with a patchwork quilt filled nearly a quarter of the space. The only other furniture was a small table and a single chair. Julia motioned toward the chair, and Amelia felt a stab of sadness for this woman who'd likely never had a need for a second chair until this very moment. Julia sat down on the bed, the gift in her hands, and slowly pulled on the ribbon until the small vase was revealed. With a single finger, she traced the curves of the vase as if she were holding a priceless item.

"Thank you."

"You were the only person in Small Fork who didn't come to stare at me," Amelia said. "Boone has gone to Abilene to send a telegram for me, and I've been minding the store. I do believe every resident of Small Fork has suddenly run out of flour and cornmeal."

"We don't get many strangers here," Julia said, still holding the vase in her hands.

"Next time you come by, I'll get some flowers for you from Dr. Kitteridge's garden."

"Oh, no, you can't do that."

"Why ever not? I'm sure he wouldn't mind."

"Then you don't know Dr. Kitteridge."

Amelia smiled. "Don't tell me he's as particular about his garden as he is about his store."

"Even more."

Suddenly, a memory flooded her, of Carson snapping off a rose from someone's Mayfair garden without a second thought and presenting it to her with a flourish.

"We'll simply have to get him to change his mind. There's no sense having a vase if you cannot put flowers in it."

Julia stood and placed the vase in the center of her little table where it looked rather forlorn, in

Amelia's opinion. "I don't think you should," she said, staring at the vase as if she were trying to picture flowers in it.

"I suppose he does like things just so," Amelia said.

"He doesn't like my house. It's too cluttered, he says. I think it makes him nervous."

"He's very different from his brother. Have you known them long?"

Even though most of her face was covered, Amelia could tell the other woman smiled. "Oh, yes. I've known Carson since we were children. Boone was always more serious. But Carson was . . ."

"Special," Amelia supplied. And then, without even knowing that she was feeling sad, she burst into tears. Embarrassed, she recovered quickly, laughing at her foolishness, but the damage had been done. Julia stared at her in dismay, clearly uncomfortable.

"I'm sorry," Amelia said, still laughing. "I suppose I owe you an explanation." And then she spilled her entire story to Julia, ending with her opening up her trunk and finding her money gone. "And that's why I'm still here. If it wasn't for that, I'd be on a train home by now."

"You traveled all the way from England for *Carson?*"

Why was everyone so shocked, Amelia thought with a bit of irritation. She supposed if she had met Carson for the first time here, she wouldn't have looked at him twice. Or if she had, she likely would have wrinkled her nose at the wild-haired giant whose clothes were stained, and whose breath smelled like sour whiskey. "In hindsight, traveling here was a mistake."

"And then he lit out?"

"Yes. Which is why I'm returning home. I do believe he never intended to marry me. I was simply a diversion for him during his stay in England. He *can* be charming," Amelia said, looking down at her lap.

"It was a terrible thing to do to you."

Amelia darted a look at the older woman, realizing there were much, much more terrible things a man could do to a woman. "Yes, it was. But I'll get over it. I'm going home as soon as my brother sends me funds, and then this will all become just a grand adventure, something to tell my grandchildren one day."

"And I can tell everyone about the time an English lady came to my house," Julia said.

"And watered your floor with her silly tears," Amelia added, laughing.

Soon after, Amelia said good-bye and promised to visit again before she left.

"Maybe you can tell me about England. I don't know anything other than Small Fork. I've never been anywhere."

Amelia agreed and walked from the small house feeling lighthearted for the first time since her arrival.

# Chapter 7

Boone knew it was a mistake to leave his store in the hands of someone who didn't realize just how important it was to keep everything in its place. He hadn't worried about Julia, for George had promised to keep an eye on her. But when he walked into his store, he broke out into a cold sweat.

Everything was wrong.

"You're back," Miss Amelia said from behind the counter, a smile on her face. He hardly noticed her smile, the genuinely happy welcome. All he could see was that everything was in disarray.

He wasn't certain when it had become so important to him to keep everything in the store precisely where he wanted it. He hadn't been like that when he was a child helping Mr. Johnson. Back then, the store had been a rambling hodgepodge of items shelved by size, not by what they contained. A customer might find linseed oil next to a jug of honey or a bag of salt. But Roy could find everything . . . eventually.

Boone darted a look at her and tried to stop himself from shooing her out of the store immediately. "I hope my brother gets the telegram within days. I'm certain he can arrange someway to get the money to me quickly. Did you have a good trip? I so do appreciate your doing this for me."

All the while she'd been talking, he'd been trying to set things aright. It looked as if a bull had rampaged the place, leaving everything helter-skelter.

"What are you doing?" she asked, sounding exasperated. "I spent hours last night arranging everything just so, and now you're doing it all again. Well, perhaps not hours. But it's perfectly fine."

A sheen of sweat shone on his hands as he carefully put everything on the shelves precisely the way that was necessary. He did it because he had to. Because if he didn't . . . he didn't really know what would happen if he didn't. He simply had to.

"I must say, you certainly are particular," she said.

"It's all wrong," he muttered, carefully aligning the cans so that they were exactly the same distance from the edge of each shelf—the length of the first joint of his index finger. He didn't even dare look at the ribbons and fabrics at the back of the store, which were no doubt in complete disarray.

He felt her come up beside him and wished she'd go away. He knew he was strange to care this much. He'd been made fun of for years because of his meticulous nature.

"Boone?"

He stopped, slightly irritated with her interference.

"I already straightened them." She sounded slightly annoyed, but he didn't care. He only wanted to fix everything she'd managed to put in disarray while he was gone. He should have known better than to leave his store in the hands of someone else.

"They are not properly organized."

Amelia felt completely unappreciated. She'd worked hard to make the store neat and clean for his return. She'd taken a feather duster and swept it over every single item in the store. Amelia had never dusted a thing in her life. She felt rather proud of herself for doing it without uttering a single complaint. She certainly hadn't heard the words "thank you" come out of his mouth yet. "Perhaps they were not properly organized when you left," she said, and nearly laughed at his unveiled look of disbelief. He'd been holding his index finger at the edge of each shelf and moving the items precisely, so that they all lined up perfectly. He even tested the items that clearly had not been moved.

How maddening.

"Every single person in this town came through the store while you were gone when they realized I was behind the counter." He kept his focus entirely on the items, gazing with a single-minded intensity that was rather fascinating to watch. He had a nice profile, and his lashes were strikingly long for a man. Carson had those same lashes, but his were blond and less noticeable. "You didn't have any patients. I did see Julia, however."

"Hmmm."

At that moment, he reminded her of her brother when he was looking at a rare book. He was so completely focused on his task, her dress could catch fire and he no doubt wouldn't notice. Amelia had always been one to tease, and saw no reason why she shouldn't now. So she nudged the nearest jar of preserved peaches one-quarter inch back, a little poke, while she stared daggers at his profile. His only response was to place his finger upon the shelf and move the preserves so the jar was aligned with its neighbor.

Poke.

"I do not find you amusing, Miss Amelia," he said, straightening out her next victim.

"I am not trying to be amusing," she lied, grinning at him. Not that he'd notice, since he was still focused on the jars. Poke. "I am trying to be annoying."

His nostrils flared, and it was obvious he was trying valiantly not to get annoyed. She'd thought he would simply ignore her, but when she went to poke her third bottle of preserved peaches, his hand shot out and grabbed her wrist before she could make contact. He didn't squeeze her wrist, but she could feel the strength of him just the same, as if she were being lightly held by iron.

He stared at her, his gray eyes hard as steel, and without a hint of amusement, he said, "Please stop."

They were inches apart, so close she could feel his angry breath against her forehead, so close she could see the gold specks in his beautiful gray eyes. She noticed again just how thick his eyelashes were. His eyes swept her face, touched on her mouth, and he dropped her hand.

Amelia smiled up at him, extended one finger, and held it against the next jar.

"Don't you dare," he said, but this time she

thought she detected a glint of something other than annoyance in his eyes. Laughter perhaps?

"And what if I do?"

Again, his gaze slipped down her face to her mouth and back, as if drawn there against his will. He gave her a look of pure exasperation, as if he were baffled by her childlike behavior. Amelia let out a soft laugh.

"You won't do anything, will you?"

"I'll dunk you in the fountain," he said, as if proud that he'd come up with such a brilliant idea.

"You wouldn't. Not for simply moving a jar"—she could feel the cool smooth glass beneath the tip of her finger—"like this." She nudged it, let out a squeal, leaped back, and found herself slightly disappointed when he simply sighed and fixed the jar.

"You're no fun," she said. "A stodgy old man like my brother." It was no fun antagonizing someone if they did not react. Amelia let out a sigh, crossing her arms and meandering away from where Boone worked.

"I could help," she said.

"No. Thank you." He was studying the shelf, making certain all the items were aligned. As if it mattered. Amelia had been bored to tears ever since her arrival. Other than her visit to Julia, she'd spent most of her time alone. There were no shops in Small Fork, no theaters or museums, or even a book to read. The only books Boone had in his home were medical journals, and she wasn't yet bored enough to start reading them.

She'd gone to visit Paula earlier, but the woman had taken her baby and young son to visit her family in Fort Worth. She watched Boone work, amazed that someone could care so much about something so insignificant. His movements were measured, careful, his gaze intent on his work. Boone was probably even more handsome than Carson, or he would be if he ever smiled. He seemed to be rather a cold fish. Certainly, he was not a great conversationalist. No wonder he wasn't married.

"Do you have a sweetheart?" she asked to fill the silence, more than out of any real curiosity.

"No."

"Have you ever?"

"No."

"Do you want one?" she asked, her voice tinged with laughter because it was clear to her she was annoying him.

"Not particularly."

Amelia tilted her head. Was she, perhaps, in the presence of a confirmed bachelor? He was far too young and far too handsome for that fate.

"I suppose you don't have much chance to meet women here," she said. "I adore balls and parties and dinners. Not that I got much chance to attend any of those before my engagement." She let out an extremely unladylike snort, and smiled when she saw him grin at the noise.

"I'd just had my come-out, you see. London is spectacular. Well, when it's not raining or clogged with smoke and fog. Did you know that people die in the fog? It gets so thick, it kills people. Kills them! I was only fifteen and in Meremont, but I read about it in the *Times*. I wrote to my brother that I never wanted to go to London. Ever. I was so frightened. And then, only a few years later, I was begging him to take me." She paused. "Am I bothering you?"

He seemed to consider her question carefully before answering. "No."

"Shall I tell you about London?"

"If you wish."

"Well, I've only been twice and not for very long. It's very noisy and dirty. Not where we live, though. But . . ."

He looked up, questioning.

"I do believe I'm a country girl at heart. I adore balls and such, but I think I can admit to you that by the time we left London and returned to Meremont, I was so sick of it all. You have no idea what it entails being an earl's sister. It's exhausting. All those visits and smiling at people who bore you to tears, who talk and talk and say nothing at all." Amelia burst out laughing and Boone smiled at her.

"I'm not doing that to you, am I? Talking and talking and boring you?"

"No. I'm just not used to having anyone to talk to."

"Oh." She noticed his cheeks turning slightly ruddy, as if he were embarrassed to admit such. "I'm afraid I will talk your ears off if you let me. I'm used to having people to talk with, you see. I've a whole house full of children to entertain." Her voice faded a bit. She missed her stepcousins fiercely.

"Small Fork doesn't have many children."

"I've only seen one. Carson told me the streets were filled with children playing. He lied about that, too."

"Carson likes making people happy," Boone

said. "He just can't stand it if someone is angry with him."

"And so he'll say anything."

Boone stopped his work, and turned fully to Amelia. "I'm sorry for what my brother did to you."

Amelia gave him a halfhearted smile. "I am too. Hopefully, my brother will send me funds, I'll go home, and this will simply be a wonderful adventure." She felt a tickle along her temple and grimaced when her hand came away dripping. "I must say I'll not miss the heat."

"It's not hot today."

It was scorching, the air in the store stagnant and oppressive. She was constantly moist, constantly feeling trickles of sweat where she'd never felt them before, moving down her back and between her breasts. Her dresses were nearly soaked by the end of the day, when finally the air cooled and she could find some relief.

"In Meremont it's always cool. Deliciously cool. We live by the sea and the air in the summer just drips with the scent of it. I used to sit on a cliff overlooking the water and stare out and wonder what America would be like. It always seemed to me to be the best of all places."

"It's not?"

She shook her head. "I'm sorry. Perhaps it's only that I've seen it from a dusty train. And it's not at all what I expected. It's so . . . big."

"That's Texas."

"It goes on forever. More and more land, leading to nowhere. I don't mean to sound so disagreeable."

As he moved from one place in the store to

another, she followed, chatting away, not really caring if it was, for the most part, a one-sided conversation. "I guess it takes getting used to.

"Why don't you want a sweetheart?" She'd always bothered her brother about finding a wife, especially when she'd suspected he had a secret love. Her suspicions were realized when she discovered her brother had almost fallen in love on a visit to Newport, Rhode Island, only to leave the poor girl behind in America. It wasn't until Maggie showed up in England that she realized her brother had, indeed, fallen in love.

"Guess it's too much trouble," he said.

"You don't plan ever to get married?"

"Don't see why I should."

"For one thing, you can't have children," Amelia said. "Don't you want a family? Don't you want to fall in love?"

"I never really gave it a thought."

She looked at him as if he were a foreign creature. What person wouldn't dream about love and family and children running about? Her brother might have claimed to not want to get married, but he'd always known he would. Boone truly didn't seem to care one way or the other. If fact, it was almost as if marriage was something he'd never thought about. "You can't be serious. Surely there's someone you've met or seen or imagined that you could marry."

He stared at her and slowly shook his head. "Nope."

"No one?"

"I don't think I could take all the chatter."

She opened her mouth as if angry, then gave into

laughter, wondering if Boone was trying to be funny or if she just found him so. He smiled, so she realized he was just teasing her.

"Truth is, not too many unattached women travel through these parts, and I just don't have the inclination to go off someplace looking for a wife."

"That's a much better answer. I thought that perhaps you truly were made of stone." She hugged her arms around herself. "Ever since I was little, that's all I've ever wanted. A home, a husband, a place that was mine. I suppose it may be because my parents both died when I was quite young, leaving me alone. I've never really felt like I had a home. Just a big old drafty house filled with furniture and servants." Amelia let out a sigh just thinking about those long, lonely days she'd spent while Edward was off in the Light Guards and she'd been left to wander around their house by herself. "I don't ever want to be alone again. Don't you get lonely here? It seems like the loneliest place on earth to me."

"Yes," he said, carefully moving a small sack of beans to the right. "It can be."

That night, Boone taught her how to light the stove and Amelia let him, thinking all the time that this was one particular skill that she would never need to master. Still, she watched him, and when he told her how to regulate the temperature, she paid attention. They fried up some steak and boiled potatoes and carrots, even though Amelia had always disliked cooked carrots.

She had much more fun cooking than she'd thought she would, and told Boone that.

"It's only fun because you've never done it before," Boone said.

Amelia was beginning to relax around Boone. He was far different from any man she'd ever known. He didn't flirt with her as Carson had, or tease her like her brother did. He was difficult to read, and she found herself studying him in an effort to know what was going on behind that serious expression of his. His eyes, it seemed, were the key. Because he rarely smiled, she found herself staring at his eyes to see whether he was annoyed or amused.

"It's true, I've never cooked before in my life," Amelia stated.

"You don't say."

She made a face, which he ignored.

They ate on the little table across from each other, lit by the sun, which was still high in the sky and making it unbearably hot in the small kitchen.

"I think tomorrow night I shall eat sitting in the fountain," Amelia announced. She was literally soaked with sweat and decidedly uncomfortable, while he sat across from her as if he were sitting on a block of ice. He just stabbed a piece of meat and shook his head as if baffled how anyone could be uncomfortable sitting in the oven that was his kitchen.

"I meant to tell you earlier that Dulce has abandoned me. She wouldn't listen to reason even when I explained to her that it's even more improper for me to be in this house with you alone. Especially at night. She seemed to think that with Carson gone, I didn't have any need for a chaperone."

Boone had been looking at her but he dropped his gaze to his plate.

"Would it be terribly inconvenient for you to go to the hotel at night? At least until we can find someone else or convince Dulce to return?"

For some reason, Boone's face tensed, the muscles along his jawline bunching as he sawed at another piece of meat.

"It's not that important," Amelia said, not knowing why Boone was angry. "It's not as if you're going to ravish me on the spot."

He dropped his fork and knife suddenly. "And why wouldn't I?" he said, sounding almost angry.

"I'm sure you wouldn't," she said cautiously, still not understanding his anger.

"Do you think I don't want to? That having you in my house isn't a temptation?"

Amelia felt her cheeks go scarlet. "Is it?"

"Why wouldn't it be?"

This was the strangest conversation she'd ever had. "You certainly don't act as if I'm a temptation. Not that I want you to, but . . ." She bit her lip. "I'm not quite certain what you want me to say."

Boone stood up abruptly. "A man would have to be dead not to see how pretty you are."

"Thank you," she said rather uncertainly, because he still seemed angry.

"You're beautiful. The most beautiful woman I've ever seen, and you're sitting across from me. And your lips. Aw hell," he said, swiping a hand through his hair. He let out a self-deprecating laugh. "Now you know why I'm not married."

"I suppose that wasn't the most eloquent speech," Amelia said. "You're no Lord Byron."

He stood staring at the stove, turned partly away from her. "I'm a gentleman. At least I try to be. You don't have to worry about me making any kind of advances toward you."

"I'm not worried. At least I wasn't until you told me I was a temptation." She gave him a shaky smile, but he was still turned away.

"You aren't. I'm not." He let out a strangled sound. "All right. You are."

"Perhaps I should go to the hotel?" she asked softly.

"That hotel isn't fit for a lady. I'll go."

"I hate to force you from your own home," Amelia said, feeling awful. "I know it was my suggestion, but now I feel just horrid." She was only doing what she thought she ought, but somehow it had come out all wrong, as if she were afraid of him. To be honest, he didn't really frighten her in the least. It was rather flattering that he thought her a temptation. "It's the appearance of it."

"I understand."

Amelia stood and gathered the plates, bringing them to the sink. "Since you cooked dinner, I'll wash the dishes. Agreed?"

"Agreed."

Amelia set about filling the sink with water, then poured in a kettle of boiling water from the stove to warm it a bit. "Back home we have hot and cold running water. I used to take the most wonderful baths." She felt herself blush, because the image of her naked in a bathtub was not at all the thing she should be discussing with a man.

"I have a big ol' copper tub if you want a bath."

The thought of sinking into a tub of cool water

sounded wonderful. "I'd love a bath," Amelia said. "Could you?"

"I'll set it up in the kitchen and then I'll go on to the hotel. That way you'll have your privacy." He cleared his throat as if he were uncomfortable talking about such a thing. He got out a large pot and filled it with water, then put it on the stove to heat.

"I won't need much hot water. The air in here will heat the water fast enough," she said, laughing.

While she did the dishes, he dragged the tub into the kitchen and started filling it with water. For a moment, Amelia was struck by the comfortable intimacy of the two of them working together in the small sunlit kitchen. She wondered if Boone had ever fixed a bath for a woman. If she believed him about never having a sweetheart, then he likely hadn't.

"This is very nice of you," she said, as he poured the fourth bucket of water into the tub. She ran from the room to retrieve the scented soaps she'd brought from home. She loved her lavender-scented soap, and had feared Texas wouldn't have it.

"Smell," she said, holding it up to Boone's nose. He took an obligatory sniff.

"Nice."

"I do love good soaps," Amelia said, breathing in deeply. "I didn't see any in your store."

"I don't think most ranch hands would appreciate smelling that pretty," he said.

Amelia giggled. "You never know. You could start something new."

She placed the soap and a towel on one of the kitchen chairs where it would be easy to reach, and watched as he poured the steaming pot of water from the stove into the tub.

"I'll head over to the hotel now."

"Good night, Dr. Kitteridge."

Three Legs lay in one corner, and when she looked at him he thumped his tail, no doubt hoping she'd toss another piece of steak his way.

"I've nothing more for you." *Thump thump thump.* At least she had the dog to keep her company. "I don't like being alone." The dog rested his head on his paws and looked up at her as if understanding every word she said. "I suppose I've nothing to worry about. It isn't as if this is a busy town with strangers walking about looking for naked women to accost while they're taking a bath."

She eyed the tub warily, suddenly torn between the wonderfully soothing water and her unexplainable fear of being naked and alone. She'd finally made up her mind that she was being silly, when she realized she had a problem. Her dress hooked up the back.

"Oh, bother."

She looked at the bath with longing and began tackling the twenty-five hooks that held her dress together.

Boone walked across to his store early the next morning, secretly hoping Amelia would still be abed. He'd felt like a fool the night before, and if he'd been a drinking man it would have been a good night to get stinking drunk. As it was, he had to suffer with cursed clarity at just how stupid he'd acted. He could feel his face heat just thinking about what he'd told her, how he'd acted.

He wished for the first time in his life that he'd spent more time in the company of women. He couldn't recall ever having a conversation with one other than Julia. He didn't know what to say, how to act. Obviously.

Carson came out of the womb flirting. It was as natural to him as breathing. But Boone was a different story entirely. In college, every student, every professor, was a man. He'd kept to himself, making few friends, studying instead of going out into town. He'd wanted to make Roy proud, and so he'd put every ounce of energy he had into getting good grades and becoming the best doctor he could. He'd graduated a year earlier than the other students, anxious to get home and help Roy out with the store.

He wasn't certain just how it had happened, but somehow he'd gotten to be a grown man without even so much as holding a woman's hand.

He'd lain in that hotel room torturing himself with thoughts of Amelia in that bathtub, the golden late-day sun bathing her in soft light as she moved the soap that smelled like heaven slowly over her breasts. Always when he'd thought about a woman, she'd been some faceless body with all the right parts. But Amelia was painfully real, agonizingly beautiful, and today she would smell like lavender.

Boone entered the building through the store, making his way back to his apartment. He smiled when he entered the empty kitchen; the bath was still there and filled with water. It was tangible proof that for a little while, someone else was in his home.

Then he stopped still, his heart hammering in his chest. Her dress lay on the floor in a heap and it was obvious it had been viciously ripped.

"Oh, Jesus, no," he whispered, holding the dress in his hands, staring at the torn cloth. A knife lay on the kitchen table and he nearly collapsed from fear.

"Miss Amelia!" he shouted, moving out of the kitchen and throwing open the doors as he went. "Amelia!"

He reached her room, opening the door with force, only to find her sitting up sleepily, her blond hair tousled, her cheeks flushed from sleep. And her neck red and raw, as if someone had tried to strangle her. He took a step toward her, his concern overcoming any relief that he'd found her alive, and she instinctively pulled up the blanket to cover herself, even though the gown she wore was hardly provocative.

"What's wrong?"

"Your dress. It was ripped. I thought . . ."

"Oh. My dress. I forgot. I couldn't get it off and the bath looked so lovely . . . I ripped it." She giggled. "I never thought I'd sacrifice a gown for a bath."

"*You* ripped it?" He let out a breath of pent-up air. "The next time you rip a dress from yourself, I would ask that you please discard it so that I don't think you've been murdered in my house."

"I'm sorry."

"If you weren't accosted, what happened to your neck, then?"

She put a hand to her neck and winced. "Again. My dress. It's wool. Light wool, but not the thing to wear here. I think the heat and the wool combined to make my neck quite red. It was my last clean dress, you see. Dulce helped me get into yesterday but there was no one to help me out of it last night. And I certainly couldn't ask you." She grinned. "Not with you already so tempted."

"I'm not that tempted," he said, irritated that she would bring up his foolish words.

"Oh." She put on a pouty face as if disappointed that he could resist ravishing her, which forced a smile from him, the little imp.

"Get dressed and I'll see to your neck," he said. "You do have something to wear, don't you?"

"I'll find the least offensive item." She smiled again, her teeth straight and white. It really wasn't fair that everything about her was so completely appealing. He found himself wishing, just for an instant, that he was a different sort of man. The sort who would flirt and court a woman. And he wished she wasn't planning to go home quite so soon.

Amelia entered his office wearing a high-neck cotton blouse that had been nearly ruined on the crossing. It was stained and so Amelia had deemed it unwearable, but now she was glad she'd saved it.

"Please take a seat."

Amelia smiled slightly, hearing his "doctor" tone, which was so different from the one he'd just been using when he thought she'd been accosted.

"Unbutton your blouse." His back was turned to her as he gathered some sort of ointment and gauzy material.

She undid four more buttons and opened the neckline a bit to expose her neck, lifting her chin when he turned around, so that he could have a good look at her rash.

He put a gentle hand beneath her chin, moving her head this way and that to get a better look at the raw area, his gray eyes intent on her wound. "I would suggest no more woolen dresses," he said, frowning. "You're actually bleeding in one spot."

"I thought it hurt a bit more than it should."

He rested one hand on her shoulder and began applying a soothing balm on her neck so gently she hardly felt it. His fingertips moved in a slow, circular motion on her skin, and it felt so lovely, she closed her eyes. His fingers moved from just above her collarbone to below her chin, almost as if it were a caress.

"You need to pull your blouse down a bit so I can get to the back of your neck."

She opened her eyes and undid the buttons, feeling strange, as if she were undressing for a much different purpose. He'd done nothing, said nothing to make her feel like anything but a patient being helped by a doctor, but for some reason, she felt oddly liquid, and frighteningly aroused. She shrugged the blouse down, revealing nothing more enticing than her beribboned chemise and the top of her loosely laced corset.

What is wrong with me, she thought. A man looks at me, touches me, and I'm ready to . . . to . . .

"Move your head forward a bit. It's quite raw back here."

She dipped down her head and he moved aside the strands of hair that had escaped her loose bun to apply the salve. She could feel her breathing growing more languid, and yet she was aware of every time his fingertips touched her skin. It felt exquisite. She let out a small sound and he froze.

"Did I hurt you?"

She could only shake her head, her cheeks blazing red with embarrassment. He is a doctor, she told herself, applying medicine.

"Almost done?" she choked out.

"I am hurting you. I didn't think this would sting, only soothe the burn."

"It doesn't sting." She swallowed, mortified that she could actually feel herself growing more aroused with every touch.

He came around to the front of her. "Miss Amelia," he said, clearly not believing that he wasn't hurting her.

She looked up at him, her mouth open slightly, her breathing shallow. "It doesn't sting."

He looked momentarily confused, then his eyes flickered, and his gaze dipped to her mouth as if drawn against his will.

"I should put on gauze, to stop the chafing." He said it, but he didn't move to the gauze, didn't move at all. It seemed as if they stared at each other for several minutes, though it couldn't have been more than a few seconds. Amelia felt herself moving forward, and realized she wanted to kiss him, wanted him to kiss her.

She jerked back, horrified by what she'd been thinking, feeling. Boone was Carson's *brother*. She couldn't be thinking such thoughts about him. She hardly knew him, hardly even liked him.

"The gauze?"

He blinked twice, then retrieved the gauze, wrapping it around her neck quickly and efficiently, stepping back as soon as he was done. "I would suggest you wear your collars unbuttoned for a few days to allow your neck to heal. I'll be out in the store."

He turned, leaving her alone to wonder what was wrong with her. She'd met hundreds of men in her life, had danced with them, allowed them to hold her hand. One even tried to kiss her, but she hadn't allowed him to, mostly, she had to admit, because the thought of kissing that particular gentleman gave her the giggles.

It was only when she met Carson that she realized what desire was, how it could consume a woman, make her want to do all sorts of wonderful forbidden things. Carson had made her feel like a desirable woman, and she'd thought that meant they were perfect for one another.

Disconcerting as it was to admit, she had the same humiliating reaction to Boone. It wasn't as if she were a woman of loose morals. She *had* let Carson take certain liberties that no proper girl should have, but she'd been in love and convinced that she and Carson would marry.

She had absolutely no illusions about Boone. And yet his touch sent her body shivering with pleasure. She didn't like it. Didn't like it at all. It made her feel out of control, as if she had absolutely no say in who she was attracted to.

She only prayed Boone didn't know what was happening to her body when he was treating her rash. How mortifying if he suspected.

From Boone's office she could hear the inviting

sound of the garden's fountain gurgling gently. She went out, wetting her hands and pressing them against her flushed cheeks. There had to be something wrong with her. She still felt aroused, her senses heightened, and she knew if Boone were to come out to the garden, she would allow him to kiss her. And more. She would allow it because she wanted it. And she shouldn't. A proper young lady shouldn't be thinking about kissing a man she hardly knew.

"Miss Amelia."

*Oh, Lord.* She turned and smiled politely. "Yes?"

He stood uncertainly in the doorway. "Did you sell a vase? One with flowers? It's missing, and there is no notation in the ledger."

Amelia almost sagged with relief. For one terrifying moment she'd thought that perhaps he'd known what she'd been thinking. "I bought it. For Julia. I thought she'd appreciate something so pretty. I'm sorry, I did forget to put it in the ledger."

He grinned at her, an unexpected reaction to be sure. She wished he wouldn't smile, for it only made him all that more handsome. "You gave that vase to Julia?"

"Yes. I thought it was lovely."

"I'm sure she thought it was. She made it. Julia has a kiln behind her house. She makes pottery, and I sell some pieces in my store and ship some to Mr. Johnson's old friend in Fort Worth."

"She didn't say a word," Amelia said, laughing.

"It was very kind of you to give it to her just the same," he said quietly.

"She's a lovely woman. I plan to visit her again before I leave. I'm certain I shall be here for several weeks at least." She let out a sigh. "I did mean to ask you if you requested a reply from my brother so that I at least know he received the telegram."

"I did. Because there's no office in Small Fork, it will come in the mail. We get mail on Tuesdays and Fridays when the train runs."

"Oh, bother. I could have an answer sitting there and not know it."

"Is it so bad here then?"

"Yes," she said grumpily, then laughed. "I know you must think I'm extremely ungrateful, but I do wish I could simply blink my eyes and be home."

Just then, they heard Agatha calling for Boone.

"If you don't mind, I'd like to talk to Agatha and try to get her to convince Dulce to come back. Once I get the money my brother is sending, I'm certain I'll be able to pay her quite handsomely. I do feel awful about forcing you from your home."

Twenty minutes later, Amelia was feeling nothing but pure frustration.

"She won't come back," Agatha said. "She told me so herself. Not for all the tea in China."

"But why?"

Amelia had asked before, but Agatha had pressed her mouth closed.

"She doesn't like me," Amelia guessed.

Agatha sighed. "It's not you, honey. Dulce don't like nobody telling her what to do. You're used to people listening to you, and Dulce is used to not listening to a soul."

Amelia looked helplessly at Boone, who shrugged, his only contribution to the conversation. "I hate to force Boone from his own home, but he won't let me stay at the hotel."

"That's no place for you," Agatha said, nearly repeating what Boone had told her.

"I don't mind staying at the hotel. George owes me for the time I sewed him up, so I'm not even paying."

"You can hardly call the place a hotel. I'll have you stay with me before you go there," Agatha said.

Boone stared at the older woman, completely surprised by her unexpected generosity. Agatha had a tiny house; it wasn't a house that could easily accommodate a guest. Where would she put Amelia—on the kitchen table?

"You're making the hotel seem rather intriguing, you two," Amelia said.

"It's got rats," Agatha blurted out. "I didn't want to say anything and spread rumors about the place. I wouldn't want George to know I've been talking bad. But, that's it. Rats."

Amelia wrinkled her nose. "Rats? Out here?"

"Big ones. I saw a real big one there just yesterday," Agatha said, and then it dawned on Boone exactly what she was saying.

Carson was back in town.

# Chapter 8

"What are you doing back here?" Boone said after finding his younger brother knocking back a whiskey.

"Drinkin'," Carson said with a careless grin. By the looks of him, it wasn't his first whiskey of the day, and it was barely noon. Carson's eyes were more than bloodshot. He had the look of a man who'd given up entirely, with hair a greasy mass hanging far below his shoulders, and a scraggly beard that should have been scraped off his face weeks ago. Give him a haircut and he would have looked exactly like their old man not long before he'd puked blood all over the town's main street and died. It made the bile in Boone's stomach churn to see him looking so much like their father.

"You look like hell," Boone said, gazing at his brother. He was twenty-four years old but looked far older.

In answer, Carson reached into his pants pocket, digging deep, and took out a wad of cash, throwing it to Boone carelessly. "Thanks for the loan."

Boone gave Carson a hard stare before looking down at the bundle of money in his hand. "What did you do, rob a bank?"

"Haven't sunk that low yet, big brother." He was still grinning so Boone shook his head, exasperated with himself for not smashing Carson's face and with Carson for using his considerable charm on him. No wonder women fell at his feet; he had a way of turning people's rage into bewildered acceptance in a few seconds, even when he looked not much better than something you scraped off your boot. "Turns out, Fort Worth's full of people who like to gamble and lose."

Boone pulled back a beat-up wooden chair and sat next to his brother, laying his hands flat on the table. "She's still here, you know."

"That's why I'm here and not across the street. She waiting for me to come back?"

"She's waiting for her brother to send her money so she can leave as fast as possible. Apparently her maid helped herself to Miss Wellesley's cash." Boone held up the money. "This might help her on her way."

Carson emptied the bottle into his glass and took another long pull, frowning as the last drop splashed into his glass. "I'm real sorry for what I done to that girl. You probably won't believe me."

"I know you're sorry she showed up here. I know you're sorry you're stuck here waiting for her to leave."

Carson stared into his drink. "Yeah. That's about right."

"She didn't deserve what you did to her. I'm pretty sure she loved you, and thought you loved her."

"Stupid girl."

Boone would have smashed his fist into Carson's face if he hadn't detected an underlying sadness to that seemingly cruel answer. He wished Carson didn't get to him, but he always had. Even when they were kids, all Carson had to do was look at him with his angel-blue eyes and Boone would do anything to protect him from their monster of a father.

"Make me understand, Carson," Boone said, even though he suspected he knew why Carson did what he did. Carson was afraid he was like his father, that if he had a wife and kids, he'd beat them down until they either left or died.

"Can't."

"You sure as hell should try."

Carson shrugged, then stared at his brother with those bloodshot eyes. He took another drink and placed the glass down hard. "Leave me the hell alone. I don't have to listen to your shit. I wanted to fuck her and she wouldn't let me," he said, finally sounding as drunk as he no doubt was. "The end. And then she's stupid enough to follow me halfway across the world without me askin' her to, making me some kinda villain when all I was doin' was trying to get a fancy piece of tail."

"You're disgusting."

"You wouldn't say that if you could get it up." And then he grinned, almost begging Boone to hit him. God above knew Boone wanted to, could feel his fists curling and tightening, could feel the rage making the veins in his temples throb.

Boone shoved away from the table before he murdered his little brother.

"Run away, Boone. Goddamned coward."

Boone stopped, closed his eyes, then continued walking out the door, the sound of his brother laughing drunkenly behind him.

Amelia took up a place in the mercantile where she could keep an eye on the hotel and watch the entrance. She knew what Agatha had been hinting at, that Carson was back and holed up in the hotel. Against her will, she allowed herself to imagine Carson, looking fine and clean, following behind Boone when he returned. He'd beg her forgiveness, promise never to leave her again, promise to make their lives happy. Even though she knew with absolute certainty that Carson was not the man she'd thought he was, she still allowed herself to dream, to escape for a time the pain of him discarding her.

It was what she did. A curse. She dreamed up things in her head that somehow turned into hope, and which nearly always ended with her feeling ridiculous. How many times had she done this to herself, set her dreams so high, so beautiful, that they could never come true?

She told herself Carson was a cad, a man who'd used her for a bit of distraction in England. And yet, when Boone emerged from the hotel alone, her eyes pricked with tears as if she'd really believed Carson would follow behind, hat in hand, ready to beg forgiveness.

Sometimes she just hated herself.

Before Boone came through the door, she watched him cross the street, his strides long and sure, his face set and angry. Apparently the confrontation had not gone well. She hurried to the back of the counter, pretending as if she was just waiting for a customer. The place was deserted most of the time, and other than that first day when nearly the entire town showed up to get a glimpse of her, they'd only had a handful of customers each day.

"How's Carson?" Amelia asked when Boone returned.

He looked at her as if mildly surprised she'd figured out Carson was back, then took a deep breath. "Drunk." He was angry.

"He thought I'd be gone, no doubt," she said, using great effort to act as if she didn't care whether Carson hoped she was gone or not.

"No doubt." He began straightening shelves that didn't need straightening, then seemed to make himself stop. "If you want to go home on the next train, I have the money to send you."

As tempting as the offer was, and Lord knew it was tempting, Amelia knew she couldn't ask Boone to part with so much money. It was clear to her that the mercantile wasn't making money, and he certainly wasn't getting rich from his practice.

"No, I couldn't. But I thank you for the offer. No doubt my brother has received the telegram and is already sending the funds I need. He has an extremely efficient staff. They'll know where he is even if I do not."

"You don't mind being stuck here?"

Amelia smiled. "Oh, I do mind. Very much. But I will use this opportunity to teach myself a lesson in impulsive behavior."

"So, staying here is a punishment."

"Yes, in a manner of speaking. If I ever consider acting so impulsively again, I shall only remember my time here and be dissuaded from that action."

He narrowed his eyes at her. "I think that was insulting to all Texans."

"I didn't mean it to be," she said lightly. "It's Texas I don't care for, not Texans."

"It's the same."

"Oh posh," she said, waving a hand at him. "It isn't the same. You, for example, are a very nice man who has been only kind to me. Well, mostly kind when you're not insulting my intelligence." She grinned at him when he scowled. Teasing Boone was nearly as much fun as teasing her brother.

"You have to admit, coming to Texas for Carson isn't a sign of high intelligence."

Amelia would have been insulted if it weren't for the glint of humor she thought she detected in his eyes—and the painful fact that what he said was probably true. It wasn't readily apparent that he was teasing her, but she was getting better at reading him.

"And it's also probably not a sign of intelligence that I didn't accept your offer for funds so that I could remove myself from your onerous presence as soon as physically possible."

Goodness, he almost grinned. "Onerous, hmm?"

"Extremely."

Amelia smiled at him. She couldn't help herself, for it was clear he was trying quite hard not to smile himself.

Just then the bell tinkled on the door, and a man walked in looking harried. Amelia studied him curiously, because other than Boone, he was the only man she'd seen in town who was dressed like a gentleman.

"Afternoon, Jason."

The man nodded. He was young and handsome, with slicked-back hair, a neat mustache, and sideburns that bracketed his strong jaw. He wore a blue jacket with a deep burgundy vest beneath, decorated with the fanciest buttons Amelia had seen since leaving England. In fact, the suit looked decidedly English.

When he spotted Amelia behind the counter, he came to an abrupt stop. "Ma'am," he said, giving her the smallest of bows. Even that little gesture of respect made her homesick.

"Have you met Lady Amelia? She's visiting from England."

"No, but my wife . . ." He stopped speaking abruptly, as if he'd gotten something stuck in his throat. "Paula mentioned her." He finished, looking miserable.

"How can I help you?" Boone asked, as if also aware that the man standing in front of them was suffering from some unknown ailment.

"It's my wife," he said, and Amelia thought the young man just might cry. "She's left me. Or rather, she's left Small Fork. I need to bring her back."

"Sorry to hear your troubles," Boone said cautiously.

"She hates it here," Jason said, and Boone darted a look at Amelia.

"It's a difficult place to live for women," he said, his tone neutral and calm.

"She's gone back to Fort Worth to her parents and wrote me . . ." He dug a letter out of his trouser pocket. "She's not coming back. She says so right here. But I can't leave. I'm the branch president here. My employers put great faith in me, and I cannot abandon my position." He turned to Amelia. "You're a woman; would you live here?"

"Not except under extreme duress," she said frankly, and received a dark scowl for her honesty from Boone. "I'm only being honest. Why, there's no school, no church even. Where would she shop? Or luncheon? There's no theater, or even a town square to sit in. There are no *trees*, for good-ness sakes."

"We've got trees," Boone said, interrupting her.

"I suppose I meant trees that offered shade from this incessant heat," she said, and smiled just to ir-ritate him. Then she turned to Mr. Brentwood. "Perhaps most difficult for your wife is that there are no young women she can relate to."

"There's Dulce," Boone said, and she assumed that was his idea of a jest.

"I meant nice women with whom she could take afternoon tea," she said, giving Boone a dark look because it appeared he was not taking Mr. Brent-wood's plight seriously. "Frankly, I'm surprised there's even a bank," Amelia said.

"It's because of the ranchers. They petitioned for one after getting robbed a few times bringing their money to Hanover." The man truly did look as if he was going to cry.

"What about the ranchers' wives and their daugh-ters? Surely not every man in this town is a bachelor."

"They stay out on their ranches for the most part," Jason said, shaking his head. "It's a long trip

into town, and they don't come but when they
need supplies."

"You need to have something in this town that
would be remotely attractive to a woman. A shop. A
real restaurant. An opera house." She wasn't certain, but it almost sounded as if Boone snorted.

"Well, none of that's going to happen in the next
day or so, and I want my wife back," Jason said, his
frustration showing. "I came here to tell you that
I'm shutting down the bank for a week so I can retrieve my wife and children. If you have any business to conduct, I'd appreciate if you could
conduct it before the next train comes in."

"As a matter of fact, I'll be making a deposit tomorrow," Boone said. "I won't make the mistake
of keeping my money here until Carson leaves."

Jason darted a look at Amelia, and she felt her
face heat with embarrassment. She wondered if
everyone in town knew of her humiliation.

After Jason left, Boone closed up the store,
pulling down a shade.

"I think I would die of boredom in a month if I
had to live here," Amelia said, completely unaware
she was being extremely critical of the town where
the man in front of her had lived all his life.

"Most people are too busy to get bored. Not too
many pampered ladies 'round these parts," he said,
suddenly sounding nearly as Texan as Carson did,
drawing out his words.

Amelia lifted her chin. "I daresay I don't know
what I could possibly to do pass the time."

"Cooking. Laundry. Gardening. Cleaning. Women
around here find it a blessing just to be able to have
enough time to watch the sunset."

"What a completely dreadful life they must lead," she said. Even though she did, indeed, think it sounded dreadful, she'd said it aloud simply because she detected a large amount of censor from Boone. "Thank goodness I can return to my life of complete idleness."

His lips curved. "You're not there yet, miss. So I'd appreciate if it you could cook me up some supper."

Amelia smiled slyly. The biggest punishment she could think of would be to make supper for Boone. "Only if you promise to eat it." She lifted one delicate brow.

He let out a sigh. "I'll cook. But you watch."

Amelia clapped her hands and smiled. "I'm not really hungry yet. What are you making?"

"Chili. And it won't be ready for another two hours."

She furrowed her brow.

"You'll like it. Real Texas food, though I'm not the best 'round here at making it."

"I've never heard of it."

"That's because you've never been in Texas. It's the only place you can find it, to my knowledge."

She wrinkled her nose. "It doesn't have rattlesnakes in it, does it?"

Boone chuckled and walked back toward the kitchen. "No. Beef, onions, and enough spice to grow hair on your chest."

At her alarmed look, Boone laughed again. Goodness, she wished she was better at making him laugh. He looked completely lovely at that moment.

"I'll go easy on the spice. We can have rattlesnake tomorrow."

He didn't appear to be joking. "People don't really eat snake, do they?"

"Of course. But you have to make sure you cook it enough to get the poison out."

Amelia laughed uncertainly. "You're telling tales," she said, feeling foolish for believing him.

He grinned. "People do eat rattlers. If you like chicken, you'll like rattler."

Amelia wrinkled her nose and shook her head. "I don't think it could possibly taste anything like chicken. But I suppose I could try it. I seem to be quite adventurous lately."

Boone gave her the job of cutting up onions into tiny pieces, something she found was an utterly painful and noxious job. Her eyes stung brutally, and teared to the point that she was nearly blinded.

"Goodness, I never realized what Cook went through each evening," she said, wiping the tears from her face.

Boone just shook his head, slightly bewildered to be in the presence of a human being who'd never cut an onion.

"Roy used to make this chili for me," Boone said.

"The man who owned this store?"

Boone nodded as he sliced up a slab of beef.

"You lived with him?" she asked, remembering what Agatha had told her about Boone being raised by the old store owner.

"For a time."

Amelia made a face at his back. She was getting rather annoyed with his cryptic answers. "Did

Carson live here, too?" she asked, even though she knew the answer.

"No."

"He was raised by wolves, perhaps?"

"Close enough."

Amelia let out a little growl and he looked up, a completely innocent look on his face. "Either you may participate in this conversation or else I will proceed to talk about something you have absolutely no interest in. Like flower arranging. My stepaunt taught me all there is to know about it, and I will share every bit of information she imparted to me."

Boone's only answer was to let out a sigh.

"Roses." Amelia said with a nod, and cleared her throat as if preparing for a lengthy diatribe. "They are often the centerpiece of arrangements because of their wonderful scent, hardiness, and variety. One shouldn't overcrowd a rose arrangement with other competing scents, as that would . . ."

Boone stopped chopping and turned around. "My father beat the living hell out of me on a daily basis and I came to live with Roy. Carson stayed with my father because he wouldn't let him leave. You want more detail, then talk to Carson."

Amelia felt a sudden wave of regret, so strong her stomach actually felt a bit queasy. She wouldn't have asked if she'd known the answer would be so horrid. "Oh." She stared at his back as he began cooking the meat, his movements angry and tense. She'd known all was not quite right with Boone's childhood, but she'd had no idea it had been so awful. In her experience, parents loved their children and whipped them only when they were very, very bad. Her own father had swatted her behind when she was five years old because she'd wandered into the path of a speeding carriage without bothering to look into the street. And then he'd hugged her so fiercely she couldn't breathe. It had been her one and only spanking, and she still remembered it.

What could a little boy have done to deserve to be beaten daily? Boone, who was so kind and quiet. It didn't make sense.

"Did he beat Carson, too?"

"No."

"Why you, then?"

Boone let out a sigh and stopped stirring for a moment, tilting his head so she could just see his pained expression. "I guess it was because he loved Carson. He was a cute kid."

Amelia stared down at her onions, feeling her eyes prick with tears that had nothing to do with the vegetable she'd been cutting. Amelia had been lonely as a girl, but she'd never felt unloved. "Mr. Johnson was a good man," she said finally.

"He was."

"When my parents died, my brother joined the military and left me behind. Do you know what I missed the most?"

"Talking."

Amelia laughed, and was gratified to see Boone smiling again. "Yes, talking, but it was more than that. It was feeling that I mattered to someone. Sometimes in those days I thought I could disappear and no one would miss me. Our servants were very kind, but there is a sort of gap, you see. They don't tuck you in or give you hugs. There's a distance that's always maintained. I would go months at a time without touching another human being. It was very lonely."

Boone didn't say a word, just looked at her with his solemn gray eyes and nodded, as if he understood precisely what she was saying.

"And then my uncle died and suddenly I was surrounded by children and a woman whom I now love like a mother. You see, my uncle never had children of his own and so he married a woman with six! I suppose he was hoping for number seven. Then he died, and she stayed on when my brother became earl." She laughed aloud. "It was so chaotic compared to my quiet life, but I loved it. We were constantly running about, having adventures, playing games. Their favorite was statues. Do you know it?"

"No."

"The children run about crazily until someone shouts 'statue,' and then you must freeze as if you've instantly become a statue. It's great fun, because you must stay frozen for as long as possible or you lose the game. I was dismal because I always started laughing. You should try it."

Boone felt his cheeks flush slightly. "I don't think so."

"You must. It's a parlor game."

"There you go. I don't have a parlor."

Boone watched as she made a face at him. Following her expressions was nearly as entertaining as listening to her talking. As she chattered away, he showed her the various spices for the chili, and felt warmth flow over him, like a comfortable old blanket that had been missing but was finally found. He liked having her here with him, talking away and not even caring whether he talked back. She baffled him, going from melancholy to laughing in a matter a minutes.

While the chili cooked, they went outside and sat by the fountain, and she continued to talk about this or that. He swore he would recognize every member of her family if they walked through the door, so vivid were her descriptions. He found himself liking her brother, feeling sorry for poor cousin Janet who couldn't keep any food down, and wishing he could meet the mischievous Mary.

Boone pulled the small table out into the courtyard, and she'd clapped her hands in delight as if he'd offered her the greatest gift. She ran back into the house and grabbed the chairs and he felt a tug on his heart so strong, it scared him to hell. He had a terrible feeling that, though he'd felt alone most his life, when she was gone, he'd really understand the meaning of loneliness.

"I do realize Small Fork doesn't have a lot of inhabitants, but I have noticed your practice doesn't see many patients," she said, as he was spooning out the chili.

"By the time I see them, they're already dead most times," Boone said, and enjoyed watching the shock on her face. He chuckled, and even to his ears it was a rusty sound. "Texans are fiercely independent and are disinclined to come see me until it's usually too late. I did set a couple of legs before the drives this year, but people in these parts mostly tend to themselves."

To his surprise she clapped, as if delighted. "Oh, I adore Texans," she gushed, laughing. "My brother would send for the doctor if I had the sniffles. I allowed it after what happened to my parents. You see, he came home from school sick and gave the sickness to them and to me. They both died, of course, and I nearly did. After that, Edward became rather overprotective of me. I still can hardly believe he allowed me to travel here with just a maid. I know if he discovered that Anne abandoned me in New York, he'd be on the next ship."

"I think I'd like your brother," Boone said darkly.

Amelia waved a hand. "Men should realize that women are perfectly capable of taking care of themselves." After a thoughtful silence, she added with her characteristic honesty, "Although perhaps I'm not a good example of that." She gave him a sheepish grin, then looked down at her chili as if it were yet another insurmountable obstacle.

"It's good," he urged. "And not nearly as spicy as usual."

She bravely dipped her spoon in and took a rather delicate mouthful, her eyes widening in happy surprise . . . until the heat kicked in. "Oh," she said, swallowing. "Oh, goodness. I do believe my mouth is on fire." She waved a hand in front of her face as if that would keep the heat at bay, while Boone poured her a glass of water.

"It's not hot," he said.

She narrowed her eyes at him. "You keep saying that, about the weather and now this. It *is* hot." Then she smiled. "But also rather good. I think I might actually like this."

"Praise the Lord."

She took another spoonful, squeezing her eyes shut and taking another drink. "I don't know quite why, but I find I like the heat. The chili, not the weather." She held up her hand to stop him. "And it is hot, Dr. Kitteridge, no matter what you say."

"Boone." He was grinning at her like an idiot, like a man who'd never been completely charmed by a beautiful woman before. Which, in fact, he had not. As he watched her take spoonful after spoonful of his chili, her eyes watering with the heat of it, he felt his heart give another odd and painful tug.

When they'd finished, they went back inside and washed the dishes together, Amelia washing and Boone drying, like a couple who had been doing such mundane things together for years.

Amelia was finding she liked doing little chores; it made her feel useful in a place where she felt utterly useless. She'd never given much thought to how her homes had been cleaned. Of course she'd seen the servants and appreciated what they did, but never thought of it beyond the general acknowledgement that the work was being done.

"Do you think you could sweep the floor while I go get the table and chairs?"

"Of course," Amelia said, taking the broom from him with a smile. As soon as he was out the door, she frowned. It was the first time in her life she'd held a broom. She knew how it worked; she'd simply never done it before.

And so, she began sweeping, bringing the dust and bits of debris into a pile with remarkable ease, and sweeping it up into the dustbin. It was, dare she think it, fun. Her brother would fall over laughing if he could see her now. Feeling ridiculously proud, she held the door open for Boone so he could maneuver the table through.

"When I get home I think I shall shock everyone with my newfound domestic skills," Amelia said.

"I hope I haven't been working you too hard," Boone said, and Amelia couldn't tell whether he was being sardonic or not, so she peered up at him suspiciously. He was teasing her, she could tell from his eyes.

"I'm not completely useless, though I'm certain you think that's the case." She was slightly miffed. Just because she hadn't done physical labor didn't mean she was not a capable woman.

"I was just teasing. From what you told me you were running your brother's household from the time you were twelve years old."

Amelia was instantly appeased and inordinately happy that he'd actually been listening to her as she'd prattled on about her everyday life back home. "I don't know what I shall do when I return. I will become one of the most dreaded creatures in London society." When he gave her a questioning look, she answered. "I shall be an unmarried relative living on the kindness of my brother and his wife."

"I suppose I should ask you to explain. But I'm not going to," he said, making Amelia laugh.

"Are you saying, sir, that I talk too much?"

"My ears are getting a bit worn out. I'm not used to so much noise."

Amelia was delighted. "You are getting rather good at teasing, Boone."

His cheeks turned ruddy, and that made her smile fade. For some reason, every time his cheeks flushed it made her heart wrench a bit. Perhaps it was because he was so unused to ordinary things, like teasing or calling a girl pretty. My goodness, some men could spout poetry for hours without a hint of self-consciousness. But give Boone the barest compliment or hint of flirtation and he blushed. It seemed impossible that a man as handsome as Boone Kitteridge would be so unused to female companionship, but clearly he was.

"I have something to show you," he said, and he gave her one of his rare smiles. "I didn't want you to leave Texas thinking only bad things about it."

"I won't, I promise."

He ducked down so he could look out the window. "Follow me."

Curious, Amelia did. When she reached the courtyard, she let out a gasp. The sky was a breathtaking mix of the most vibrant colors she'd ever seen in her life. Even the sunsets she'd seen across the Irish Sea could not match the one she was gazing at. The light bathed the courtyard in pink, making everything soft and lovely, almost magical.

Amelia grasped his left hand, overcome with happiness at the site of something so exquisitely beautiful. "Thank you, Boone," she said, holding his large hand in both of hers. Amelia didn't give the slightest thought to holding his hand, until he slowly pulled away from her grasp, leaving her feeling foolish and somehow forward.

She cleared her throat. "It is lovely. Thank you," she said, suddenly awkward when she'd never felt that way with him before. She held her hands tightly together in front of her and moved slightly away from him, feeling confused and in a small way, hurt.

Next to her, Boone let out a sigh and wiped a

hand through his wavy brown hair. "It's just that I'm not used to . . ."

"I'm sorry," she said, interrupting him, but she had no idea what she was sorry for.

"I'm not used to being touched," he said, his eyes still on the sky.

"Oh."

He looked down and she watched him quickly clench and unclench his fist.

"I promise I won't touch you again. Not without warning anyway," she said with a teasing note. She dipped her head to see his expression. He smiled, but it looked like such a sad smile.

"Boone?"

"What."

"I'm going to touch you again," she said, with a teasing lilt. "On your arm. And then I'm going to kiss your cheek. A small little kiss to thank you for showing me this beautiful sunset." He darted her a quick look but remained silent. "Are you ready?"

Again, his mouth curved in a smile.

She touched his arm and got on her tiptoes to kiss his cheek, but instead found her lips against his. It was her turn to pull back. "That was cheating," she said, suddenly finding it difficult to breathe. It was such a small kiss, really, not one that should shoot desire through her like a bolt, but it had—right to her toes.

"I suppose I should have warned you first," he said without even a hint of apology in his tone.

She gulped. "Yes, that would have been nice."

He looked down at her, his gray eyes intense with an expression she could hardly read. "Miss Amelia, I'm going to kiss you."

A little thrill went through her, and she lifted her chin. "All right."

And he did, bringing his mouth against hers, a slow, wonderful kiss that made her knees instantly weak. Carson's kisses had been full of blatant lust, but Boone's was more like warm, dark chocolate spreading slowly through her. Delicious, and beyond divine. He didn't touch her, didn't draw her against him, though she would have willingly gone if he had, but touched only her lips with his.

He pulled back after only a few seconds, an oddly happy expression on his handsome face. "That's better," he said.

"Better than what?" she said, her brain quite foggy, her lips still tingling from what was nothing more than an innocent kiss. Except it didn't feel innocent.

"Better than I imagined," he said, his voice low, and Amelia shivered as her body became intensely, embarrassingly, aroused.

"I think I'll be heading to the hotel now," he said, but he didn't move, and she knew he wanted to kiss her again. She shouldn't want him to, but she did.

"I wish you didn't have to." Oh, goodness, that sounded very much like a wanton invitation, and it was her turn to blush. "I mean, I feel badly that I'm taking your home and forcing you to . . . I didn't mean that I want you to stay or . . . I wouldn't want you to think that I . . . ." She stopped miserably. "You should go," she said, finally.

"I will. I'm finding you far more tempting than I should, Miss Wellesley."

After he'd gone, Amelia went back to the kitchen and sat down at the table, her hands folded in front of her. She shouldn't have kissed him. Shouldn't have flirted at all. Boone was not used to such easy banter, and she did not want him to get the wrong idea about her, about them. Flirting had always been such a natural part of who she was, she had never really given it much thought. Perhaps it was because in London society, flirting was a pastime, as much as playing statue or shopping.

Did he really find her so tempting? She didn't want him to. She didn't want to like his kiss or think him handsome, either, but she did.

She let out a little groan. Why was nothing turning out the way she'd wanted it to? Why couldn't it have been Carson watching the sunset with her from their front porch? It was a mistake, spending so much time with Boone. She was starting to like him too much; she found him far too attractive. The kiss was a mistake, and must not be repeated.

Boone stepped into the saloon and wished, not for the first time, that he was a drinking man. Wouldn't it be nice to disappear for a while, to forget about what a complete idiot he was? Carson wasn't at the bar, for once, and he was glad. He couldn't face his brother just minutes after kissing the woman he'd been engaged to marry.

Instead he saw Enrique Benavente, Agatha's husband, pulling back a whiskey. Enrique, or Ricky as he was known to George's regulars, was a good enough man, though about as lazy as a man could be and still run a chicken farm. He'd grown rather fat in the past few years, a rarity among Texans, who were known for their sinewy bodies brought on by hard lives. Maybe when he was younger he'd had an ounce of ambition, but now he left that particular trait to his two grown sons, both of whom seemed happy enough working from dawn to dusk to eke out a living.

"Hey, Doc."

"Enrique." Boone gave the older man a sharp look; he didn't look well.

"I've been meaning to tell you that one of my boys claims he saw Sam Benson over in Hanover. Still mean as a snake, he said."

"That so," Boone said with deceptive calm. He'd warned Julia's husband not to get within fifty miles of Small Fork, and the tiny town of Hanover was just ten miles away. "Maybe I'll head on over there and have a little talk with him."

"You be careful, Boone. He's a rough character."

"I'm used to rough characters," Boone said softly, and Enrique's cheeks flushed slightly. Everyone in town, if they'd been there for any length of time, knew of the terrible things that had happened to Boone.

"Speaking of rough characters, I'd appreciate it if you don't tell Agatha you seen me here," he said with his mild Spanish accent. "I'm supposed to be sick."

"Are you?"

"Just ate something that don't agree with my stomach," he said, rubbing his chest and flexing his arm. "Too many spicy beans."

The truth was, Enrique didn't look at all well. His face was pale and had a grayish cast. Boone sighed. He didn't know when these people would see him as a doctor who could help them when they got sick. Boone sat down next to the older man, not offended in the least when Enrique ignored him. Everyone in town knew Boone didn't drink—something that was seen as a flaw and not a virtue by most.

"Your arm hurt?"

Enrique immediately stopped rubbing it. "Naw."

"Your chest?"

"Just too many spices. Comes and goes."

Boone stared at Enrique and wondered whether he dared suggest what he was thinking: the man's heart was in trouble and he needed to be in bed, not at a bar drinking. The man was sweating unnaturally.

"Enrique?"

He took another drink and winced, and Boone had a feeling it wasn't the whiskey that had brought on that pained expression. "Agatha made those beans too spicy," he said, putting a fist against his chest.

"Enrique, I need for you to lie down. I don't think it's the spicy food. I think it's your heart."

The older man looked at Boone like he was crazy. "I'm as strong as a bull. Never sick in my life. Why, just yesterday . . ." He stopped talking in mid-sentence, and his face grew deathly pale. He gasped for breath and clutched his chest, letting out a vile curse. He squeezed his eyes shut, both hands fisted against his chest. "Okay. It's better. It's nothing," he managed. He opened his eyes and actually managed to wave George over to pour another drink.

"We've got to get you home." Boone saw raw fear in Enrique's eyes.

"Yeah. Maybe you're right. Just let me catch my breath." The man sat at the stool for a few minutes before getting to his feet gingerly. "I'm feeling better."

"It's your heart, and you're not better. Not yet." Boone had recently read an article written by a New York doctor who was able to tie obesity to deaths from heart disease. The doctor had lectured at the Academy of Medicine not long ago about ways for the overweight to reduce their flesh. Boone would talk to Agatha about treatment, and hopefully she could convince her husband to change his ways.

"I have something I could give you," Boone said, walking slowly beside Enrique, ready to help the man should he need it. "It's been used quite successfully on patients in Ireland, and I feel it has promising results."

"All I need is a good night's rest," Enrique said, but there was a bit less bravado in his tone.

"Let me get my landau," Boone said, practically forcing the man to take a seat on the bench outside the hotel. Three Legs was on the porch, and his tail thumped against the boardwalk.

George stuck his head out. "You okay, Ricky? Don't want to be losing my best customer."

Enrique smiled grimly. "I'm perfleshy fine. An' I don' need any gringo doctor telling me I'm not fine."

Boone halted in his tracks. Either the effects of alcohol had come on suddenly, or Enrique was suffering from more than just a heart attack. His words were slurred, and he slumped suddenly to one side.

"Enrique?"

"I don't feel ri . . ." and he slumped over completely, stopped only by Boone's fast action. He called for the barkeep, and the two of them laid him down on the bench.

"He dead?" George asked.

"No," Boone said, feeling the man's pulse strong in his neck. "But you best go get Agatha. And his sons."

"Aw, no," George said. "I was just joking about losing him." He wiped a hand across his bearded face, looking as if he were the cause of whatever was wrong with his friend.

Boone stayed with Enrique, feeling helpless. A small crowd gathered around him, mostly old men who stood talking quietly, secretly wondering about their own mortality. "You men watch him. I need to go across the street to get my bag," he said, then ran to his office, assuming they'd follow his orders. He exploded into the kitchen, making Amelia scream in fright. She was sitting at the table in near darkness. Hell, he'd forgotten all about her.

"Agatha's husband just collapsed outside the hotel. I need to bring him here. Could you get the room off my office ready for him? The linens are in the cabinet. Lighting a few lamps would help, too."

He didn't wait for a reply, just left her there, stunned and wide-eyed. Even with such an emergency on his hands, he had time to appreciate the fact that he'd actually surprised her into silence. He found the crataegus oxyacantha quickly, glad that he was as meticulous about storing treatments as he was about everything in his life.

The crataegus would treat the heart problem, but now Boone was far more worried that Enrique had also suffered from apoplexy, which had no known successful treatment. In medical school he'd learned that the outcome of such an event was not hopeful for many patients.

He turned to find Amelia behind him, her arms loaded with clean linens, looking worried. "Is it serious, do you think?"

He nodded, putting everything he needed neatly in his bag.

"Is he going to die?" she asked, her voice small and filled with a strange terror. As far as Boone knew, she'd never even met the man.

"I'll know better in a few minutes."

She nodded shakily, then disappeared into the tiny room he'd added for just such a serious patient. Boone didn't have time to wonder about her strange reaction as he headed out the door.

Enrique was surrounded by men, and to Boone's surprise he was sitting up and talking, his voice only slightly slurred. Perhaps it had just been the drink. Then Boone noticed the right side of his body was slightly off. Even his face seemed to sag slightly on the right side.

"I need you men to help me get him to my office," Boone said.

"He ain't exactly skinny," one man grumbled.

"Hell, I don't need any help," Enrique said, and actually attempted to get up, only to find the right side of his body wasn't cooperating.

His two sons, big strapping men, pushed through the crowd, with Agatha and Dulce hurrying up behind. When Agatha saw her husband sitting up, but with something clearly wrong, she threw herself on him, sobbing uncontrollably. Enrique put a gentle hand on her back, patting it, and telling her he was fine. But his voice was unnaturally slurred, and he couldn't move his right hand at all.

"What's wrong with him?" Dulce demanded, as if someone were to blame.

"It's his heart. You boys support his shoulders, and we'll get him to the office," Boone said to Agatha's sons, who hovered in the background stoically.

"We brought the buckboard," his oldest son said. "We can bring him on home."

Boone looked at Agatha with her head buried against her husband's neck, and he nodded. If the man was going to die, and he just might, it was best he did it at home surrounded by his family. "We'll get him home and talk there. You boys bring that buckboard right up to the boardwalk." It would be no easy task to get a man as large as Enrique Benavente up on that wagon.

"I'll help."

Boone turned to see Carson standing beside him looking relatively clean. He smelled of booze but wasn't outwardly drunk, so Boone nodded silently, accepting his brother's help. As they helped the stricken man up, the crowd separated and Boone saw Amelia standing in the street, worrying her hands in front of her, her eyes riveted on Carson. Even as he struggled with the near dead weight of Enrique, Boone felt a sharp, almost painful pull as he watched her watch Carson. She didn't spare him a glance. Not one.


Amelia watched as the buckboard drew away and the small crowd headed back into the hotel. Carson had seen her in the street, and for a terrible moment she felt an overwhelming need to go to him. She almost willed him to look at her, to see the pain he'd caused her. But when he did look up, his expression was completely unreadable.

"Hey Amelia," he said, nodding toward her but not taking one step in her direction. They stood awkwardly for a few minutes, with Boone watching them from the side.

"I have to go to the Benaventes'," Boone said, looking from one to the other. "You're not planning to hurt him, are you, Amelia, 'cause I'm going to be busy tonight and I won't be able to patch him up."

Amelia gave Boone a grateful look.

"I don't suppose a sharp slap to his face will warrant medical attention," she said, and Boone smiled. He looked as if he were going to say more, but he took up his medical bag and headed for the stable to retrieve his horse.

"I'd deserve that slap," Carson said, solemn for once.

"Yes, you would."

"I just wish you weren't so damned pretty," Carson said, taking a step toward her.

Amelia held up a hand. "Don't," she said sharply. "Don't you dare try to charm me right now."

He tilted his hat back on his head and put his hands low on his hips, looking for all the world like that cowboy she'd dreamed of having. His hair was pulled back off his face, and it looked like he'd shaved in the past day or so. Unbelievably, she felt a tug on her heart, which only made her angry with herself, and with him.

"Honey, I know better than to try to charm you,"

he said in that slow drawl she'd fallen in love with in England.

"Good. Because I cannot be charmed by you anymore. The damage has definitely been done."

"I'm sorry about that, I truly am," he said, and for a moment he actually looked sorry. "Does that mean I can't get a kiss from my girl?"

"I'm not your girl," she spat, feeling a rage build in her so swiftly it nearly blinded her. She might be the world's biggest fool, but she would not fall for his insouciant charm again.

"Now don't be getting all mad," Carson said, holding up his hands as if fending her off. "A man can be sorry, can't he?"

Amelia felt her nostrils flare. "And are you sorry?"

"I am."

"You should be," she said with a decisive nod.

"I heard you're heading home soon."

"Not soon enough."

Carson smiled at her and she refused, absolutely refused to smile back. Why couldn't she hate him? She wanted to, she knew she should. Not two minutes before, she could have happily killed him. And yet all it took was one of his smiles and an "I'm sorry," and she could feel her insides melting.

"I don't want you to hate me, Amelia, though I understand if you do," he said, his voice low and sincere.

"I don't hate you," she said softly, her throat closing painfully. "But I don't love you, either." She said it, but wondered if she was lying to him and to herself. She truly didn't know how she felt, beyond the anger and the hurt. Carson was her first love, the man she'd thought she'd spend the rest of her life with, the man she'd thought would father her children. She'd counted on that, dreamed about it, and now everything was gone. "Good night, Carson."

He gave her a crooked smile that reminded her of Boone. "Good night, darlin'."

Amelia hugged her arms around herself as she walked back to the store. It was nearly dark now, just a glow on the horizon hinting that the sun had been up not long ago. In the distance she heard something howl and she shivered, even though it was still warm. She'd heard that howl before but forgot to ask if there were wolves about, and found herself running to the door and closing it quickly behind her, her heart beating frantically as if a wolf were breathing down her neck.

Laughing at her own foolishness, she locked the door and made her way through the dark store toward the apartment, wishing she weren't alone. She didn't like it, but with Dulce refusing to stay with her, there wasn't much she could do. She wished she could forget about propriety for once, and let Boone stay. She'd feel safe and not quite so alone. Then again, she might not be as safe with Boone as she'd thought.

That kiss. She wished it had never happened. She didn't want to have to worry that Boone wanted to kiss her. Or that she wanted to kiss him.

None of it mattered. She'd be home soon, in her own bed, in her own room. She'd go to balls and the opera in London, and she'd meet another man whom she would no doubt want to kiss.

She touched her index finger to her lips and smiled.

\* \* \*

Boone entered his office quietly, carrying a turned-down oil lamp so as not to disturb Amelia. It was three o'clock and he was bone tired. Enrique was sleeping, and though his voice was still slurred and his movements on his right side were uncoordinated, Boone didn't think the man would die. At least not that night. Perhaps in time and with treatment, he would recover enough to live out his years in comfort.

Boone took the medications from his bag and replaced them carefully on their shelves, making certain each label faced front and each was precisely where it should be. He was still working when he heard her bare feet on the tile behind him.

"I'm sorry I woke you," he said without turning.

"You didn't. I couldn't sleep. How is Mr. Benavente?"

Boone put the last of the medications back and turned, almost reluctantly, to answer her. *Damn.* She was so beautiful. She wore a thin, white, high-necked nightgown and wrap; her blond hair was loose and bed-messy. Despite her claims that she hadn't been sleeping, she looked like she'd just woken up. She had a rosy-cheeked drowsy look that made his groin tighten. He turned away, embarrassed that he was unable to control his obvious lust, and pretended to look for something in the cabinet behind him. "I think he'll recover with the right care," he said gruffly.

"How's Agatha?"

*Please go to bed. Please.* "She's crazy with worry. She'll be fine."

"Boone?"

He closed his eyes. "Yes."

"I'm sorry about that kiss. I shouldn't have allowed it."

Boone swallowed heavily. "No. I suppose not."

"As a gentleman, you are required to say you are sorry, too," she said, laughter tingeing her voice.

He turned back to her, unable to find humor in the fact that he was falling in love with her, that he wanted her so badly he could hardly speak. "I'm not sorry."

"Oh."

Her mouth was so soft, so sweet, and at the moment was shaped perfectly for another kiss. Boone clenched his jaw and shoved his hands into his pockets in a desperate attempt to stop himself from reaching out and pulling her into his arms.

"I'm leaving," she said, as if that explained everything. Which, in fact, it did. "I'm going home," she said more forcefully. "There's nothing here for me. I'm going home."

Boone took that cruel blow to his heart like a man. He smiled. "It was just a little kiss," he said, as if mystified why she was making a to-do over such an insignificant thing as that one, perfect kiss.

"Well, yes. I know."

He stood there, looking at her as if he were wondering why she was still pestering him. "Good night, Miss Amelia," he said, still smiling at her as if bemused by her confusion.

A little crease formed between her eyebrows. "Good night."

When she was gone his smile slowly faded. He wasn't an idiot. He knew what she was saying oh so politely: Don't you get any ideas in your head, Boone Kitteridge. I'm not yours, and I never will be.

He understood. He understood enough to feel familiar humiliation wash over him. She'd been flirting with him, and he'd mistaken that for real interest. He had so little experience dealing with women, he was so naïve about such matters, that he'd actually hoped, in the recesses of his heart, she might . . .

Stay.

# Chapter 9

Amelia stood behind the counter drumming her fingers against the smooth, pristine wood. The store had been unusually busy that morning, and Boone had warned her that men were returning from the cattle drives and would likely be stopping in for various sundries.

She didn't mind, for at least it gave her something to do while she waited for the train. She'd hoped she'd get some word from Meremont's staff, at least informing her that they were attempting to get word to Edward. It was likely far too soon for a reply, but she couldn't help hoping.

All morning men came in, looked at her with surprise, quickly pulling their hats from their heads and slicking back their hair. Amelia took their reactions in stride, and in fact, enjoyed flirting with a few of the more charming of them. They were real cowboys, wearing chaps and spurs and well-worn, sweat-stained cowboy hats, and talked in a slow drawl that she was becoming familiar with.

But now the store was quiet and she was growing

rather bored. She perked up when she heard the sound of the train approaching in all its noisy, smoke-spewing glory. She ran to the door to watch, as if she'd never seen a train before, and dreamed of the day she'd get on and head home. She'd never leave Meremont again, never complain about missing balls or suppers in London. She'd stay in her room, wander the grounds, visit her stepaunt, and play with her cousins. Perhaps she'd marry a neighbor, someone she'd overlooked, someone who never lied and truly loved her. The word "home" had become a silent prayer that she said over and over. If she were home it would be as if she'd never been foolish enough to fall in love with a man who didn't love her, as if she'd never come to Texas. That train, now giving a final groan as it came to a stop, was her tie to cool sea breezes, to green grass and shady trees.

From the corner of her eye, she spotted Boone crossing the street from the hotel, and she backed away, feeling awkward in front of him. He must think her a terrible flirt, and perhaps worse, because she'd allowed him to kiss her. It had been a lovely kiss, she had to admit, but entirely improper. She was behind the counter before he pushed the door in.

"I'm expecting some supplies today, so I'd appreciate it if you could stay on in the store for a bit more," he said, not quite meeting her eyes. Apparently he was feeling a bit awkward as well.

"How's Mr. Benavente?"

"Well enough to complain about my orders to keep him in bed," he said. He handed her his bag, meeting her eyes for a brief moment. "Could you put this in my office?"

Amelia took the large bag, surprised at the weight of it, and headed back to the office, putting it on his table. When she returned to the store, Boone was still there, a strange look on his face.

And behind him, unaccountably, stood her brother and his new wife.

Edward was so relieved to see his sister seemingly alive and well, he let her water his shoulder for a few seconds before pushing her gently back so he could get a better look at her. Despite her tear-ravaged face, she looked quite well. And her ring finger quite empty.

"Oh, Edward, I've missed you so much," she said, tears streaming down her face. "What are you doing here? How ever did you receive my telegram so quickly?"

"I received no telegram. I came as soon as I realized my errant little sister had forged a particular letter," he said darkly, and watched as Amelia lowered her head. "And since I don't see a ring, I'm assuming that you and your Mr. Kitteridge have not yet married. You've been here nearly two weeks, now."

"It seems much longer," she said, giving him a watery smile. "I sent the telegram so you could send me funds to return home. Anne stole my money, you see."

"She didn't," gasped Maggie.

"She fell in love with a sailor on the ship and

stayed in New York City," Amelia said. "At the time I was happy for her."

"Why were you coming home?" Edward asked, trying not to let his growing rage show.

Amelia immediately ducked her head again, but not before giving the man standing quietly behind the counter a quick look. "Carson has changed his mind," she said softly.

Edward felt his entire body stiffen with rage. How dare that man ask for his sister's hand and then renege?

"Where is Kitteridge?" he barked.

"I'm Boone Kitteridge," said the tall man standing behind the counter. He held a quiet strength, his gray eyes level and completely emotionless— until they flickered to Amelia. "But I'm assuming you're looking for my brother, Carson."

"Indeed I am."

"He's not here," Amelia said quickly, her facing flushing. "It seems there was a terrible misunderstanding." Edward's heart wrenched a bit when his sister gave him a brave and tremulous smile. "He never did plan to send for me. I don't think he ever planned to marry me at all."

"The hell he isn't," Edward said, nearly shouting.

"Edward." He felt his wife's gentling hand on his arm. "Let's find out what happened before we do anything rash." As always, Maggie's touch instantly soothed him. "Amelia's safe and well and that's all that matters at the moment."

Just then, Amelia remembered her manners. "Edward, may I introduce Dr. Boone Kitteridge. Boone, my brother, Lord Hollings, and his wife, Lady Margaret Wellesley."

A doctor? He thought he'd remembered something about Carson's brother being simple and childlike. Apparently Carson's mendacity had no bounds.

"Please call me Maggie," the countess said, smiling. "I keep looking around for someone else in the room when I hear that title."

"Would this be the same brother Mr. Kitteridge spoke of?" Edward asked.

"Yes." She looked sheepish.

"On behalf of my brother, I would like to apologize for what's happened here," Boone said. "I assure you, Amelia's been kept safe and well."

"I shall be the judge of that, Dr. Kitteridge," Edward said, his voice cool. While he had no issue with Dr. Kitteridge, he very much wanted to throttle the man's brother. "Is Carson in town?"

"Are you carrying a weapon?" the man asked, seemingly without humor.

"He's not going to kill him," Amelia said, then hesitated. "Are you? Oh, Edward, I'm no worse for the wear. We'll take the next train and be home before we know it, and this will all be behind us."

Edward gave his sister a sharp look. She couldn't really be thinking that she could return to England now. Her reputation would be in tatters. Though he would have liked to kill Carson, he knew it would be far better for everyone if the man simply married his little sister as promised.

"I suggest we retire to the estate and discuss this with level heads," Edward said.

At his words, Boone coughed. He almost appeared as if he were trying not to chuckle.

"Carson wasn't completely honest about his situation," Amelia said cautiously.

"What do you mean, Amelia?" Maggie asked, coming to her side and gazing gently at her. Amelia simply dropped her head in abject misery, and Edward watched helplessly as tears splattered onto the cool, red tiles.

"My brother lied about just about everything," the doctor said, and it seemed to Edward that he was nearly as angry with Carson as Edward was. "There's no ranch. My brother earns most of his money gambling."

"Oh, Amelia," Maggie said, pulling Amelia into her embrace. His sister started sobbing against Maggie's shoulder, and curiously, the doctor took a step toward the two women before stopping himself.

"I'll go get Carson," he muttered, as if the sight of Amelia's tears had been the last straw. Or perhaps Dr. Kitteridge realized that if Edward found his brother first, he'd beat the living hell out of him. As the doctor passed Amelia, he pressed a handkerchief into her hand, his expression unreadable. It was, no doubt, not the first handkerchief he'd had to give his sister.

Maggie looked up at Edward, clearly feeling the same helpless rage he now felt. Amelia had gotten herself into an untenable situation, one that had no good resolution. She could either stay here and marry a complete cad, or return home and resign herself to spinsterhood. Neither solution seemed sound.

"Do you still love him?" Edward asked, his voice gentle.

Amelia looked at him, the heartbreak clear in her eyes, even as she shook her head angrily. "I hate him," she said feelingly. "But . . ." And she began to sob again. "Why did everything have to be such an awful lie? I just want to go home, Edward. Please. Take me home." Maggie hugged the girl, her own eyes filling with tears.

"Oh, honey, who knows why some men do what they do?" Maggie asked. "Why, your own brother broke my heart. Remember? And now we're married. Perhaps things will work out with Carson, as well."

Edward scowled at his beautiful wife, completely unsure whether he wanted things to "work out" with the scoundrel who'd broken his little sister's heart.

Boone swore beneath his breath with every step he took toward his brother. If he were a different sort of man, he'd probably enjoy seeing the look on Carson's face when he was informed that his future brother-in-law, an English earl, was in Small Fork. But he was far too concerned for Amelia to care about his little brother at the moment.

He entered the saloon and stalked toward the stairs, not even sparing George a look.

"How's Ricky?" he asked.

"About the same. But you'd best have Sutter prepare a coffin for my little brother."

"The two fancies that stepped off the train?" George yelled, then gave the empty stairs a frustrated look. This town had had more excitement in the past weeks than in the five previous years, and he didn't know what was going on.

Boone opened the door to Geraldine's room without knocking, took two long strides to his brother, who was still lolling about bed at eleven o'clock in the morning, and grabbed him by his long, greasy hair, hauling him up without a word.

"What the . . ."

Boone didn't even let him get out the curse. "Lord Hollings and his lovely wife are in my store. Get your ass dressed and cleaned up and get ready for your wedding, little brother."

Carson's answer was to vomit.


"I'm not doing it. They can't make me. You can't make a man get married against his will," Carson said as they crossed the street.

"You can tell that to Lord Hollings," Boone replied grimly. His brother still reeked of Geraldine's perfume, but at least his hair was pulled back and his face wasn't completely grizzled and he did have on a clean shirt. A pure miracle, that was.

Boone walked in ahead of Carson, keeping the door open for him, then shutting it and pulling down the closed sign after him. The earl and countess were standing by Amelia's side, two angry sentinels staring daggers at his younger brother. Amelia stood between them, looking so sad it tore at Boone's heart. Her eyes were red-rimmed, her cheeks pale, her lips pressed together as if she were fighting tears. Hell, if Hollings didn't punch his brother, he would. He positioned himself behind the counter, away from the others but close enough should someone need assistance. At the moment, he wasn't sure whether he would help Lord Hollings beat his brother, or try to stop him.

"Mr. Kitteridge," Lord Hollings said, his voice clipped, like a pick chipping against ice. "Explain yourself. Explain why my little sister is crying. Explain to me, if you can, why she is not married after you asked for her hand in marriage. Explain to me why you lied about your income, your wealth, even your brother."

Carson swallowed and Boone would have felt sorry for him if he wasn't so angry.

"I suppose," Carson said, drawing out the words. "I'd never seen any girl as pretty as Amelia, and lost my head for a bit."

To his disgust, Boone saw Amelia's expression soften, as if she were falling for Carson's smooth-talking ways.

"And your heart? Did you lose that as well?" This from the countess.

Carson didn't hesitate. "No, ma'am. No."

Amelia let out a little sound and Boone flinched.

"I didn't send for her. She came on her own," Carson said, losing his apologetic tone.

"I'm quite aware of that," Lord Hollings said. "However, it was also clear that the two of you had an understanding. Amelia believed in her heart that she was traveling to Texas to marry her fiancé. She informed everyone she knew of this fact. She cannot return to England and hope to live anything like a normal life. She is, to put it perfectly clear, ruined."

"But that's not true," Amelia said, her eyes wide with disbelief. "I'll simply say that . . . that . . ."

"What? That you traveled to Texas, unescorted, and then were spurned by this man? What do you think society will say or think? You've been here for two weeks, Amelia, two weeks without a proper chaperone. It doesn't matter if you've behaved properly or not, the appearance of it all is extremely damaging."

"I don't care."

Lord Hollings let out a puff of frustration, and Boone was, frankly, surprised that he seemed to be trying to convince Amelia to marry Carson, despite knowing he'd lied about nearly everything.

"But you will care when you are not invited anywhere, not even by your friends. You will care when you see their children, their homes, their lives, while you will be a spinster with a sullied past." Lord Hollings took a breath. "I blame myself. I never should have allowed him to court you. I should have listened to my instincts. I am to blame, and I will have this fixed."

Amelia shook her head, denying everything her brother said. "It is my fault, and I alone will suffer the consequences. I don't want to marry. I just want to go home."

"Amelia," Maggie said softly. "You say that now, but someday you will feel differently. There will be stories about you, most of them unkind. I know what it's like to pretend none of it matters, but once you are tied to scandal, it is impossible to escape. And it hurts, terribly so. I can tell you truthfully that I never would have married if I'd remained in this country. You must know that no respectable family will allow their son to court you now. I know it seems terribly cruel to say to you when you've done nothing worse than follow your heart, but you cannot believe it will all just disappear." The countess gave Carson a pleading look. "Surely, the two of you must share something upon which you can build a marriage."

Carson looked on, a growing expression of panic on his face. "I'm sorry for what I did. I didn't mean for her to come here. It was all a big mistake," he said, his voice shaking with emotion. "But I can tell you that I'm not getting married. I'm just not, an' you can't make me."

Amelia's face tightened and Boone's gut wrenched. How could his brother be so cruel?

"Well, someone is going to bloody hell marry my sister, by God," Lord Hollings shouted, and Amelia squeezed her eyes shut as if in pain.

Boone stared at his brother's mulish expression, at the raw despair on Amelia's face, and opened his mouth, truly not knowing what he was going to say until he said it.

"I'll marry her."

# Chapter 10

Four sets of eyes turned to Boone in disbelief, and Boone wished he'd just kept his damned mouth shut.

"Oh, Boone," Amelia said, clearly angry. "Don't be ridiculous."

Carson let out a bark of laughter, quickly stifled, and Boone could feel his cheeks flush with almost painful humiliation. What a fool he was to say such a thing.

"My outburst was meant to be rhetorical," Lord Hollings said thoughtfully.

"I was just . . . I don't know what I was thinking," Boone said, nearly wincing at how absurd he sounded.

"Boone saves things," Amelia said, staring at him. "He has a three-legged dog and a one-eyed cat. He's *nice*." She said the last as if it were some sort of horrible affliction. All Boone felt was intense relief that Amelia hadn't taken his proposal seriously, that she'd thought he was simply trying to save her from a desperate situation. It would be far worse if she knew the truth.

"Nice is good," the countess said, looking amused.

"I don't need saving," Amelia said, even though everyone in the room would've disagreed.

"I think we've discussed the situation enough for now. This is all quite unexpected, and we're all tired. At least I am," the countess said. "Could you direct us to the nearest accommodation, Dr. Kitteridge? We can stay wherever Amelia has been staying."

Boone nearly grimaced. He didn't want to admit that Amelia was staying in his home, for no doubt that would seem exceedingly inappropriate. At the moment, though, he didn't have a choice. "I've been staying at the hotel; Amelia's been staying here."

"In a store? Alone?" the countess asked.

"I have an apartment out back. And she did have a chaperone while Carson was here."

"She quit," Amelia grumbled. "She didn't like me."

"Dulce doesn't like anyone," Carson put in cheerfully. All he got for his comment was a collective glare from everyone in the room.

"You've been staying in a single man's home alone?" Lord Hollings asked, then wiped a hand over his face as if this bit of news was simply more than he could take.

"It's been completely proper," Amelia said. "Well, not completely. But as proper as we could make it without throwing Boone out of his home entirely."

Boone wanted to remind her of the kiss, but

didn't think she'd much appreciate his input at the moment.

"Boone would never touch Amelia," Carson said. While Boone was somewhat gratified by his brother's defense, his manhood didn't appreciate the blow. "My point is," Boone said forcefully, "that the hotel is completely unsuitable. It only has three rooms, and one of those is occupied. I would be happy to have you stay in my home until you leave on Tuesday."

"That's when the next train departs," Amelia put in rather mournfully.

"Well, if you're all done here, I'll be headin' back to the hotel," Carson said heartily.

"I'm not done with you, sir," Lord Hollings said.

Carson tilted his hat back on his head, and although he still smiled, his eyes had grown hard. "I'm done," he said, jabbing a thumb against his own chest. "You understand? I'm done." Lord Hollings stared after him with mute, helpless rage.

"By God, he's lucky we're not still in England," he said. He stood with his fists clenched, his entire body taut as if he were straining to hold himself back from murder.

"This is a disaster," the countess said, looking worriedly at Amelia. "I feel I should accept some of the blame, as well. This is far worse than I imagined."

Lord Hollings abruptly turned to Boone, who watched as Amelia fell into her sister-in-law's embrace, fresh tears falling down her face. "Was that proposal serious?" he asked.

"No!" Amelia shouted.

"Yes, sir, it was," Boone said quietly.

"No, Boone. I won't let you. I won't marry you.

I don't love you, and you don't love me. I'm not even certain I like you." She smiled to temper her words, but it did little to ease the meaning behind them.

Boone clenched his jaw and pretended her words didn't wound him, but hell, they did tear a bit at his heart.

"Where can we have a private conversation?" Lord Hollings asked.

Amelia stood clutching Maggie, feeling completely helpless as her life spiraled away from her. "This can't be happening," she whispered. "I just want to go home. Why won't you let me go home?"

It was as if she hadn't spoken. Her brother followed Boone out of the room and at that moment, she hated both men. Her brother for taking Boone's proposal seriously, and Boone for making it. She could never be happy here.

"Maggie, make him listen. I hate it here. I hate everything about it." She'd thought Maggie would continue to embrace her, but the older women grasped her shoulders and gave her a hard shake.

"Enough," she said harshly. "You've made your bed and now you must lie in it. You cannot blame anyone but yourself for your foolish decision to follow Carson here without word from him. You knew your brother was against this, but you carried on and on as if you'd die if you couldn't be with Carson. And your brother gave in, against his better judgment, because he believed Carson had made good on his proposal. Following Carson here without his sending for you was completely foolhardy." Maggie took a calming breath and gentled her tone. "I know what it's like to desperately love a man who leaves you. Of all people, I do understand. But now *you* must understand the repercussions of your decisions."

Amelia stared at Maggie, her blue eyes looking huge in her tear-ravaged face. "You're right," she said, closing her eyes. "Oh, why did I do it? Why? It was as if an insanity came over me. I missed him so. I loved him and when he didn't write to send for me, I went a bit mad I think. And now I'm here and I just want to go home." She swallowed. "But I can't, can I?"

Maggie shook her head. "Not without terrible consequences." She sighed. "Boone is handsome. And a doctor is a perfectly respectable profession. Do you care for him at all?"

"I hadn't really given it much thought. I suppose I enjoy his company," she said hesitantly. She couldn't admit to Maggie her rather strong physical attraction to him, that kiss that melted her bones. But she'd never thought beyond that kiss, never thought that Boone might be harboring stronger feelings for her. She certainly didn't have any. He was Carson's brother and she'd had fun teasing him, but that was the extent of their relationship. Now she was supposed to marry him? It was all rather horrifying.

Edward followed Dr. Kitteridge down a nondescript passageway ending in a courtyard that was about as surprising as the doctor's proposal had been. Here was a shaded rectangle of color, with a bubbling fountain of crystal water. It was a small bit of paradise in an otherwise gloomy landscape.

He didn't know what to make of the man or the proposal, but he'd seen small indications that Boone's interest in Amelia went beyond his sister's claim of altruism.

"Much cooler here," Edward said, pulling at his collar. By God, he'd thought Newport hot, but this was unbearable. Dr. Kitteridge gave him a bemused look.

"Your sister complains about the heat, too," he said. He looked toward distant mountains shimmering weakly in the heat of the midday sun, his expression thoughtful.

"Do you love her?"

The doctor continued staring at the mountains. "Seems I'm going in that direction," he said with great reluctance.

"I see."

"I think she could make me happy. The thing is, I don't know if I could make her happy. I'm pretty much the opposite side of a coin compared to Carson, and she loves him fiercely. Maybe she would be better off going back home."

Edward cleared his throat. "I wonder if you could answer some questions, Dr. Kitteridge."

"You can call me Boone. Everyone does."

This Kitteridge brother had a slow, almost melodic way of speaking, as if every word were carefully chosen. He truly did seem the polar opposite of his brother. "Yes. Boone. How old are you?"

"Twenty-eight."

Edward raised his eyebrows. He'd thought the other man a bit younger. "I thought you were Carson's older brother."

"I am. By four years."

Edward tried to hide his surprise. He never would have thought Carson only twenty-four years old. He looked a decade older than that. "And you are a doctor."

"I received my medical degree from Tulane University in Louisiana three years back. I inherited this store and have my offices in back."

Edward smiled. "So your father was a merchant, then," he said, using a lofty word for the rather small establishment.

"My father was the town drunk," Boone said without inflection. "The man who owned this store raised me from the time I was ten years old." Boone finally turned toward Edward, his dark gray eyes like flint. "What exactly are you trying to determine, sir?"

"Whether you would be suitable for Amelia. She is the sister and granddaughter of an earl, and has been raised as a lady. I've already made one terrible mistake, and I don't want to make another."

Boone let out a humorless chuckle. "Amelia doesn't want to marry me. Shouldn't that decide the matter for you?"

"Letting my sister decide what is right for her has thus far been disastrous. I have failed in my duty to her and have been far too lenient, but Amelia has always touched a soft spot in my heart. I don't think I should make the same mistake again." Edward looked at the man, wishing he could see inside to his soul. He loved his sister and wanted her to be happy. But he truly couldn't see her happy in this place or with this man, if he were to be honest. Boone was entirely too serious for his little sister, and he feared she'd wilt living with such a dour man in a place like Small Fork. "Would you consider moving your practice?"

For a moment, Edward thought he detected some strong emotion in the other man's eyes, but it was quickly masked before he could be certain. "I've never considered such a thing," he said carefully.

"Yes, but would you? Frankly, sir, from what I've seen of this town, it does not seem to be a very welcoming place. It's not at all what Amelia is used to, not what she expected, to be sure."

Boone felt a sudden surge of unexpected joy. To leave Small Fork, to start new—it was something he'd thought about deep in the night when he awoke, sweating hard, his throat still hurting from his screams. But the plain fact was he could not leave Julia alone, unprotected, at the mercy of this mean place. He had no doubt, none at all, that once word reached her husband that Boone was gone, Sam Benson would return and finish what he'd started. And Julia wasn't well, her wounds still needed tending, and who would do that if he were gone?

"I don't see the need to leave, sir."

Edward gave him a sharp look. "Even if it meant my sister's happiness? I could use a young physician in Hollings. The one we have now is quite old and ready to retire. You'd be kept busy with your practice and Amelia would be close to her family and all that she loves."

Boone swallowed down the hope forming in his throat. England seemed about as far away from Small Fork as a man could get, but he couldn't leave. Not now. "I appreciate the offer," he said, meaning it with every fiber of his being. "I'd like to ask you a question, if I might."

Edward nodded his consent.

"Would Amelia's life really be that terrible if she returned home alone?"

Edward looked grim. "I'm afraid it would. Though things are changing, women of our class have very few options if they do not marry. My sister has a joy about her. Usually," he added, for Amelia had seemed less than joyous this day. "I would hate to see her alone, a spinster without a home of her own. She loves children, and I know she's always dreamed of a family. She's been alone much of her life, you see. Our parents died when she was quite young, and she lost a sister she adored, as well. I would like to see her well married and happy."

"I don't want you to force her into anything," Boone said. He'd never thought to marry, to have children of his own. An unnamed dread nagged at him, made it impossible for him even to picture such a thing as children running about his feet, a wife in his bed. God, he wished he hadn't said anything about marriage. What a stupid fool he was to think for even a moment that he could have a normal life. "Let's just forget I said anything. Amelia can do better than either me or Carson. She'll just end up hating me for forcing this on her."

Edward looked at the man and felt a strong empathy. He knew what it was like to love a woman desperately and believe that woman did not love you. Unrequited love was hardly romantic; it was the purest torture. "To be honest, I don't believe my sister is capable of such a dark emotion as hate."

* * *

"I hate him," Amelia said fiercely.

"That's a sin, dear," Maggie said dryly.

Amelia gave her a dark look. "I feel as if I was one step away from putting my foot on a ship to go home and he's thrown up a hundred-foot barricade. I just know Edward's talking to him right now and arranging our wedding day and honeymoon. Perhaps they're agreeing upon how many children we shall have."

"Would that be so terrible?"

"I want to go home."

"Yes, dear, I know. What if you did? With Boone?"

Amelia gave her a frustrated look. "But I don't want to marry Boone. I don't love him and he doesn't love me."

Maggie waved a hand at her as if that didn't matter in the least.

"I want what you and Edward have," Amelia said, hoping to appeal to Maggie's sentimental side.

"No," Maggie said. "You want what you thought you had with Carson, which was a fantasy."

Amelia scowled, mostly because she knew Maggie was right. "I don't love him."

"Yes, you keep saying that," Maggie said, implying that she was protesting too much. "But I do not believe the nonfeeling is mutual. I suspect that Boone may indeed love you."

For some reason, Maggie's words made Amelia's heart beat a bit faster. But what rubbish. Boone had kissed a pretty girl at sunset because . . . because . . . "Why would you say such a thing?"

Maggie shrugged. "Just intuition. The way he

gave you that handkerchief, the way he took a step toward you when you started to cry, as if he wanted to be the one to comfort you. The way he shot daggers at Carson when he refused to marry you. Honestly, Amelia, if he's not in love with you, he's halfway there."

"Hmph."

"Yes, indeed," Maggie said, smiling in victory. "And if that is the case, think how crushed he must have been when you told him he was being ridiculous."

"Oh, but he couldn't have meant it," Amelia said, somewhat uncertainly. "I'd feel positively beastly if he did mean it. I'm certain he was simply trying to save me. What did he look like when I said that?"

"Honestly? I thought he looked rather crushed at first," Maggie said gently. "He did make a good recovery, almost as if he was expecting such a reaction."

"Now I do feel beastly," Amelia said. "I would never want to intentionally hurt him. He may come across as rather gruff, but he's extremely nice. Too nice, really. He never even charges his patients, and there's one woman who's been getting all her groceries for years for free."

"And the three-legged dog?"

Amelia nodded. "He really is very nice."

"And handsome."

It was Amelia's turn to shrug, as if she hadn't noticed just how beautiful a man he was, which of course she had. She was a living, breathing woman, after all.

\* \* \*

That night, when everyone had found a bed, Amelia lay in her room staring out the window at the unimaginable number of stars above her. She couldn't sleep, her mind going over and over the day's events. She hadn't had a moment alone with Boone, who had barely been able to meet her eyes when she did find him looking her way.

They'd eaten at the hotel, before it became filled with the rowdy cowboys that were starting to flood home from the cattle drives. Even at this moment, though her bedroom faced away from the hotel, she could hear someone banging on a piano that clearly needed tuning, and the loud, drunken singing of men. They seemed a harmless lot, but Boone didn't want to expose his guests to their revelry.

Boone. Since he'd proposed, she kept imagining what her life would be like with him, whether she could come to love him. And she realized as she lay looking at the stars, that she would. How could a woman not love a man as good and kind and handsome as Boone? It would be a calmer, gentler love than she would have had with Carson, certainly.

Carson. She scowled into the night. Carson, she reminded herself, had never loved her, so any comparison between the brothers was fruitless. She seemed to have lost control of her life the minute Carson Kitteridge walked into the ballroom at the Christmas Ball just eight months before.

As if that thought conjured him, Carson slipped into her room, nearly frightening her to death. "What are you doing here?" she whispered harshly, sitting up, her heart racing.

Carson sat at the foot of her bed, his hands braced

on his thighs as if he was ready to lunge up at a moment's notice. "I've come to say good-bye. I'm headin' west to California, and I won't be back." He let out a breath. "Ever."

Despite her resolve to remain unaffected by this man she thought she'd loved so desperately, her eyes pricked with unshed tears. "Good-bye, then."

"Before I go, I need to say something. I need . . ." He paused as if forming his words carefully, which was so unlike Carson. "I need to say I'm sorry. And I need to tell you something about Boone."

"I won't marry him," Amelia said, even though she knew, deep down, she would. But the broken part of her heart still hoped that Carson would magically turn into the man she'd thought he was.

"I think you should," Carson said quietly, and Amelia's heart broke all over again. "I think you should because you'll never find a better man than my brother. And because he deserves to be loved."

"But I don't love him," Amelia said.

"You should," Carson said with uncharacteristic fierceness. "If he asks, you say yes. And act happy. And make sure he never knows you don't love him. Can you do that for me?"

Tears spilled over, and Amelia wondered if Carson had any idea how painful it was to hear him urge her to marry another man. How could he be so utterly unfeeling? "I don't know if I can marry him, but if I do, I will, of course, do as you say," she said honestly.

"I want to tell you a story," Carson said, hiking one knee onto the bed so he could face her. "My father loved me somethin' fierce. I was the apple of his eye and I loved him back just as much. But I'm ashamed of myself, I truly am. Because my father hated Boone. To this day, I don't know why and I expect I never will. Boone was the good one, the one who made sure I was fed, who cleaned up my messes. He tried so hard to please my father, but he never could. Ever.

"My father would beat Boone almost daily and say the most awful things. And Boone would just try harder. And I watched and figured Boone deserved what he got. I was just a little kid and my daddy was always nice to me. He'd lift me up on his shoulders and carry me around town and Boone would be trailin' behind us. I didn't know any better, you see."

Amelia made a small sound, but Carson ignored her and kept talking.

"One night we were all eating supper and my father was in a rare good mood. I remember feeling so happy that he wasn't yelling at Boone. I must have been six or seven and I let out some gas."

Amelia could see Carson smiling in the darkness.

"Well, my daddy put down his fork and laughed and laughed. And we both laughed, even Boone, and it was the best sight I'd seen in a long time." His smile slowly disappeared. "I don't know what he was thinkin', probably that he wanted to please my daddy, I don't know, but Boone lit off some gas himself. And my father backhanded him so hard, he flew off his chair."

"Oh, no," Amelia gasped. "Poor Boone."

"Yeah. He just got back up on his chair and finished eating. He didn't even cry, but he was shakin' so hard he could hardly get the food to his mouth. I remember thinking for the first time that what my daddy had done was so unfair. I'd never felt that before. Guess I was too wrapped up in being the favored son. Not long after, Boone moved in with Mr. Johnson and I hardly saw him at all."

Carson turned silent, staring off into the darkness.

"Why did you tell me this?"

"You have to know what makes a man to understand him," he said simply. "He never deserved all those bad things, but I have a feeling that deep down inside, he thinks he did. I just want something good for him, just one good thing."

Amelia let out a small, sad laugh. "And you think I'm that good thing?"

"You could be." Carson leaned over and kissed Amelia's forehead. "Good-bye, Amelia." And then he stood and walked from the room, closing the door quietly behind him.

# Chapter 11

Amelia sat in the kitchen with her brother and Maggie playing piquet to pass the time. In Small Fork, the amusements were few and far between. In the fall, one of the ranchers held a Harvest Ball that all the ranchers from miles around attended, but few people in the town proper went. It was a hard-scrabble life for most, trying to eke out a living from a harsh land that its inhabitants would die protecting.

Amelia simply didn't understand Texans, and probably never would. Julia, for example, had told her during her last visit that she would never leave Small Fork, and especially not Texas. "Why would I?" she asked, as if Amelia were asking her to leave paradise.

Paula Brentwood was back, unhappy as ever, with her equally unhappy husband, who'd dragged her home from Fort Worth. She'd been in the store that morning and Amelia had been so happy to see her. She hadn't said a word that she might be staying in Small Fork as Boone's wife, because other than blurting out his proposal, Boone hadn't formally asked her.

She hadn't seen Boone yet that day, for he'd gone over to the Benaventes' to check up on Enrique and hadn't yet returned. Amelia was about to deal when she heard the distinct tinkle of the store's bell.

"It seems Boone has a customer," she announced, then went into the store, hesitating slightly when she realized it was Boone.

"Good morning," she said, trying—and failing—to sound normal.

"Morning." He took off his hat and scrubbed at his hair, mussing it up in a boyish manner.

"How is Mr. Benavente?"

"Failing." That one word held so much pain, it made Amelia's heart lurch. "I don't think he'll last the day."

"How is Agatha?"

Boone shook his head as if angry. "Not good. Not only is her husband dying, but Dulce hightailed it off, chasing after Carson."

"Oh, dear."

"I swear I hope she finds him. No two people deserve each other more than that pair." He gave her a sharp look as if suddenly remembering that she herself had "hightailed it" after Carson not long ago.

Boone began wiping down the pristine counter. "Any customers this morning?"

"Just Mrs. Brentwood looking rather glum. I must say I was happy to see her, though I don't think she was as pleased to see me."

"Guess this isn't really the place for some women," Boone said, his words full of hidden meaning.

"No. It isn't," Amelia said softly.

Some emotion flickered in his eyes before he turned away, neatly folding his dusting cloth and putting it in a drawer. "About that proposal . . ." he started.

"You don't have to explain. I know you didn't mean it," Amelia said quickly.

Boone turned to her, his eyes burning, and for a moment Amelia thought he looked furious. "I did mean it," he said.

"Oh."

"I'd like an answer."

Amelia swallowed. "Now?"

His mouth curved just a bit. "Now is as good a time as any."

Amelia looked around her helplessly, seeing her world shrink to the size of this tiny town, this neat little store, this one man. She felt as if she were being squeezed and squeezed into a box with all sides closing in on her. "I can't," she said finally, and watched as his eyes grew dull and cold.

"All right then. The next train out is tomorrow. Start your packing."

Amelia let out a laugh. "I didn't mean I can't marry you, I meant I can't give you an answer right away."

Boone felt relief wash over him.

"We need to talk over some things first," she said pertly.

Then she smiled up at him and he felt the urge to drop to his knees and beg her to stay with him. He just might have if he'd truly thought it would work. For the first time in his life, he had a tormenting glimpse of something sweet and wonderful, but he wasn't such a fool to believe the dream could come true.

"First," she said, pulling back on her index finger, "that was not a proper proposal you made. I'm afraid even if the answer was yes, I would have to say no simply on those grounds. Second," she said and pulled on another finger, "as much as I admire your ability to live, work, and conduct commerce all in the same building, I would like to have a separate house, if possible."

Boone grinned, feeling himself fall more and more in love with every word she uttered. "That all sounds acceptable."

"And finally," she said, as if he hadn't said a word, "I have to find out if you can kiss properly." She raised an eyebrow as if she were issuing a challenge.

"I think I could try," Boone said, feeling his cheeks flush like some schoolboy. "I don't suppose that other kiss counts as proper?"

"It was quite adequate," Amelia said primly. "But I do believe you can do better."

Boone had never flirted with a girl in his life, and he wasn't sure how to go about such a thing. "I think you'd better show me what you mean," he said slowly, saying the first thing that came to mind.

Her eyes widened. "Here?"

"No one's in the store."

"But someone could walk in any moment."

"Then we'd better get hidden," he said, leading her behind a shelf. "Now. Go ahead with your lesson."

Amelia narrowed her eyes. "You're making fun of me."

Boone had been smiling, but his grin slowly faded. "Amelia," he started, then floundered, ducking his head down. How could a man go about telling a girl that he was completely without experience when it came to lovemaking? What was it about Amelia that made him even consider such an admission?

"Go on."

"You're the only girl I've ever kissed."

It was as if he'd just told her he had two heads, that's how stunned she looked. "But you're so handsome," she blurted, then covered her mouth. "Well, you're not offensive," she amended. "All right, you're quite stunning and surely you know it."

His grin was back. "Stunning," he said, liking the sound of it.

"Not that stunning," she said, her eyes sweeping his face as if examining a painting. Her expression changed then, from teasing to something more serious. She reached up and touched his cheek with soft fingertips, and his eyes fluttered closed for a moment. If such a simple touch could affect him so, he wondered what making love to this woman would do. "No, I'm wrong again. You *are* beautiful."

Her lovely mouth curved up into the gentlest smile. "I'm going to kiss you now, Dr. Kitteridge."

She rose up on her tiptoes and, putting her hand to the back of his neck, drew him down for a kiss, drew him toward heaven. She smelled like summer should, clean and fresh and pretty, and she felt like a woman should, soft and warm and lovely.

He moved his mouth against her, pure instinct,

pure male need, artless and hungry. The only thing he knew was that he wanted more, wanted to kiss her forever, wanted to taste her and touch her and bury himself inside her. He let out a moan and thrust a hand against the wall to keep from falling as he felt the first timid touch of her tongue against his. Her hands clutched at his neck, pulling him close, and she let out sounds that nearly drove him mad with need.

He was growing painfully hard and tried to resist the urge to pull her against his arousal, but she was so pliant, so willing, he found himself putting one hand around her lower back, the other still braced on the wall, and pulling her toward him.

"Oh, Boone," she breathed against his mouth. "Touch mc."

"Where?" he asked, nearly in a panic. Where should he touch her that was even remotely proper? They were in his store, after all, and anyone could walk in on them. He hadn't thought past the idea that he wanted to kiss her. But this was more than a kiss, this was blatantly, wonderfully, frighteningly carnal. "Where should I touch you?" he said, not recognizing his own voice.

"Wherever you want," she answered, kissing his neck, moving against him.

*Wherever I want? Is she insane?*

"What I want to do and what I can do are completely different things," he said, breathing harshly.

Amelia stepped back flat against the wall, looking horrified. "Oh, goodness," she said, holding her hands against her cheeks. She looked at him as if he were some sort of magician who had cast an evil spell upon her. Then she giggled, gazing up at him.

"Oh, Boone, that was quite, quite wonderful. I do believe that was a proper kiss."

And then something came over him, or perhaps it was just the rubbery feeling in his knees, but he fell to one knee and pulled her against him, his face turned, his eyes shut.

"Marry me," he said, lifting his gaze to her, not caring that his eyes burned, that he was laying his heart at her feet.

"Yes, I will marry you."

A woman would have to be made of stone to reject such a proposal after such a kiss. And as Amelia had found out, she was not made of stone.

Her physical reaction to his kiss was nothing less than astounding. Had she really begged him to touch her *anywhere?* If he had, she would have welcomed it, helped him, led him down a path that could only end one way. When he got down on one knee and asked her to marry him, it seemed so right.

But now, standing awkwardly beside a man she hardly knew in front of her brother and his wife, she felt all the uncertainties come flooding back.

"Boone has asked me to marry him and I have agreed," she said, unaware that her voice sounded strained, as if someone were holding a knife to her throat and forcing the words from her mouth.

Maggie let out a squeal and rushed over to Amelia, pulling her in for a hug. "I'm so happy for you," she said, as if the announcement were a total surprise. Then she turned to Boone and pulled him in for a rather awkward sisterly hug. "Welcome to the family."

"You've made the right decision," Edward said, far more formally. He shook Boone's hand solemnly.

If anyone thought it odd that the engaged couple looked strangely unhappy, no one said a word.

"We could go to Abilene and get married there," Boone was saying, which made it all more real. "Or I can fetch a preacher from Hanover."

She wished he would kiss her again to make her feel that wonderful sense of rightness. A creeping panic began to envelop her, a silent scream that she had just agreed to change her life irrevocably. She would live in Texas with the man standing next to her, a man she didn't love, but who could at least kiss well. When Edward and Maggie got on the train to leave, she would likely never see them again. She wouldn't see her little cousins; they'd never know their aunt.

For some reason, those thoughts hadn't occurred to her when she'd left England all those weeks ago to marry Carson. Which was why it was perfectly understandable when she burst into tears and threw herself into her brother's arms, completely unmindful of how this would make Boone feel.

"Pre-wedding jitters," Maggie said with false cheer.

Edward held Amelia, patting her on her back while she shed copious tears. "It's been a trying two days," he said weakly.

Boone stood there like a fool watching the woman he was going to marry sob into the shoulder of her brother not seconds after announcing, rather reluctantly he thought, that they were getting married. Where was the woman who'd been so willing in his arms? At least he'd thought she'd been willing. Perhaps her brother was putting undue force on her to wed him, and he was simply gullible enough to believe she wasn't horrified by the thought.

"I'm not crying because of Boone," Amelia said, her voice watery. "I'm crying because I'm going to miss you and the children. It's so final. I never thought about it, not really." She looked at Boone, her blue eyes wet with tears, her dark lashes spiky. "Oh, Boone, what you must think?"

Boone shook his head and lied. "I'm not thinking anything."

She gave him a stern look. "Yes, you are. But you're wrong. I do want to marry you."

Though he wasn't convinced, Boone accepted her words at face value. "I have to go check on Mr. Benavente. Can you watch the store for me?"

Amelia gave him an uncertain smile. "Of course."

After he'd gone, Maggie looked at Amelia with a bit of exasperation. "You have to start being more aware of how your actions affect others," Maggie said. "Men are far more fragile than we women would wish. Honestly, if I give your brother the tiniest frown, he thinks I've fallen out of love."

"Not true," Edward said. "It takes a scowl, not simply a frown."

"I shall be a terrible wife," Amelia moaned. "And of course, Boone shall be the perfect, kind, thoughtful husband. I shall make him miserable."

Edward laughed. "Do you know he told me the opposite? That you would make him happy, but he would likely make you unhappy?"

"He said that? It would be nice if we made each other happy," she said with a hint of melancholy.

"I'm certain you'll both be happy," Edward said, but his words sounded forced and his smile didn't reach his eyes.


In August when the sun was the hottest, all the businesses in Small Fork, such as they were, closed down for a few hours. During that time, people ate cold lunches and tried to do as little as possible. Maggie, Edward, and Amelia sat by the fountain and held their hands in the cool water, periodically bathing their faces and necks.

"It's rather hellish, is it not?" Edward asked.

"I'm getting a bit used to it," Amelia said, sounding amazed. "When I first got here, I actually fainted. Can you imagine me fainting? Of course, I was wearing wool and a corset. I've learned that summer muslin is the only fabric one should wear in Texas. Boone's not bothered a bit by the heat."

"It's like sitting in an oven," Maggie said.

"I do hope for your sake that Boone considers my offer to move to Hollings."

"What?" Amelia asked, feeling a thrill of excitement.

"He didn't tell you?"

"No. He didn't," Amelia said, her heart sinking slowly. Certainly if Boone planned to move to England he would have mentioned it when he'd asked her to marry him.

"I spoke out of turn."

"Yes, you did," Maggie said, glaring at her husband.

Feeling depressed, Amelia let her hand trail in the water. "I think I shall visit with a friend of mine, if you don't mind."

"We'll be here. Cooking."

Amelia laughed, appreciating that her brother was trying to make her feel better. "I'll return when you are medium well. Perhaps one hour?"

There was something wonderfully calming about Julia Benson and her little fairy-tale house. Amelia had been to visit her new friend twice now, and this time Julia opened the door and stepped back without a word.

"What has happened?" Julia asked, when Amelia sat down in her only chair.

"It seems I'm engaged," she said, sounding rather stunned.

"Carson came back?"

Amelia felt her cheeks blush. How unseemly it would look to people to have her marry the brother of the man she'd come to marry. "No. Someone . . . else."

Even with her scarf on, she could tell Julia had a puzzled expression.

"For goodness sakes, Julia, it's Dr. Kitteridge."

"Boone?" she asked, as if there was more than one Dr. Kitteridge living in Small Fork.

"It seems that is the best solution to my dilemma. I cannot return home without a husband and he did propose. Twice."

Julia lowered her head slightly and became quite

still. "You're leaving. With Boone?" She clutched her hands together in her lap so fiercely, Amelia frowned.

"No, we're staying here," Amelia said, suddenly wondering if Julia had more than a doctor-patient attachment to Boone. It would certainly be understandable, given how kind Boone had been.

The older woman relaxed visibly, making Amelia's heart wrench for her. If she were in love with Boone, no doubt her heart was breaking to hear news of the engagement.

"You would certainly miss your doctor," Amelia said evenly.

"Yes, I would. But it's more than that," Julia said, rising and going to the home's only window. "Boone does more than care for my face. He protects me."

Julia stood in silhouette, the late afternoon sun glowing around her, the bright glass pieces making her look almost as if she were standing underwater in a fantastical colorful pool. The vision of her was in stark contrast with her tense body, the terrible way she clutched her arms around herself.

"He protects you? From whom?"

"As long as Boone is here, my husband won't come back. He's scared of Boone."

Amelia raised her brows in surprise. "Of Boone?"

"Maybe I'm wrong. Maybe he's dead somewhere. I hope so. But I feel safer with Boone here. I'm glad you're staying, and I'm glad you're marrying him instead of Carson."

Amelia let out a laugh. "That's nice to hear. For a moment I thought you held a tendre for Boone."

"No. I'm no good for anyone anymore," she said,

and Amelia wondered again if Julia was in love with Boone.

Julia turned away from the view of the endless plains she was staring at. "Just thought I'd tell you the truth. Carson is a good man, but he'd be a terrible husband. People don't know what I see. They think just because I got hurt that I can't hear or understand what's going on." She shrugged. "People are plain stupid sometimes."

"Do you really think your husband wants to hurt you again?"

"He wants to kill me," she said simply. "He meant to the first time, and I think he won't quit 'til he does. He will, too. Someday. Even with Boone here. There are rumors he's been in Abilene, just biding his time. I've heard he was in Hanover for a time. That's just one town over. I got me a gun, just in case. And I can see people coming from any direction here."

"Why would he kill you? You must be mistaken."

"Sometimes I wish he would show up so I could kill him first," she said calmly. "So. When are you getting hitched?"

Amelia laughed, liking the way Julia so abruptly changed the subject. "I don't know. Soon, I suppose. I'm quite certain my brother wants to see me safely married before he continues his wedding trip. And Small Fork was not on their original itinerary."

"Boone'll probably go fetch that preacher over in Hanover. He comes here once a month and gives us a sermon in the hotel. Hanover's not but a two-hour ride west. You could get married tomorrow if you wanted."

"That fast? Goodness, it's a bit more complicated back home," she said.

"It's easy to get married. It's the *un*marrying that's hard," Julia said pragmatically.

Julia then urged Amelia to talk about England, the cool sea breezes, the winter storms, the snow that sometimes fell, her little cousins whom she so desperately missed. It felt good to have someone simply listen to her without saying a word. She told things to Julia she had never told another soul, about those terrible lonely days after her parents died, and her absolute belief when she was young that she was cursed.

But she didn't talk about Boone or Carson or her despair at living in Texas for the rest of her life.

# Chapter 12

Reverend Harley Beaumont was nothing like any man of the church Amelia had ever seen. He wore a leather vest, heavy spurred boots that jangled when he walked, and atop his full head of silver hair sat a large white hat quite unlike any that had ever graced the head of an Englishman.

He was big and loud and about as far removed from Reverend Peter Smythe, who presided over the tiny church in Hollings, as Amelia could have imagined. Weddings, it seemed, were a rare event in these parts, and cause for celebration. He'd brought along his wife and four strapping sons to be witnesses. Amelia had a feeling her wedding was in some way supposed to act as a bit of an incentive to the sons to get themselves married. The oldest of them, still single, had nearly as much gray as his father.

Because Small Fork didn't have a church, Amelia and Boone were to get married in his courtyard, which was probably the prettiest setting within a hundred miles.

From her room, Amelia could hear the reverend's voice booming out directions. They were expecting quite a crush of people, given the rarity of the event and the prominent place Boone held in Small Fork. Such a wedding would have taken weeks to prepare back home, but here, it seemed that everyone within miles had dropped what they were doing just so they could attend.

Amelia cocked her head. "Did I just hear a violin?" she asked Maggie, who was struggling to do something with her hair. She'd gotten quite proficient at dressing hair when the Pierces had lost their fortune and had to do without a maid.

"I believe there is a small orchestra setting up," Maggie said through the hairpins in her mouth. "Or at least several people with instruments," she added wryly after a particularly grating squeak. She jabbed in a few more hairpins and let out a sigh. "Your hair is so slippery, I cannot do what I planned."

"I wish I had your curls, Maggie," Amelia said, eyeing her sister-in-law with a bit of envy. Maggie's dark curls looked lovely no matter how she wore her hair.

"If I had a curling iron," Maggie said wistfully. "At least you have a lovely dress."

Indeed, lovely dresses were nearly all that Amelia had. She wore an exquisite green-foam silk gown she'd worn once during her one and only London Season. It sat slightly off her shoulders, revealing just a bit of the creamy skin below her neck. It was one of her more modest gowns, appropriate for a young, unmarried woman.

"There, I give up," Maggie said, stepping back to

get a better look at what she'd been able to accomplish. She sighed. "You look lovely, Amelia. Truly, truly beautiful."

"I wish there was a mirror somewhere in this house. Can you believe a home without a mirror? The only one I know of is the tiny one Boone uses for shaving, and that will hardly do. I suppose I'll just have to trust you." Amelia looked down at herself, remembering just how lovely she'd looked in this gown, and laughed. After Carson had left England, she'd rarely made the effort to look beautiful, for she didn't want to attract any male attention. She'd actually had a row with Edward until she'd agreed to wear this gown, never imagining it would one day become her wedding gown. Suddenly, ridiculously, there were tears in her eyes.

"Oh, Maggie, am I doing the right thing?"

Maggie looked as if she might cry, too, which certainly didn't help Amelia feel any better. "You know, Amelia, I am a bit of an expert at reading people, and I have a good feeling about Boone."

"You do?"

"And I had a bit of a bad feeling about Carson. But it wasn't my place to say anything, not really, and you were so in love, I thought perhaps my feelings were wrong."

Amelia shook her head. "What I'm feeling has nothing to do with Carson. It has everything to do with Boone. I hardly know him. I hardly know if I like him or not. He's so quiet, and I have the feeling he thinks I'm completely frivolous."

Maggie laughed lightly. "You'll simply have to teach him otherwise. You do know that the

Duchess of Bellingham had similar doubts before her marriage."

"I had heard." The duchess was an American heiress forced to marry the impoverished duke.

"She not only had misgivings, she was ardently in love with another man and disliked the duke completely. And yet, you've seen them happy. Rather nauseatingly happy, given how opposed she was to the marriage."

Amelia tugged lightly at the intricate lace of one sleeve. "My friend Julia was forced to marry a scoundrel and he tried to kill her." Even Amelia knew she was being completely ridiculous, so she shook her head as if to erase such a thought. "I know Boone is a good man. But what if I never come to love him? What if he never comes to love me? Wouldn't that be horrible?"

"You would still have your children to love," Maggie said, sounding infinitely sensible. "Speaking of children."

Amelia gave Maggie a curious look, then smiled. "Oh! Are you . . ."

"No. No, not yet," Maggie said quickly. "What I am rather awkwardly trying to talk about is tonight. With Boone. In bed."

"Oh."

"Do you have any questions?" Maggie asked, sounding very much like she prayed Amelia would have none.

"I don't think so."

"The most important thing to know is that Boone will know what do to and it can be wonderful. I don't know what you've heard, but you must know that the physical love between a husband and his wife is rather spectacular."

Amelia could feel her cheeks flush. She'd never spoken to anyone about what happened in the marriage bed. "What if the man . . ."

"Yes?"

"What if the man doesn't know what he's doing?" Amelia asked in one quick breath.

"Well then you shall both have a wonderful time discovering what makes you happy."

Boone was sweating profusely, and he felt as if he was going to be quite sick. He eyed the kitchen sink, judging whether he could reach it in time should he feel the need.

"Here," Edward said, staring in sympathy at his future brother-in-law. "Drink this."

Boone looked up to see Edward holding a small glass filled with a dark amber liquid. "I don't drink," he said.

Edward looked at the drink in his hand, shrugged, and downed it with one swallow, gasping as the fiery liquor went down.

"Good God, no wonder you don't drink," he said, shuddering. "That is the most hellish concoction I've ever put in my mouth." He went over to the bottle and sniffed.

"I believe it's Kentucky whiskey."

"Remind me not to go to Kentucky," Edward muttered. "There, you see? It did help. You are looking much better now."

Boone grimaced. "You're sure Amelia's okay with this wedding?"

"I'm sure."

"She doesn't feel forced? You didn't force her, did you?" Boone, already filled with misgivings about their marriage, felt nearly paralyzed with uncertainty. What could he possibly give this girl? She was a member of the English aristocracy, and he knew enough to realize she was marrying far beneath her class. Her brother was an earl, which meant she'd likely lived in a home that was far more impressive than anything he could build for her. She would miss her home, her family. She hated Texas, and surely she would come to hate him, as well. Oh, Lord, his head felt as if it were about to explode.

"I must be honest with you, sir. This is not the life, nor the husband, she dreamed she would have when she left England. But I wouldn't let her marry you if I thought you were not up to the task. And to answer your question, no, I did not force her to marry you. If you want my honest opinion, frankly I'm surprised she agreed to your proposal so easily. It's not like Amelia to do anything she doesn't want to, which can only bode well for you."

Edward's words did little to calm Boone's doubts. Outside, people were gathering for the wedding. He could hear the reverend's voice, the sound of fiddles tuning up, which meant dancing and yet another thing for him to dread. He looked out to the courtyard and smiled for the first time that day, seeing so many of his patients and customers milling about wearing their Sunday best. Someone had thought to set up a table, which was laden with food for a wedding feast.

Edward took out a pocket watch and snapped it closed. "It's time for you to head out," he said solemnly.

Boone stood with the Reverend Beaumont in front of the fountain and waited for Amelia to appear, when a sudden and sickening thought occurred to him. What if she changed her mind? What if he were left standing there like some fool waiting for his bride? He wouldn't blame her if she did. Certainly, even if her brother had not forced her into this, circumstances had. She'd acted skittish and distant toward him ever since that kiss, and he'd tortured himself with doubts about his ability to please his future wife. Perhaps he'd enjoyed the kiss far more than she had. Perhaps when she'd begged him to touch her, he'd been going about it so wrong, she'd felt obliged to take it upon herself to guide him.

His stomach clenched and he willed himself not to get ill.

"The ladies always take their time," Beaumont said with false bravado, which only served to increase Boone's anxiety. He could almost hear his father's voice in his head. *"What did you expect, you little shit, that you could have a girl that pretty? You?"*

And then, like a vision, she appeared at the doorway on her brother's arm, smiling as if she were happy, as if this wedding was something she welcomed. Boone nearly fainted with relief.

She walked the few steps toward Boone with her brother, then kissed him on the cheek before turning to her groom and offering him a brilliant smile.

God help him, but he felt his eyes burn with unshed tears as he smiled back.

They both turned toward the preacher, who boomed out the vows so everyone in the small courtyard could hear, and within minutes, Boone was slipping a simple gold ring on her finger. It had been in his store waiting for an owner for as long as he could remember.

Amelia stood before him, staring at that ring, and then looked up at him, her eyes shining. "We're married," she said, as if stunned by such a strange development.

"Kiss 'er, Doc!" someone yelled.

Amelia got up on her tiptoes and kissed him lightly to the hoots and hollers of the men around them. A wedding, Texas-style.

Within minutes, the couple was surrounded by well-wishers, the fiddlers started playing lively music, and the whiskey and tequila started pouring.

Amelia couldn't believe how many people, total strangers to her, had shown up at her wedding, bearing small gifts and large platters of food. She'd expected a tiny ceremony attended only by her brother and Maggie, not this raucous gathering.

"You are the most beautiful bride I've ever laid eyes on," Agatha said, hugging her tightly.

"Oh, Agatha, you didn't have to come, but thank you so much," Amelia said, feeling close to tears that this woman had left her dying husband to see her wed.

"Poor Enrique doesn't know if I'm there or not anymore, I'm afraid. Besides, I haven't missed a wedding in Small Fork in thirty years. 'Course, there haven't been too many of them," she said, laughing.

It was good to see Agatha smiling again.

Amelia saw Boone looking rather out of place in the midst of a group of back-slapping men, all with nearly empty glasses in their hands. But Boone was smiling and shaking his head at something. That's when Amelia saw Julia hovering near the fringes of the crowd, and she made her way over to her friend.

Grasping her hands, she said, "I'm so glad you came."

"I am, too, but I think I'll be headin' home now. You look beautiful, Mrs. Kitteridge," she said.

Hearing herself called Mrs. Kitteridge should have sounded strange, but Amelia had been calling herself that in her head for months—even if it was for another Kitteridge man. "Thank you. I'll be by to visit in a few days, if that's all right with you."

"Are you two going on a wedding trip?" she asked, with strange intensity.

It took only a moment to realize Julia lived in fear of Boone leaving her, even for a short time. Even though Julia fought to hide her anxiety, Amelia knew the other woman was hoping they were staying put. "We've nothing planned."

Julia shook her head apologetically. "I've been hearing things, is all. Probably nothing but rumors." She smiled and gave Amelia a quick hug. "I'll see you soon. I hope you like your gift."

Amelia clapped her hands together, delighted. "I adore gifts! Dare I hope it's one of your vases?"

"My favorite so far."

Julia left and Amelia turned to see Boone smiling

at her in a way that made her feel self-conscious, as if she'd been doing something extraordinary by talking to Julia.

He moved to her side, not an easy task with so many rowdy men hampering his path.

"There'll be plenty of time for the wife later, Boone," yelled one of the rough-looking men. "C'mon and have a drink with us."

"You all start the dancing," Boone shouted back and to Amelia's surprise, they moved away from the crowd and started swinging each other around in time to the music, appearing to be having the time of their lives. The only three single women in the crowd were already taken, and looked rather exhausted by the exuberant dancing.

"When shall we have our dance, Dr. Kitteridge?" Amelia asked saucily. Boone's cheeks instantly turned ruddy, a clear sign he was feeling uncomfortable. "Do not tell me you cannot dance. Why I shall file for annulment on the spot."

She said it to be funny, but Boone looked bothered by her words.

"I'm only jesting. Surely you know that," Amelia said gently. Boone could be prickly about the most unusual things, which only reminded Amelia how little she knew her husband.

"I never learned how to dance. I didn't have much chance to socialize when I was younger."

Amelia recalled what Carson had told her about Boone's childhood, and then felt terrible for making him feel self-conscious. She'd just assumed that Boone could dance because Carson had danced, if not well, with enthusiasm. "I don't expect it's a necessary skill for a physician," she said. "In fact, I don't expect there are many formal balls in Small Fork to hone one's dancing ability."

Boone looked down at her and something in his eyes made her heart catch for just a moment. He gave her a crooked grin. "I seem to be lacking in quite a few skills required of a husband."

"Nothing that cannot be overcome with proper tutoring." She laughed when his eyes widened with surprise, but she couldn't help herself. She adored flirting; it was one of her better skills, and she certainly didn't mind using it on her new husband.

"I am a fast learner," he said, in that measured way he spoke. She wished he talked more, for she loved his accent, the slow, clear way in which he spoke, as if every word had its own hidden, subtle meaning.

The party continued, growing more and more raucous, and Amelia found herself dragged into a dance more than once. After a few startled moments, she relaxed and began to enjoy being thrown about the dance floor with such abandon. During one dance, she saw Boone, head bent listening to another man, his face intent, and Amelia wondered what could be so serious a topic on his wedding day.

The last few days he'd been kept busier than usual with his practice, thanks to the very men she was dancing with now. Ranch hands were a rather careless lot when it came to their health, it seemed. One young man was watching rather mournfully from the sidelines on crutches, with his leg in a splint.

Eventually, her brother claimed her for a dance, and it was like going from a tumultuous sea to a calm pond. "I daresay Boone cannot dance any worse than my partners thus far," Amelia said, laughing up at her brother, who was positively elegant in his formal attire. He knew he stood out, but he announced it was only befitting to dress his best at his sister's wedding.

"I feared for your life," Edward said dryly.

"They are all lovely men. They just need a bit of refinement. Perhaps I should open up a school for Texas gentlemen to teach them a bit of deportment and other necessary skills."

"I hardly think they need to know the proper way to bow working on a ranch," Edward said.

"Everyone should have basic manners, Edward. Just look at you. If you hadn't had the proper education, you wouldn't have been ready to take on the earldom."

"With my fine employees, a lap dog could do what I do."

"True," Amelia said, just to needle him. No doubt her big brother had expected her to protest.

"I have learned quite a bit and am taking on more work," he said, sounding almost peevish, which only caused Amelia to laugh aloud.

"I'd forgotten how easy it is to tease you," Amelia said. "I've given Boone fits in my efforts to make him laugh. He's a hard nut to crack, though."

The fiddlers stopped their rather buoyant waltz and Amelia begged for a rest, much to the disappointment of several young men.

Boone immediately went to her and pressed a cool glass of lemonade into her hand. She looked particularly flushed from the dancing in the day's heat. A fine sheen of perspiration covered her face, making her hair cling to her cheek in wet strands. Another woman might have looked simply sweaty, but Amelia seemed to glow with happiness.

"Oh," she said, looking down into her glass with delight. "Is that ice? Truly? Thank you. I feel as if I might faint." She pressed the cool glass against her forehead and let out a sigh, a sound very much like the one she'd made when he'd kissed her.

Boone felt such a rush of lust, it took him a moment before he could speak. "It's the last of the ice until winter," Boone said. "The warehouse is nothing but a soggy puddle of sawdust about now."

"This is the best wedding present," Amelia said, meaning it.

"You look like you are enjoying yourself."

"I am," Amelia said. "I do love to dance. I could dance all day and all night if it weren't so dreadfully hot. I wish you would try. These men certainly have had no formal training."

Boone stared out at the men who were so exuberantly dancing about. "I don't like to look foolish," he said.

Amelia frowned. "I don't know who looks more foolish, then. These men with their enthusiasm or you, who refuses to dance with your bride." Her words came out far harsher than she'd meant, perhaps because she truly was disappointed not to dance with her husband on her wedding day.

"Just one disappointment in what I suspect will be many," he said, and moved away from her, his body stiff with anger.

Amelia watched him in disbelief.

"Not your first lovers' spat already?" Maggie asked, coming up beside her.

"If I must spend my life walking on eggshells, this is going to be an extremely contentious marriage," Amelia said darkly.

"What ever did you say to him now?"

"Me? Why do you assume I said something to him?"

Maggie smiled. "Because I cannot imagine Boone saying anything unkind to you," she replied gently.

Amelia let out a puff of air. "I do believe he is upset that I love to dance, and asked him to partner me even though he explained that he does not know how." Amelia pressed her lips together. "And I very well may have insinuated he looked more foolish *not* dancing at his wedding than he would dancing."

"Oh, Amelia, you didn't."

Amelia gave her friend a mulish look. "I didn't mean to sound quite so shrewish as it came out," she said. "Honestly, the man is entirely too sensitive."

"Of course he is, my dear. He's fully aware you do not love him, that you would rather have returned home in complete ruin than marry him while he, himself, has fallen in love with you."

"He hasn't," Amelia gasped.

"You cannot be that blind. The man looked like he might be ill when your entrance was delayed by only a few minutes."

Amelia shook her head slowly, feeling true anguish at the thought that Boone loved her. "He cannot love me," she said. "That only makes things far, far worse, you see."

"I'm afraid I don't understand."

"It's only that I don't love him at all," she said not unkindly. "Not one bit." Amelia looked up too, too late. She didn't see the warning look on Maggie's face, didn't understand that hand upon her arm urging her to stop talking.

"Don't worry," Boone said, as if he were trying to ease her mind. "I already knew." He even tried to smile.

# Chapter 13

Boone went through the motions the rest of the day, smiling when he should, shaking men's hands and slapping backs. He even kissed his new wife when the men, drunk on tequila and whiskey, started yelling for him to do so. He made it look good, too. He took her in his arms and crushed his mouth against hers, making her gasp in surprise as he thrust his tongue into her mouth. Then he smiled at her as if it was something he did every day, and pretended to enjoy the catcalls from the drunken men.

"That wasn't very nice," Amelia whispered harshly.

"Wasn't supposed to be, darlin'." He said it just as he'd heard his brother say it to her, and even pretended not to care when her face went deathly pale. The thing was, he wasn't that man, he didn't want to hurt her. He did love her and it killed him inside to know, without a doubt, that she didn't love him, that she perhaps even pitied him for his love.

What an idiot. Two kisses and a wedding and he'd thought that maybe she loved him, maybe someone would finally love him. He cursed silently to himself, hating that he could be so pathetic.

"Give her time," the countess had told him earlier when she'd pulled him aside. He pretended he didn't care that his bride had told someone on her wedding day that she didn't love him. He knew she wasn't being purposefully cruel or hurtful when she'd said those words.

By the time the sun set, most of the men had gone to sleep off their drunk or to the hotel to keep it going. The only ones remaining were Lord Hollings and the countess, for they had nowhere else to go. The courtyard was a mess, and Three Legs was rooting along the ground, hoping to pick up a few scraps dropped from plates.

"That was one of the liveliest weddings I've ever attended," Lord Hollings said heartily. "We don't have this tequila in England. I could make a fortune importing it. Lovely stuff, this."

"I think we should leave the tequila where it belongs," Maggie said dryly. "I'm afraid you're not used to it."

"I am feeling a bit under the weather," he said. His wife laid a hand on his arm and he looked down at her with such open devotion, it only made Boone more depressed. Clearly, the couple in front of him loved each other and didn't care who knew.

"Our wedding was far more sedate, wasn't it?" the countess asked.

"Wouldn't have been if we'd had this," Lord Hollings said, holding up his near-empty glass.

Maggie took it from him and set it on a nearby table. The other man shrugged goodnaturedly, then placed a rather sloppy kiss upon his wife's mouth. She giggled, and led him toward the house, wishing the bride and groom a good night, leaving Amelia and Boone alone for the first time since they'd said their vows.

"It was a lovely wedding," Amelia said softly.

"Was it?"

"Yes, it was. I thought so anyway."

Boone let out a rough sound. "I find that hard to believe."

She lifted up her chin. "Believe what you will. I'm going to bed."

"Alone?" he asked harshly, and watched as she stiffened.

She looked back. "Not by choice."

It took three strides to reach her, and she lifted her chin higher, only her eyes giving away the alarm she felt. "It was your choice to marry me. No one forced you to. You could have gone home. You should have gone home," he said, letting his words hang in the cool night air. To his disgust, all he wanted to do was kiss her senseless. "But you didn't."

"No. I didn't."

"You should have," he repeated, then turned away and walked into the inky black night, away from her, away from his mockery of a marriage.

Boone didn't go far. After perhaps a hundred yards, he stopped and looked toward the distant mountains, black as sin against the night sky.

He'd known she didn't love him, so why did it bother him so much? It was damned unmanning, but he couldn't rid himself of the feeling. He couldn't drink it away, that was for certain. He couldn't slam his fist into a wall, he couldn't scream out his rage. He could only keep it inside with all the other pain that was eating his gut, making his entire body shake with it.

He scuffed the dry dirt with his shoe, the only sound other than the distant noise from the hotel and the faint rustling of the prairie grass in the wind. He wondered what England would be like, with its cold, damp air, crowded villages made of stone, where the memories that haunted him would be so far away.

*"It's only that I don't love him at all. Not one bit."*

She'd sounded sad. Amelia would. She was a kind person who likely felt awful that he'd overheard her rather brutal honesty. *Not one bit.*

He stood staring at the mountains for a long time, wondering whether he should stay away from his bride, give her a way out, a way home. If he didn't touch her, their marriage could be quickly and cleanly annulled. She could go home, probably to face ruin, but no one would ever have to know she'd been married. He would stay here, carry on, live his life.

That thought was so bleak, he pushed it away. He didn't want to lose her; he didn't want her to leave him. He wanted her to stay even if she didn't love him, even if she wasn't happy. He wanted her for him. It was perhaps one of the most selfish thoughts he'd ever had in his life. He simply couldn't bear the thought of his endlessly lonely existence if he let her go.

His marriage would be consummated; he would give her no escape.

* * *

Amelia sat in her bed, wondering if she was supposed to be sitting in his. And wondering if he would come to her at all, which made her decision to be in her own bed rather wise.

She'd turned her oil lamp down low and stared at her closed door, listening intently for sounds that would indicate he was coming to her.

She wasn't sure whether she hoped he did or prayed he didn't. All she knew was she felt terrible about what Boone had overheard. She wasn't even certain whether it was the truth. She didn't dislike him. In fact, she liked him quite a bit. Each time she thought about his overhearing her talking with Maggie, she felt a physical pain. She might not love Boone, but she certainly would never intentionally hurt him, and it was obvious that she had.

Even after these weeks with him, he was such a stranger to her. She didn't know what made him laugh or smile. She didn't know whether he could sing or play an instrument. She didn't know whether he enjoyed sweets or swimming or playing card games. She knew nothing of him, so how on earth was she supposed to know whether she loved him or not? And despite what Maggie said about Boone loving her, she truly didn't know whether he did or not. She knew only that she had the capacity to hurt him.

Amelia realized she could not trust her own judgment in such matters as love. Hadn't she thought Carson loved her? Of course, Carson had actually *told* her he loved her, and she'd believed it with all her heart. She had a feeling if Boone ever uttered those words to her, they would hold far more meaning.

The only thing she knew for certain was that her body loved it when he touched her. Or looked at her. Which was one reason she was sitting up in bed partly hoping he'd come to her.

They had kissed only a few times, but it was enough to know that his touch sent her nearly over the edge. It was disconcerting, to say the least. And rather nice.

She let out a puff of air and glanced at her lamp. She was debating whether to finally put it out and try to get some sleep, when her door opened. Boone stood there, a wild look about him, as if he'd been in a fierce wind storm and had just blown in. He stared at her, his eyes burning with an intensity she'd never seen, and she shivered beneath his gaze.

He entered the room without a word, slid the braces from his shoulders, and began unbuttoning his rumpled white shirt. He slipped it off, letting it fall to the floor, revealing a powerful chest lightly sprinkled with hair. Silently, he pulled off his shoes, then his pants and underclothes in one movement, leaving him completely naked and standing before her, staring at her.

He was clearly aroused, and Amelia flicked her eyes downward, curiosity overcoming her complete shock at seeing a man naked before her. Boone was a large man, even taller than Carson, but he seemed like a giant to her, standing unclothed in the shadowy lamplight in her tiny room.

She understood what happened to a man who

was aroused, that his man parts grew larger and harder. But that was all she knew for certain.

"Take off your clothes."

Amelia smiled. "You." And she lifted her arms over her head to help him.

That one word seemed to act as a catalyst, for he was on her bed in a single stride, pulling her toward him with near violence. But instead of being frightened, Amelia threw her arms around his neck and welcomed him as he brought his mouth against hers in an almost desperate way. He fisted her nightgown in his hands and drew the garment over her head, tossing it aside, hardly breaking their kiss.

Ah, the feeling of skin against skin was an unexpectedly delicious sensation, and she let out a sound that she hardly recognized as coming from her. His body was so completely different from hers, his muscles hard and velvety beneath her seeking fingers.

"I'm going to touch you," she said, then brought her hand boldly to his arousal and grasped it. His erection was quite fascinating, she realized, staring down at what she held. Hard and impossibly soft at the same time. He let out a groan that sounded almost pained, but Amelia knew better. He pushed her down onto the bed and covered her with his large body, pulling her close against the hard planes of his form. His hands stroked her from her neck to her thighs, learning her, molding her beneath him. And then he touched one breast, his eyes shining with lust. He stared at her breasts, touching her lightly with his fingertips, before he brought his mouth down upon one nipple and drew her into his mouth, almost as if he couldn't stop himself. And he suckled her, causing such an exquisite feeling between her legs, she cried out.

He moved to the other breast, a starving man not knowing which delectable morsel to put in his mouth next. And then, while he made love to her breasts, one hand moved between her legs and it was her turn to groan aloud. Amelia arched up into his hand, mindless of her actions, only knowing that everywhere he touched made her feel such intense pleasure, she simply could not remain still.

She was wet between her legs, but she didn't care. She only cared that he keep touching her there, oh, God, there. "*There,*" she said, gasping. And he did, he touched her and moved his hand against that perfect, wonderful spot. A finger slid into her, invaded her, filled her, and she only shook her head back and forth and begged him aloud not to stop, not to stop, because it felt too good. It felt as if she were going to scream.

And then she did, long and loud, her body arching, her toes curling, hips undulating, hands pulling his head up so she could taste him. Slowly, ever so slowly, she came back to herself, to the rather embarrassing realization that she'd acted rather unlike a lady in those last few moments.

She breathed into his neck, her hands on his slick back, and kissed his salty skin. "That was quite unexpected," she said at last.

Still silent, he ravaged her mouth again with his, long, wet, drugging kisses, and Amelia wondered whether he'd been joking about his lack of experience. He certainly seemed to know precisely where to touch her, how to make her body catch fire.

Boone pushed himself up, so that his knees were

between her bent legs, his arms straight down by her shoulders. He stared at her, not quite believing this responsive, beautiful woman was his. He didn't care if she ever came to love him, as long as she gave him this.

All his dreams, all his fantasies, didn't come close to the reality of having her beneath him, crying out with pleasure. He had to restrain himself, had to stop himself from licking and kissing and touching every inch of her. He was a starving man at the most sumptuous feast in creation, and he could not stop himself from wanting to devour every morsel. He hardly recognized the man he became with her, but he liked that man, liked his sureness, his confidence.

With one hand, he reached down for his member and guided it toward the junction of her thighs, not looking anywhere but at her lovely face. The tip of him entered her, hot and wet and perfect, and he thought he just might die from the pleasure of her heat. Gently, he pushed forward, his entire body trembling from the restraint it took not to simply thrust forward. He was so damned close already to that shattering release.

"It's all right," she said, and moved her hips slightly, giving him permission to push inside.

He did, closing his eyes against the most agonizingly intense pleasure he'd ever experienced in his twenty-eight years. She let out the smallest sound when he drove past her barrier and he kissed her face, over and over, her cheek, her mouth, her nose, as he buried himself deep inside his wife. His wife.

If he moved, it would be over, and he didn't want

it to be over. So he remained still, throbbing, hovering between pain and pleasure, letting them both get used to the feeling of him inside of her. He pushed up to see her face, and she smiled at him, and that was his undoing. He began thrusting, fiercely, his body taken over by raw need. Finally, he came, pushing his head down beside hers, letting himself flow into her, letting himself pulse until he realized he was still alive and lying with his wife.

He lay there, catching his breath, happier than he'd ever been in his life, happier by far than he'd ever thought he could be. She lay beneath him, her hands lightly caressing his sweat-slick shoulders.

Boone pulled out, already wondering when he could make love to her again.

"Wasn't that wonderful?" she asked, sounding unsure, which was quite unlike her.

"Yes, ma'am. It sure was."

And then, he got up and pulled on his pants and left, returning moments later with a wet cloth. He gently pulled down the covers that she must have pulled up, smiling a bit when he felt momentary resistance.

"Oh." She looked entirely mortified that he was going to wipe up the blood and semen drying on her inner thigh. "I hadn't realized making love would be quite so messy." He gently cleaned her and moved the covers over her naked body once again with a small amount of regret. He wished he had hours and hours just to stare at her, to memorize every curve, every tiny birthmark, every feminine bit of her.

"You're all right?" he asked.

"Yes. Fine. Thank you." She looked up at him, her

blue eyes uncertain, and he wished it was different between them. He wished he could stay and hold her all night. But, of course, he couldn't.

"Good night, then."

He turned to go, the joy seeping away.

"Boone."

She sounded rather exasperated, so he turned to her.

"Where are you going?"

"To bed. I'm beat."

Her cheeks flushed slightly. "I thought, perhaps, we could sleep in the same bed."

Boone swallowed, a slight bit of panic twisting his gut. "I don't think that's a good idea," he said slowly, as if saying the words that way would stop them from hurting her. "I don't sleep well and I'd just keep you awake."

She smiled briefly. "Certainly. I understand."

"It's not that I don't want to stay here, it's that . . ."

She held up her hand, her eyes flashing. "It's fine, Boone. I understand. In fact, most couples do not share a bed at all. Ever. My own parents had separate rooms and it worked out wonderfully. They did have three children, after all."

Boone stared at the floor. Why the hell was she doing this? Why was she making him love her even more? Part of him wanted to beg her to come with him to his bed, to lie next to him, to wrap her arms around him and keep the demons away. But he feared even she could not. Not only were his nightmares violent, he would sometimes wake up standing, punching the air, stalking around his room in confusion. He'd punched Carson more than once in his sleep when his brother came into his room to make sure he wasn't endangering himself. Carson could take a punch; he was a big man. But Amelia. One punch could kill her.

It would be humiliating, not to mention terribly frightening for her and potentially dangerous.

"I've never slept with another person in my bed before," he said. "I have nightmares."

Amelia had known the physical part of her marriage would be tolerable, but she hadn't expected the complete rapture of their union. She hadn't expected the pleasure to be so completely intense that she'd scream out in joy. And now she didn't want it to be over. He moved toward her door as if she was chasing him, and doubt began to filter into her haze of contentment.

"Boone."

He stopped, his entire body tense. "What?"

"We don't have to sleep just yet. Can't we just . . . talk for a bit?"

When he turned, she lifted the covers and it seemed to her he reluctantly moved toward the bed and awkwardly joined her. The bed was small, but they moved together, facing one another. Amelia placed a hand on his cheek, liking the beard-rough feel of it, the pure masculinity of the lines of his face. "There, that's not so bad, is it?"

His lips lifted and she smiled at him.

"I need to ask you a question and you must promise to answer honestly." He nodded, his gray eyes intent on hers. "Were you joking with me before, when you told me you'd never kissed a woman?"

"No," he said, sounding a bit stiff.

"Well. You're quite good for someone with no practice."

"You inspire me," he said, finally, and Amelia smiled. It was the perfect thing to say, really.

She closed her eyes and moved her hand on his chest and heard him breathe in sharply. Then she moved one finger slowly across his lips and felt him smile. Leaning on one elbow, she placed a gentle kiss where her finger had just been. Then on his shoulder, then his flat nipple. She moved her hand across his belly, finding herself completely fascinated by the hard ridges of his stomach, the strength they signified. And then she felt his erection against the back of her hand and it was her turn to smile. With the very tip of her index finger, she touched the velvety tip of him.

"Amelia," he breathed.

"I find you fascinating," she admitted, moving her hand and touching the area beneath his arousal, the sac that seemed to tighten with her caress. "You're very different from me, you know."

"I had noticed," he managed. He lay still, not touching her, and Amelia wondered if he were simply waiting to see what she would do next. Honestly, she wasn't certain. Then she got a bit of her own inspiration. Where she'd touched him, she placed her lips, giving him a gentle kiss.

"Is that proper?"

"Not at all," he gasped, jerking his hips and pressing her down gently.

"I suppose I'm not all that proper," she said, kissing him again and reveling in the fact that the smallest thing could bring him such obvious pleasure.

He let out a strangled sound, and he pulled her up for a searing kiss. And another. And another.

Until they were joined together again, until they were both sated and smiling in the darkness.

"Now," she said, once they'd both come back to earth and were breathing normally. "You may go to bed."

He gave her another kiss, and left, leaving behind a heated spot that quickly cooled, even though the air was still warm.

# Chapter 14

Amelia awoke to find a note on her pillow. She smiled at his whimsy, until reading the brief note:

> *Called to fire at Worcester Ranch. Many men injured.*
>
> B

Her first thought, of course, was for the poor injured men. Her second was that the note was completely devoid of any tenderness. Amelia smiled at her silliness. He'd probably left in a hurry, and the fact he'd left her a note at all was very considerate. What a ninny she was.

She stretched, aware of muscles aching that had never ached before, and smiled again. Married life was wonderful, she decided. Just the thought of what had happened the previous night made her want more. If she wasn't already married, she certainly would have been considered a shameless hussy.

By the time she reached the kitchen, Maggie and

Edward were already sitting at the small table nibbling on eggs and bacon.

"It smells wonderful. Who was the cook?"

"I was," Maggie said happily. "I found it necessary to learn after all our servants left, and have retained a good amount of knowledge, it seems. I can do up some more eggs for you if you want."

"I'll just have a peach," Amelia said. "They're wonderful. Boone says Texas is famous for peaches."

Maggie raised an eyebrow. "And how is Boone? Still sleeping?"

Amelia blushed for no apparent reason. "Apparently there was a fire last night at a local ranch and some men were injured. I have no idea when he left or when he'll return."

"I do hope he returns by tomorrow. Your brother and I will be taking the train."

Amelia let out a sound of disappointment. "But surely you can stay a bit more. You cannot leave so soon. I don't know when I'll get to see you again." She stood up and hugged Edward, who looked helplessly at his wife.

"We weren't supposed to be here at all," Edward pointed out. "It is only through your actions that we find ourselves in Texas for our wedding trip."

Amelia pouted. "But you are here now and must stay."

"We must leave," Edward said. "Or I shall grieve."

Amelia narrowed her eyes at her older brother. It was just like him to take advantage of her sentimental side by beginning the rhyming game they'd played as children.

"If you do not stay . . . I will . . ."

"Be okay," Maggie put in, laughing when Amelia

cried foul. "Amelia, you know we have to leave. We've been gone from Meremont longer than either of us wanted already."

"I know." Ever buoyant, Amelia smiled. "At least you were here for the wedding. I daresay it was more than I expected when I left Meremont."

"There you go," Edward said heartily, glad that his little sister was finally using common sense.

As it turned out, Boone was not there when Maggie and Edward climbed aboard the train that would take them on the first leg of their journey home. He'd stumbled home after midnight, exhausted from tending those who'd been badly burned in a stable fire that took the lives of ten fine horses. He still smelled of the stench of smoke, even though he'd hastily bathed before checking in on Amelia. He mumbled an apology, then went up to bed, and was snoring almost immediately, leaving Amelia staring at the ceiling as she listened to the distant rumbles. When she awoke the next morning, the day of her brother's departure, Boone was already gone. This time, there was no note.

She tearfully bid her brother and Maggie goodbye, then returned to the store, only to find two customers waiting for her to reopen. She wouldn't even be able to have herself a good cry. By the time she pulled the shade shut to indicate the store was closed, she was feeling lonely and depressed and again thinking she'd made a terrible muck of things.

It was almost as if that passion-filled night with

Boone had never happened. She stood in the middle of the kitchen staring at the cold stove and had such a fierce longing for Meremont she let out a small anguished sound. How shocked her friends back home would be if they could see her now, wearing a simple muslin dress, her hair pulled hastily back in a simple bun, her hands beginning to look more like a servant's than those of a lady.

She'd told them about how exciting her life with Carson would be, full of adventure and change, full of balls and moonlit rides around their sprawling ranch. Would they laugh? Feel sorry for her? As she thought back to how she'd gone on and on about Carson and their future life together in Texas, she cringed. No doubt her friends pictured her living in some sort of mansion surrounded by servants.

And here she stood, alone, staring at a cold stove. In England, she'd never felt useless. Her brother had relied on her to oversee the running of every aspect of a large and busy household filled with servants. Now she was finding all her skills were worthless.

"What am I doing here?" she asked the empty room. Amelia heard a soft thumping in the corner and saw Three Legs greeting her in his lazy way.

"Hello, Three Legs." The thumping increased in tempo, and the dog let out a small whine. Amelia walked to the dog and hunkered down to scratch behind his ears. "You get lonely, too, don't you?" The dog let out a satisfied groan, then lay back down, happy to have received even that small amount of attention.

Amelia grabbed another peach, one of the last of

the season, and took a bite. It was soft and sweet, and almost made being alone more bearable.

That night when Boone came home, he fell asleep at the kitchen table, a bowl of stew from the hotel cooling in front of him. That's where Amelia found him when she came downstairs to use the water closet. His soft snores alerted her to his presence, and she smiled when she saw how he'd fallen asleep, with two arms dangling down by his sides and his head resting on the table, mashing one side of his handsome face. He began muttering something unintelligible in his sleep, his brows gathering together. A bad dream, perhaps.

Amelia quietly sat down at the table and gave him a gentle nudge. He exploded awake so forcefully, it took Amelia completely by surprise when he swung wildly and blindly, connecting with jarring impact to her shoulder, and causing her to nearly stumble from her seat.

Amelia cried out, for the pain was sharp and intense, and the blow completely unexpected. Slowly, Boone became aware of where he was, but his befuddled mind was still trying to put together what had just happened.

"You hit me," Amelia said, immediately recognizing that she was not her husband's intended target. At least she hoped not.

Boone, breathing heavily, looked at Amelia, horrified and utterly confused by her statement. "What?"

"You hit me. In your sleep," she said, trying to sound calm, even though her heart was racing painfully in her chest. "You were having a bad dream."

"I hit you?" Boone asked, clearly agonized at the thought. "Oh, God, I'm so sorry. I wasn't hitting you, I was hitting . . ." He closed his eyes. "I was hitting my father."

"I'm certain he deserved it," Amelia said quietly.

Boone gazed at her as if he couldn't quite believe she was being so completely understanding. "Did I hit you hard?"

"Actually, yes," she admitted, and he winced. "But we should thank goodness your aim is so dismal. You could have hit my face and that would have been rather difficult to explain."

Boone buried his face in his hands for a moment, then pulled her to him. "I'd never hurt you knowingly. Never. I'm so sorry."

"I know, Boone," she said, her voice muffled by his shirt. "Please don't make more of this than there is. You were asleep."

Despite her words, he continued to look rather miserable.

"I think you ought to kiss it better," Amelia said, sounding serious. "You may have only hit my shoulder, but I fear the pain is shooting everywhere." Amelia tried to look like a coquette might, but she simply couldn't maintain her composure and began to giggle.

Boone smiled and rested his chin on one hand, as if enjoying a play. "Tell me where it hurts," he said, his voice low.

"Here," she said, and pointed to her elbow. Boone dutifully kissed her. "And here. This *is* where the blow hit." He kissed her shoulder with utmost care. "And here," she said, pointing to her left cheek.

He leaned over and kissed her, then moved his cheek against hers. "And here." She placed a finger on her bottom lip.

He kissed only her bottom lip, but lingered as if unwilling to pull away. "I think your lips are especially hurt," he muttered, then deepened the kiss with a low sound, purely male. He moved to her neck, and she arched back, her eyes closed, her breathing becoming rather labored for a woman who was sitting down.

She pulled away and began unlacing her nightdress while a slow smile formed on Boone's face, even as his gray eyes darkened with desire. She loved to see him smile, so she unbuttoned a few more and pointed to where her breasts were just visible beneath her cotton garment. He rewarded her with a rather wicked smile before he lowered his head and placed a series of small kisses over every inch of her exposed flesh.

"Feeling better?" he asked. "Because as a doctor, it's my opinion that such a blow could have done more damage."

Amelia bit her bottom lip and pulled her nightdress down, exposing her shoulders and all but the nipples of her breasts. She liked the way he stared at her, as if she were the most beautiful creature on earth. Her lips were parted, her breathing almost irregular. "Please," she said, forgetting about their game, forgetting everything but the feeling in her breasts and the wetness between her legs.

Boone pulled her nightdress lower, tugging it over her nipples, and then pulled one taut tip into his mouth, feeling powerfully male when she let out a cry of pure female joy.

"I can always tell what you like," he said, pleased with his discovery.

"I don't make much secret of it," she said, sounding breathless.

"You like this," he said, moving his index finger around one nipple. She fascinated him. Her body, every curve, every feminine bit of her was completely and utterly beautiful.

"Yes."

"And this," he said, suckling her.

Her only response was a whimper of pleasure.

"I think we should go to the bedroom," he said, wanting to get her completely naked and on a bed so he could continue his slow exploration of his beautiful wife.

She stood, leaving her upper body exposed to his view, and held her nightdress around her waist. In the lamplight she looked like something a master would paint, her creamy white skin, her softly rounded shoulders, her full round breasts. Boone had never in his life felt more grateful than he did at that moment to have found such a wife. The words he'd long felt were pushing against his throat.

God, he loved her.

But he swallowed, and smiled, and held out his hand to lead her to her room, where he would show with his body what he could never tell her in words.

# Chapter 15

In the days that followed, their life took on something of a routine. When she could get away from Enrique, Agatha made it her mission in life to teach Amelia how to be a proper Texas woman. Though she could not leave her husband for long hours, she did stop by the store frequently, and took the time to show Amelia something vital each time.

Amelia now knew how to make a proper bread dough, though she could not figure out why her bread was not quite as good as Agatha's, and a pie crust.

"I can open a bakery," Amelia said, after pulling out a not-too-burnt peach pie from her oven.

Boone was kept busy with his practice, something not unusual when the ranches ended their drives. Amelia would spend her time in the store, or practice her new domestic skills. It was all a novelty and rather fun. She'd always been a bright and willing student, and with her usual optimism, she tackled even the most mundane tasks with a certain amount of pleasure.

Though Amelia already knew she had to designate certain days to wash and iron clothing, she had no idea how to operate a washing machine. In her world, soiled clothes appeared once a week, cleaned and ironed and hung, and she'd given very little thought to how they came to be this way. She knew, of course, that someone was doing something, but all she'd really concerned herself with was making sure everything happened like clockwork.

Agatha had done the washing and ironing for Boone and Carson, but with a capable woman in the house, those household duties now fell to her. Fortunately, Agatha immediately understood that Amelia needed instruction.

"I never knew everything was so much work," Amelia said, cranking the washing machine's handle and making Agatha laugh.

She was determined to show Boone she could handle any task he gave her, even if it meant reddened hands and broken fingernails. Even if she missed her old life and going to parties and playing cards late into the night and singing along with her cousins as she played the piano.

It was only after hanging some sopping clothes on a windy September day that she broke down for the first time, showing the first crack in her rather thin veneer of sanguinity. She hated domestic work. She didn't want to be a servant. She wanted to play her piano and sing songs with her cousins. She desperately missed the cool ocean mist that blew up from the Irish Sea. She looked down at her hands, hands that she used to protect with soft kid-leather gloves for her daily ride through Meremont's pristine grounds, and saw a sight she did not recognize. And then the wind blustered, pulling all but one clean white shirt onto the dusty ground.

"Oh," she shouted dismally, and quickly scooped up the shirts, as if picking them up fast enough would stop them from becoming a muddy mess. "Bloody, bloody, bloody hell," she shouted. She stared at the ruined shirts and looked around, instantly aware that she'd sounded nothing like the lady she was. But no one, save the cat, had heard her outburst. Her throat aching from unshed tears, Amelia emptied the water from the washing machine, filled it, added soap and started turning the lever to move the machine's agitator. Agatha had commented on how lucky she was to have such a modern machine.

"Bloody nasty machine, if you ask me," Amelia said, thinking that if she was going to be a washerwoman, she might as well talk like one.

When she was finally done and the clean shirts were securely on the clothesline, Amelia smiled, feeling rather chagrined about how angry she'd gotten over a few dirty shirts. Maggie's words came back to her: "You've made your bed and now you must lie in it."

For the most part, her life was far better than she'd thought it would be. But there was a joy missing, one that she longed for but didn't know how to find. Since the night of Boone's dream, they hadn't made love, hadn't even touched, and she wondered if he were somehow unsatisfied with her. It was almost as if he were avoiding her. Perhaps when they had children she would feel more content, she would feel more like this was home.

She heard Paula calling and realized that Boone must have gone out and locked the store. Thankful to be pulled away from her domestic chores, she went through the house and opened up the store, smiling as she let her friend in.

Strangely, Paula was smiling, too.

"I'm just brimming with gossip," she gushed.

Since Amelia's marriage, Paula had spent quite a bit of time in the store, especially when Boone was out on calls. She would follow Amelia around as she floundered about her new chores, offering advice and some help, though she had almost as little experience with domesticity as Amelia did. Paula had grown up with servants, and as the wife of a banker, she had live-in help. Amelia would have liked to have said this didn't bother her one whit, but she was terrifically honest, and had to admit it did niggle at her a bit.

"Let's go out to the courtyard," Amelia said. "Would you like tea?"

"Just a glass of cool water is fine."

The two women settled themselves before Paula said another word. She leaned forward, her eyes shining with excitement. "Do not tell a soul, and I do mean everyone, but a Dallas businessman has been meeting with my husband and it looks as though we're going to have us an oil drill right here in Small Fork."

Amelia shook her head, not quite knowing the significance of such a thing.

"Why, goodness, that means schools, a church, electricity, and a theater are sure to follow," Paula said, her lively blue eyes dancing with excitement. "Henry Wilfred was drilling for water on his ranch and he found oil instead. That was ten years back or so and nothing much ever came of it. This Dallas man has been going around looking for good places to drill for oil, and he's heading here next month."

"So it's not definite that he'll find oil."

Paula's eyes lost a bit of their glitter, and she looked at Amelia as if she personally was responsible for whether or not the man stayed and found gallons of the stuff. "No, but at least it's hope," she said sullenly. "In Nacogdoches County they found oil, and within just a few months they had to build a school."

"I hope that does happen," Amelia said, feeling strangely detached from this discussion of future schools and theaters. She still hadn't wrapped her mind around the idea that Small Fork was her home forever.

"Hello, ladies." Boone walked to the fountain and splashed water on his face, and Amelia couldn't stop the sudden desire coursing through her. My goodness, the man simply walked in front of her and she could picture him doing all sorts of shockingly wonderful things to her.

Paula gave her a warning look for Amelia to keep mum about the oil, and Amelia nodded, hoping her friend would assume her flushed cheeks were from the warm afternoon.

"We were just talking about all the marriages in these parts lately," Paula said with forced cheer.

"Were you," Boone said, sounding a bit strained, studying Amelia's face carefully.

"Why first you two, then your brother. I was telling Mr. Brentwood just last night that if we're going to have so many weddings, we should see about having a proper church and a regular preacher. Baptist, of course."

Amelia stopped listening after Paula said the word "brother," and she noticed that Boone had become extremely still. "I'm sorry," she said, plastering a pleasant smile on her face. "Who did you say got married?"

Paula looked at her as if she were crazy. "I know it's only two, but still . . ."

"Boone and I, and . . ." Amelia prompted.

"Why, Dulce and Carson," she said, as if Amelia had gone quite daft. "Of course, I'm not sure if we can count Carson and Dulce because they didn't technically get married in Small Fork, but they're both from Small Fork, and . . ." She stopped, looking from one to the other, finally realizing that she was the only one excited about the news.

"Have I spoken out of turn?" she asked, looking mortified.

"Not at all," Boone said smoothly.

"I mean, I had heard rumors about . . ." Paula clamped her mouth shut, her cheeks flushing. "Certainly you knew they got married," she finished weakly.

"Of course, we knew," Amelia said, her smile still intact, and Paula brightened immediately, making Amelia question the other woman's intelligence. "In England, you see, elopement is simply not the thing, not at all. I must say, if I were to elope, my family would cut me off entirely. You have far more liberal views about such things in America, and I shall have to get used to that. I know they've held a tendre for each other for quite some time. We're happy for them, truly."

Amelia refused to look at Boone, absolutely refused. For it was quite apparent that he hadn't been surprised by this news and had allowed her to be blindsided.

"I didn't know that about England," Paula said, leaning forward, glad to be getting a bit more gossip. If ever there was a woman oblivious to the rather obvious nuances going on around her, it would be Paula Brentwood.

"Dulce and Carson have loved each other for years, or so I've heard," Amelia said, as if telling the other woman something in great confidence. "I really don't know Carson well at all, you see." This was true, at least. "My stop here was intended to be brief, if you recall, and if I hadn't been waylaid by my thieving maid, I never would have been *forced* to stay until my brother arrived." She hoped Boone caught the rather unsubtle anger in her tone.

Paula beamed at the two of them, apparently oblivious. "And what a good thing you did, for you fell in love with our doctor. So romantic." There was absolutely nothing but sincerity in those words. "Speaking of husbands," she said, standing up, "I believe I need to go home and feed mine. And also rescue him from our son, who no doubt is begging that he be allowed to count all the money. Like father, like son."

"I'm so glad you stopped by," Amelia said, standing as well and walking with her friend to the front of the building. As soon as Paula started walking across the dusty street to the bank, Amelia whirled around, only to find herself staring directly at her husband.

"I was going tell you."

Amelia lifted her skirts and stalked by Boone without a word, her face set. Then she turned. "Do not follow me." Of course, he did.

Boone didn't know what to do or what to say, but he followed his angry wife anyway. He'd known the news that Carson had married Dulce was going to upset her and was waiting for the right time to tell her. Like when they were old and gray.

She was in a right tizzy right now, stalking away from him, her skirts lifted just enough so he could see her ankles, which made him smile. He knew he shouldn't be thinking about ankles, or how pretty they were, or anything but how mad she was that Carson had gone off and married another woman just days after claiming he never wanted to get married. She ought to be angry, and he wouldn't be surprised if she stomped around in a snit for a while.

He couldn't help it—he felt glad Carson was married—and he wasn't going to apologize for that. He'd expected her to be angry, but he truly, stupidly hadn't expected the tears he saw running down her face.

"How could he?" she asked him, her blue eyes huge and filled with a sadness that struck him like a hard blow to the gut. "He told me he didn't ever want to get married. He told me that was why he couldn't marry me. And then . . ." She swallowed, and stopped, as if knowing what she was saying was like a knife to his heart. Boone truly hadn't thought she still loved Carson, had thought his brother's mean treatment of her had made Amelia, if not love *him*, at least hate Carson. Apparently, he'd been wrong. She still obviously loved Carson, and damn if it didn't hurt.

Amelia sat down at the edge of the fountain, overcome by grief, and buried her face in her hands. Something in Boone came to a grinding halt, that hope he didn't even know he'd been holding on to that she would ever love him. Oh, he could please her. He could make her scream in pleasure. He could make her come.

But he couldn't make her love him.

"I'm sorry, Boone," she said, her voice muffled, and as always, kind. But at that moment, he didn't want her kindness. He wanted her to stop crying, to stop loving a man who didn't deserve her love. "It's just that it was such a surprise. I hardly expected it, you see."

He thrust a handkerchief into her hand.

"Thank you," she said, still not looking at him, her voice watery. "You must think me a proper watering pot."

Boone just stared at her, not feeling sympathy or love or even anger. He felt nothing. Or at least, please God, help him not to.

When she glanced up at him, she must have seen something in his eyes, for she looked away.

"Why didn't you tell me?" she asked, her voice wooden.

"I suppose it was because I didn't want to know the truth."

"What truth?"

"That you still love him."

She started to protest, but stopped. And he wasn't

sure if she stopped because he was right or because she'd realized there was no point in arguing. *Tell me I'm wrong. Tell me. Tell me.* He could hardly breathe from the cruel hope that still stirred inside him.

"I'd be a fool to love him." She sounded bitter.

"Then I guess you're a fool."

Amelia sat for a long time at the fountain, staring at Boone's clean shirts blowing in the breeze. She'd hurt him again and felt sick, for if there was one person on this earth she didn't want to hurt, it was Boone.

She ought to tell him she was sorry, that she loved him, and she would hope he'd believe her and they could go on with their lives. It shouldn't matter that she did not love him, not quite, not yet. In truth, she didn't know how she felt. She *should* love him. She *wanted* to love him. But she knew in her heart she didn't. Not yet.

Amelia did not know if there was something missing in her, some sensible bit that would guide her in the right direction when it came to men. Carson did not deserve her love, and yet she'd given it to him. And though she was quite, quite certain she no longer loved him, the pain she'd felt upon hearing he'd married Dulce was unexpectedly stunning.

Why should it matter if he married a dozen women?

The only answer made her seem rather childish. Because he clearly didn't love *her* enough to marry her. She knew that if he were to come back and beg her to marry him, she wouldn't.

Then why had she felt so hurt when she'd found out he'd married Dulce?

"Because you *are* a bloody fool," she said, disgusted with herself.

Gathering her courage, she went in search of Boone so she could properly apologize. She didn't know what she could say to make amends, but she'd think of something. Amelia searched the house and store before giving up and deciding to wait until supper. She was planning to cook one of his favorites, a dish shown to her by Agatha, of pork and potatoes and some spicy peppers the older woman grew in her garden. Next year, perhaps, she'd have her own little kitchen garden and grow some of the peppers Boone liked. She'd do everything Boone liked if it meant he never looked at her again as he had at the fountain.

Feeling a bit guilty, Amelia made sure the store was locked and then headed to Julia's. She'd come to think of Julia's house, and Julia herself, as a bit of a refuge from her life in Texas. There, she could talk about Meremont without worrying she was hurting someone with her happy memories. She could cry about her cousins, who were surely growing up without her, she could describe the cool sea, the winter fogs, the snow in wintertime. Whenever she discussed such things with Boone, he became silent and thoughtful, as if she were somehow blaming him for her sadness.

Huge, puffy clouds gathered on the horizon, and Amelia wondered if she were going to experience one of the violent storms that sometimes hit Small Fork. Some rain would feel wonderful.

She stepped high in the tall grass, watching as

little grasshoppers jumped in front of her, whirring as they did, making her smile even though she didn't realize she still had any smiles left. Julia was like that, too, silently listening to her complain or reminisce, giving no judgment or even counsel, making her smile when she least expected it. In some ways, Amelia wished she could be more like Julia, with her calm strength. Amelia had a habit of saying or doing exactly what came into her mind before good sense told her not to.

She knocked on Julia's door and announced her presence, listening for the sound of her friend's voice bidding her to come in, but hearing nothing. On a few occasions, Julia had been out back working on her pottery, and her friend had directed her to go into the house and wait for her. Julia was a bit temperamental, like many artists, and didn't like anyone to watch her work.

Amelia opened the door, and knew immediately that something was terribly wrong.

# Chapter 16

"Who the hell are you?" came a gruff male voice.

If Amelia was startled, she barely showed it, pausing only in the act of removing her hat before dropping her hands to her sides. She knew instantly who the man was simply by the way Julia cowered on the bed, looking not like the proud woman she was, but the beaten wife this man had made of her.

"I am Lady Amelia Wellesley, a customer of Mrs. Benson. And you are, sir?" She was all haughty English lady, her chin high, her blue eyes icy. From the corner of her eye, she saw Julia shift slightly on the bed, almost as if she were cocking her ear to hear better. All the hanging glass mobiles that had made this tiny house magical had been ripped from their anchors, and her boots crunched slightly as she stepped into the room.

The room's single chair was upended, a long rifle lay across Julia's tiny table, and the floor was strewn with bits of broken glass, evidence of a violence that was terrifying. It was all Amelia could do not to run to Julia's bed and hold her friend tight, but she instinctively knew such a move would anger her husband and perhaps put both women at greater risk.

Sam Benson eyed Amelia up and down, making her skin crawl, but she maintained her haughty demeanor and looked back at him as if he were no more than an insect. She raised an eyebrow, and his rheumy brown eyes finally shifted away.

Amelia turned to Julia. "Is my vase ready?" she asked, her voice sounding amazingly normal. "You did say it would be. I suppose I could wait another day." She tugged on her gloves impatiently, and put on the beleaguered expression of an aristocrat disappointed with the lower classes. Turning to Benson, she said, "Your wife does make the most lovely vases. I ordered one for my mother, who simply adores rustic American art."

"That so?" Sam grumbled. "Well, she ain't got it."

"Oh, dear," Amelia said. "I'll simply have to come back tomorrow then." She forced a tight smile at the man and Julia, and turned to the door, praying he couldn't see that her entire body was shaking nearly uncontrollably. Just as she reached for the door handle, the man spoke.

"What the hell are you doing in Texas, anyway? You got kin here?"

Amelia took a shallow breath, the most air she could get into her lungs at the moment, and turned. "Goodness, no. My husband thought it would be rather diverting to explore the wilds of North America on our wedding trip," she said. "When the train stopped here, he thought it looked wonderfully American and insisted we stay at your saloon." She shuddered dramatically. "I do indulge the man."

"You don't know anyone in town, then?"

"Hardly. We've been here but two days."

"Then how you know Julia makes those pots?"

Amelia nearly panicked, and her cheeks flushed pink, as no quick answer came to her.

"She saw one of 'em in the mercantile," Julia said, and Amelia nearly cried with relief until she saw the look of pure violent hatred the man gave her friend. He looked at Julia the way a man would look at dog excrement on the bottom of his boot. It suddenly became even more urgent that she escape Julia's home and find Boone.

"It's been lovely meeting you, Mr. Benson. I'll stop by tomorrow for the vase, shall I, Mrs. Benson?" She tried to send Julia a silent message, but the woman's head remained bowed.

Julia gave her only a jerky nod, and this time Amelia made it to the door and calmly opened it, stepping out into the blazing hot sun of midday. Never had she been so happy to feel that sun beating down on her. Aware that Julia's husband might be looking out the window, Amelia took her time, pausing even to pretend to examine a flower as she sauntered back toward the hotel. She wanted nothing more than to lift her skirts and run as fast as she could to the store and Boone, but she couldn't risk such a move. It seemed to take forever to reach the shaded alley between the hotel and the bank, and as she did, the sound of gunfire cut through the air.

Amelia jerked violently at the sound and let out a small desperate sound before she lifted her skirts and ran to the store, groaning in frustration when she found it was locked. She banged on it hard, making the "closed" sign vibrate against the window, and nearly stumbled into the store when Boone suddenly opened it. She fell against him, clutching his shirt and shaking him.

"What is it? What's happened?" Boone said, staring down at her.

"Julia's husband," she gasped. "He's in her home. There was a gunshot. Oh, Boone, she looked so frightened. I shouldn't have left her there with him but I knew I had to get you."

Boone clutched her forearms, his gray eyes like flint. "Did he lay a hand on you?"

Amelia shook her head wildly. "No, no. I pretended I was there to buy a vase. I simply walked out. Boone, what can we do?"

Without hesitation, Boone walked behind the counter and grabbed his rifle, efficiently loading it, a grim look on his face. "You stay here," he said. "I know you're worried about Julia, but Benson's an evil man and he'd just as soon shoot you as shoot a dog."

"Why would he hurt her, why?" Amelia cried.

"Don't know," he said, cocking the gun expertly. "You go on over and tell George what's happening. I'm heading to Julia's."

"He'll kill you," Amelia whispered.

"No. He won't," Boone said, pulling her close. "He's a rotten shot."

Amelia looked up at him, her eyes glittering with unshed tears, amazed that he was actually trying to make her smile in this most frightening time. She pulled him close and kissed him, mindless of the hard line of the rifle pressing against her. "Be careful," she said, giving him one last kiss before letting him go.

They left the store, Boone heading to Julia's, Amelia running across the street to tell George what was happening. She didn't want to lose sight of Boone, as if doing so would leave him even more vulnerable. There was nothing but open space between Main Street and Julia's little shack. The only tree in sight was a small scraggly one that gave Julia a bit of shade in her garden. Boone was completely unprotected.

Amelia tripped up the steps to the saloon and shoved the door open, only to find the room completely empty. A strong smell of liquor, smoke, and unwashed male assaulted her. Not even that red-haired older woman was hanging about.

"Hello. George! It's Mrs. Kitteridge. Hello!" She moved toward a door hardly visible in the murky interior.

George stepped from the back room with a rifle in his hand. "I heard the shot. Julia?" George asked grimly.

"Yes. Julia's husband is back and Boone's heading there with a gun and he has absolutely no protection at all and he told me to come get you."

Before she'd taken a breath to give George more information, another shot sounded. For the smallest of moments, the two simply stared at one another as what they'd just heard registered on them. Then George erupted and headed for the hotel's back door, which faced Julia's house.

"You stay here," he said, and thrust out a hand, as if that would stop her.

Tears streaming down her face, Amelia ran to the

back door and let out a scream when she saw Boone lying on the ground two dozen yards from Julia's front door. She started running toward him, but George stopped her.

"He's all right. Not hit. You get back, you hear, Mrs. Kitteridge? You get back in that saloon now."

Breathing harshly, Amelia backed up until she felt the building behind her, not letting her eyes stray from Boone's prone form for even a moment. As she watched, she could see that Boone was slowly crawling toward the tiny house. It was agony to watch him inch closer and closer, completely exposed to the madman inside the house. She prayed the gunshot she'd heard hadn't struck Julia, that somehow her friend had managed to get away. Please, God, let her be well.

"You in there, Benson, you son of a bitch?" Boone called, his voice carrying clearly through the open space. Silence.

Boone looked back at George, who was a few yards behind, edging toward the door the same way her husband was. Behind her, a few townsfolk had gathered to see what all the commotion was about.

"Amelia, what's going on?" Amelia recognized Paula's voice, but simply shook her head. The woman could wait to find out what was happening. Amelia's mouth was so dry from fear, she doubted she could have spoken anyway.

"George, I'm going in," Boone called, and Amelia stepped forward, unable to stop herself. Even from a distance, she could see Boone's eyes on her, warning her silently to get back to the relative shelter of the hotel alley. It was only when she was in the shadows again that Boone stood up and approached the house, crouched over and holding his rifle, ready to shoot.

In one movement, Boone crashed through the door and the people watching gave a collective gasp. It seemed forever before he came back out, his head down. "They're both gone," he said, his low voice filled with anger.

That was when Amelia broke away from the crowd and ran to Boone, flying by George, who stood alone, his head lowered, his hand loosely holding his rifle. Amelia threw herself into Boone's arms, loving the solid feel of him, needing to have him hold her, needing to feel his strength.

"Why?" she cried. "Why would he hurt her? Oh, God, Boone, if I had stayed . . ."

"He would have killed you, too," Boone said fiercely, pushing her away just far enough so she could see his face. "He would have killed you," he repeated, and the knowledge of that was clear in his anguished eyes. He pulled her close again, almost painfully so, as if she truly had been in some sort of danger.

"She didn't deserve it," Amelia said, tears coursing down her face. "She didn't deserve any of it. I don't understand why. Why did he kill her? Why didn't he just kill himself and leave her be? She was the most beautiful person I knew. I'm glad he's dead. I'm glad."

They held each other for a long time, two bodies like one in the middle of a Texas prairie, as clouds rolled toward them and obliterated the midday sun. Boone looked up and studied the sky for a bit.

"I think we should get you home," he said slowly, his words heavy with meaning.

Amelia didn't want to move, even with the sky threatening rain. She just wanted to stand there forever, held in Boone's arms where she felt safe—the way Julia never had.

"Did you hear me, sweetheart?"

"You want to go home. I know."

She had her head pressed against his chest, listening to his powerful heartbeat until she felt his hand gently lift her chin so she could look up at him. Strangely, he was smiling down at her. "I meant home to Meremont. I meant let's get you really home."

# Chapter 17

Julia's funeral made Amelia angry all over again, but this time at the townspeople who came to show their respect. These were the same people who'd ostracized her and made Julia feel ashamed of what had happened. Amelia faced them stonily, standing by Boone. Reverend Beaumont had been brought in for the solemn ceremony, holding his Bible and letting his voice boom out so that even those who hadn't attended could likely hear him.

It lasted, perhaps, ten minutes, and then Boone, George, and the reverend shoveled dirt over Julia's coffin until there was nothing left to prove she had existed but a mound of dirt. Boone had promised her that he'd see to it a marker was made.

The small graveyard was within sight of Julia's little house, and Amelia started walking toward it, away from the grave, from the townspeople. She knew Boone followed silently behind her, but she kept walking until she reached the door, hesitating only a moment before pushing it open.

She wasn't sure what she would find when she

opened it, but some unknown force was pushing her, almost as if to prove that her friend was truly gone. She knew Boone had spent much of the day at the house yesterday, preparing the bodies for burial, cleaning up the aftermath of death.

But when the opened door revealed the sparkling, magical world that Julia had created so long ago, she smiled, even as her eyes filled with tears. The patchwork quilt that had lain upon Julia's bed had been replaced, the floor had been scrubbed clean, the tiny multicolored glass bits that made her world so beautiful clinked softly together in the morning breeze. That Boone had done this, had taken all those bits of glass and hung them again, had wiped this house clean of all the evil that had transpired there, was overwhelming.

As she watched the glass move in the slight breeze, making rainbows dance about the room, she knew, with utter certainty, that she loved her husband, this man who'd spent an entire day making Julia's world right again. Amelia turned and fell into Boone's arms, overcome with what he'd done. "I wish she could see it like this again. I wish she were here."

"I know."

"She was so frightened. All the time."

"I wanted to protect her," he said, his voice raw. "But I couldn't."

He gently pushed away from Amelia and walked farther into the room, his strong hand brushing the table as he passed it. He stood there, looking at that table, its old, marred surface where Julia had sat alone, night after night, and eaten her meals.

Amelia saw a drop hit his hand, and she turned away, unable to bear the pain she was witnessing.

"I was all she had, but I . . ." He stopped and clenched his fist. "I was her doctor."

Amelia took a step toward him, then stopped. "You were her friend. Her only friend for a very long time."

Boone roughly wiped at his face, then turned to Amelia, the rawness of his pain hurting her heart. "Let's go," he said finally, walking by her, not touching her—and Amelia didn't know why.

That night, they sat together at their kitchen table, an awful cold space between them, and Boone stared at the black night, feeling the weight of terrible guilt that he hadn't protected Julia. He'd known of the threat, he'd suspected the man would return some day, but he'd still been unable to save her when she needed it the most. Benson could have just as easily killed Amelia that day, and he wouldn't have been able to do a thing. The only thing that had saved his wife was her wit and bravery.

He squeezed his eyes shut in a vain attempt to turn off his torturous thoughts. When he was four years old, he remembered watching his mother die, remembered trying to get her to drink some water. It was one of the few memories of his mother that he had, watching her helplessly die. She was the last person who had loved him, the only person. Even Roy, for all his kindness, had never showed him more than a kind of stoic protectiveness and duty. If he had loved Boone, he'd never said it, never showed it. Roy had put clothes on his back and food in his stomach, he'd paid for his schooling, but he'd done all of it from a distance. There had never been any birthday parties or Christmas presents. There had been no hugs or tucking in at night. Perhaps the worst thing was Boone had never expected any of that, for he knew he would never be more than a boy Roy had taken in, not his son, not someone to love.

Boone thought he'd learned not to feel, but apparently he hadn't learned well enough. He'd loved his mother with all his heart, and he was in real danger of feeling that way for Amelia. He had to stop this love. Had to. He hated the agony that washed over him at the thought of Amelia being hurt. If it hurt so much to lose Julia, how much would it hurt to lose Amelia? It didn't bear thinking about.

"Boone?"

He swallowed down his fear. "Hmmm?"

"We don't have to move to Hollings."

He turned his head to look at her, hating the way his heart hurt as he gazed upon her. "Where should we go then?"

Amelia tilted her head in confusion. "What do you mean?"

He turned back to look through the window at the dark night. "I'm not staying here, so it surely makes sense that one of us is somewhere they can call home."

"I don't understand."

"I hate Small Fork," he said, knowing he sounded harsh, angry. "Likely as much as you do."

She looked positively stunned. "You do?"

"When I was in university, all I dreamed about was going away. It didn't matter where. California, Oregon, Boston, even. But I couldn't, not with Roy needing me at the store. I owed him my life. I moved back to Small Fork, knowing that someday I'd leave. I didn't want him to die, but when he did, I knew I'd leave Small Fork forever. And then Julia got hurt."

"You stayed for her?"

"I couldn't leave her. She needed me. She needed medical attention and protection against her husband." He let out a bitter laugh.

"Did she know?"

"I hope not. No, she didn't. If she had, she would have been madder than a hornet." He was silent for a moment. "Or hurt. She hated pity."

Amelia stared at him as a sharp realization hit her. She'd always known Boone liked to save things, but she had no idea the lengths he would go to put his own needs last. No doubt, he would have stayed in Small Fork for years if not for Julia's death. He'd even put his own life at risk in hopes of saving hers.

"Boone. Why did you marry me? Truly." A horrible thought had come to her, one she couldn't shake. With all her worries about her not loving Boone and her recent revelation that she did, she hadn't thought even for a moment that Boone didn't love her. Oh, she'd thought at first he was simply trying to save her, but since then she'd become quite convinced that he loved her. Even though his love had made her feel guilty, even unworthy of it, it had still given her comfort, to know that he loved her.

Even though he'd never told her as much.

Even though he never touched her, hardly even smiled, when they were not in bed.

Could it be possible that Boone didn't love her? That all he felt was such vast responsibility toward her, he was willing to marry her and stay married to her?

Boone shifted uneasily in his chair, his eyes still staring through the kitchen window. "Because you needed a husband," he said slowly. "And because I thought we would suit. And we have."

Amelia was completely unprepared for the wave of despair that washed over her.

*Oh my God, he* doesn't *love me.*

She turned her head and studied his profile, trying to gather the courage to tell him she loved him. She'd given her love so freely to Carson, gushed on and on about love, and he'd lied and told her he loved her. Boone wouldn't lie, she knew that.

And that was why she didn't tell him; she didn't want to know the truth.

"I'll go whenever you want to, Boone," she said quietly, not even knowing if he heard her, for he didn't respond.

But he smiled grimly into the darkness, an unwanted lightness touching his heart, and the weariness that had made his life so hard started to lift.

*October 1894*
*England*

They arrived in Liverpool on a cold and blustery early October day, with heavy clouds hanging down low and the River Mersey a dark, gloomy gray.

"It's not always like this," Amelia said, huddling happily into her coat as Boone shivered by the rail of the ship as they waited what seemed an interminable time for the tide to rise high enough so they could disembark upon the landing stage. "Oh, there's Edward," she said, frantically waving to her brother, who'd obviously already spotted them from his higher vantage point on the wharf.

Liverpool was a bustling port town, about as different from Small Fork as one could get. Large three- and four-story brick warehouses stretched back from the docks, obscuring any of the more picturesque parts of the city. It all looked wonderfully English. Even the smell of coal smoke, coating the chilly air, gave Amelia a feeling of nostalgia.

Liverpool was a rapidly growing city, and they could hear the sounds of construction all around them. It was noisy and chaotic, and Amelia watched for Boone's reaction as he took in the long lines of houses in the distance, cramped together, electrical lines looking like malevolent spiderwebs crisscrossing the city.

"Hollings is much more in the country. Much . . . cleaner," Amelia said.

"Please stop worrying about me. I haven't been this happy in years," Boone said, smiling down at her and making her heart swell.

It was true. Boone had never felt so excited about anything than since the day he'd stepped onto the train heading for Tulane. He felt as if his life was finally beginning.

But no matter what he said, Amelia simply would not believe him. It was maddening that she continued to believe he was moving to Hollings for her.

He loved the chaos, the noise, the people everywhere. He even loved the damp chill in the air, though he suspected it wouldn't be long before he dreamed of the dry, hot heat of Texas. His years in New Orleans, with its water-drenched air, had at first seemed wonderful, as well.

They had left nearly everything behind, but for some vital medical equipment and clothing. He wanted to take nothing of his former life with him, and in all honesty, there wasn't much to take. George took Three Legs and Agatha took Blink. His own room was barren of personal effects, the house simply a place to live. Now, they would have a home, a cottage in an English village, a place where their children could play without fear.

"We should have taken a ship that landed in Southampton," Amelia grumbled. "This wait is quite maddening, especially knowing that our carriage is waiting and we cannot get to it. We could be home in an hour's time if we could just get off this ship."

"Before you know it, we'll be there."

"I wonder where we shall live," she said, not for the first time. "I wonder what's available in the village. The doctor's house simply won't do. It's fine for an old bachelor, but you're not an old bachelor." She looked up at him to gauge his reaction. "Of course, we don't need anything too fancy. Just as long as it's ours."

Boone frowned, hating such discussions that involved money—and reminders that he had so little. Everything on this trip had been paid for with Amelia's dowry, which seemed a pretty poor way for a man to get cash. The whole idea of a dowry seemed downright humiliating, no matter how many times Amelia explained that titled families often still used them in wedding negotiations.

George had paid him two thousand dollars for his store and inventory, and he didn't want to spend it all on fancy hotels and new clothes. He'd thought he would use that money to buy themselves a nice little cottage in Hollings. But now, that two thousand dollars didn't seem nearly as much as it had when George had handed it over.

With that money in his pocket, Boone had felt rich, until he started realizing Amelia's idea of "rich" was far, far different. Until she'd rather blithely told him the gown she was wearing when she'd walked into his store that first day cost more than five hundred dollars, a stunning amount to him, but a rather modest amount to her.

"I got a rather nice price on it because it was missing some lace. Edward was very impressed. You'll see, I can be very frugal when I set my mind to it."

Boone's idea of frugal was very different from hers. He'd had a general idea that Amelia's family was well-to-do, but he was starting to feel extremely aware that she was from a kind of wealth he'd never imagined.

"Oh, look," Amelia said, pulling him away from his thoughts. She was jumping up and down a bit, like a child ready to open up a large present on Christmas morning. "They're getting ready for the gangplank. How do I look?"

Her cheeks were flushed from the wind and cold, her blue eyes sparkling, and he didn't think she'd ever looked more beautiful to him. "Like a picture," he said, and she smiled.

"A nice one, I hope," she said, teasing him. "Oh, I'm so nervous. Why am I so nervous? You're the one who should be jumping out of his skin, not me. Are you nervous?"

He laughed out loud. "If you want me to be."

She grabbed his arms and leaned into him, seeming utterly happy. "I can't believe we're home. I just can't believe it."

Boone wished he could capture this moment when Amelia was purely happy, and he realized in all the time he'd known her, he'd never seen her this way before, bubbling over with joy. This was what her brother had meant when he'd told him all those weeks ago that Amelia had a joy about her. He was finally seeing the girl she truly was, the girl Carson couldn't resist. Boone knew he certainly couldn't resist her. So right there, in front of her brother and anyone else who happened to look toward them, Boone pulled her in for a long kiss.

"My," she breathed.

And then he pulled her toward the gangplank, toward the rest of their life.

Boone drew his coat a bit closer, eying the rich-looking coach that would bring them to Meremont. The coach, a burgundy red, stood out against the mist-washed backdrop of Liverpool like a red poppy in the prairie. A man in an odd uniform stepped down at their approach and knocked on the coach's door with a sharp, efficient rap.

And then Lord Hollings emerged, wearing an overcoat with a fur collar, boots that gleamed from polishing, and a derby hat. He stepped down and embraced his sister, then shook Boone's hand.

"Welcome to England," he said, looking up at the gray sky. "Sorry about the weather."

"I don't mind," Boone said truthfully. Right now it was the sheer differentness of England that he most appreciated. There was nothing to remind him of Small Fork and his past.

Lord Hollings handed his sister into the coach and waited while Boone climbed aboard. Inside, Boone was again struck by the luxury of the vehicle, its leather seats, thick velvet curtains, and brass fittings. The walls were paneled with a dark wood, and an inlay design of the type he'd seen only once in the home of an acquaintance from school.

"I hope your trip was good," Lord Hollings said after they'd all piled into the roomy carriage. "Those Atlantic crossings can be perilous, even this time of year. My wife was in a shipwreck, you know."

"It was horrible," Amelia said. "But she was so brave about it. She not only sailed back to England, she got right on a ship in search of me. I never did thank her for that. But our sailing was lovely, even if it was interminably long," Amelia said, a silly grin still on her face. "I cannot wait to get to Meremont and get settled in. I feel as if I've been gone for years."

"Speaking of home, I've found a couple of houses for you to look at that would be suitable for you," Lord Hollings said. "They're both rather small, but I think they'll do for now."

"How small?" Amelia asked.

"We don't need much room," Boone said at the same time. Anything would do, as long as it had a bedroom, sitting room, and kitchen, and a place to set up his practice.

"I suppose you'll have to determine what small means when you see them. In the meantime, you're both more than welcome to stay at Meremont."

"It would be lovely to be in our own home by Christmas," Amelia said. "We shall have a large tree and perhaps a Christmas dinner. I have so many friends that I haven't seen in so long, I just know they'll want to visit. Of course, I don't know whether everything will be ready this year. We'll have to hire staff and that can take time. Unless we borrow some of yours," she added, teasing her brother.

"Staff?" Boone asked.

"You cannot run a proper home without servants these days," Amelia pointed out.

Boone had a feeling that Amelia was in for a bit of a shock when she realized a doctor's salary likely would not be able to pay for staff, never mind a home big enough to hold them. But it wasn't until they had reached the Meremont estate boundary, then continued to drive another half hour, that Boone realized the extent of Lord Hollings's wealth.

As they approached a large two-story stone home with mullioned windows and a well-kept garden, Boone was slightly relieved. The house wasn't much grander than those he'd seen in Fort Worth and New Orleans. They passed by the house without slowing and Boone frowned.

Apparently seeing Boone's interest in the house, Amelia said, "That's the caretaker's cottage. I've always loved it."

Boone tried not to look stunned, but he sat back in his seat and grasped his thighs almost painfully. "Just how big is your brother's home?"

Amelia seemed almost reluctant to answer. "It's quite large, actually. I thought I told you."

"No. You didn't."

"I wouldn't be overly impressed by its size," Lord Hollings put in. "It was simply one of my ancestors' ways of proving his worth to the aristocracy."

And then the carriage turned a corner, and sitting on a small crest was Meremont, the grandest home Boone had ever set eyes on. He'd seen huge plantation homes in Louisiana, and grand homes in Texas, but this was as large as a New York hotel. It made him purely ill to look at it.

"What the hell," he said softly, and let the velvet curtain drop.

"What's wrong?" Amelia asked, her overly innocent tone making him believe that she'd been purposefully vague about Meremont. What had she said? That it was a "big old house by the sea." Yes, he thought, seeing the glimmer of the Irish Sea in the distance, it certainly was that.

"You never told me you lived in a palace," he said, feeling anger wash over him. How the hell was he going to make Amelia happy in a tiny cottage when this was what she came from? No wonder she'd been so bewildered when she'd first arrived in Texas.

And he'd been ready to have her live behind the store in that rundown little apartment. He'd been so proud of his little fountain and garden. His face turned ruddy when he remembered showing her his flush toilet.

The carriage wheels sounded loud on the cobble-stone drive as the horses were brought round a huge fountain that looked more like a large pool. The house itself was a three-story, soft yellow stone building with intricate gables and a slate roof that bespoke history and money. The shrubbery was pruned to perfection, rounded and sculpted as if even the leaves had agreed to convey an impression of vast wealth.

A huge two-story bay window dominated the left side of the building, giving it an almost homey look. If it was any building other than the home his wife had come from, he would have thought it beautiful. But the sight of it only served to prove to him that he was about as out of place as a tumble-weed in New York City.

"I thought you said Meremont was relatively small," he said, nearly choking on his words. He didn't want to sound like a country bumpkin, but that was exactly what he felt like.

"It *is*. Relatively speaking, that is," Amelia said, giving Meremont a worried look, as if she was just now realizing that Boone was less than happy. "You should see the Duke of Bellingham's house. It's truly a palace."

"And this is?"

"A country house," she said with forced noncha-lance, smiling as she looked out her window. "Oh, it's far grander than the home I grew up in. That house was much smaller and not nearly as lovely, was it, Edward?"

"We English like to do things rather grandly," Edward said, sounding almost apologetic. "As I said, don't let the size of the thing intimidate you.

We only use a few rooms. Many of our homes have been sold or let out to help pay the debts of the estate. Times are difficult, even for the titled."

"That's why the duke married an American," Amelia said.

Edward made a sound.

"Oh, shush. I adore Her Grace and you know it, but it's the truth. All these titles and all these houses, and not enough to support them."

"And no one to buy them, either. Many are entailed and cannot be sold, you see," Edward explained.

"What does entailed mean, exactly?" Boone said, feeling quite lost among these English rules.

"It means a property must be passed on to the next heir," Edward explained. "It's a way to prevent properties from being broken up, leaving some poor sap homeless because of a relative's misdeeds. You see, I was untitled, being the son of a second son, but inherited the title and the entailments when my uncle died without a direct heir. I was saved from disaster only by the intelligent investments my uncle made. He was a man ahead of his time."

"The poor duke had to marry an heiress or let his estate go to ruin, you see. But it all turned out well in the end, because they are madly in love," Amelia said, sounding almost wistful.

The carriage finally came to a stop and the three stepped down. Boone looked up only to see a line of servants forming to greet them all. "Oh, hell," he said, beneath his breath.

Amelia glanced at him, a crease of worry between her eyes, and she squeezed his hand. "You'll get used to all this," she said, as if that would somehow comfort him. The fact was, he wouldn't have to get used to any of this because he'd be lucky if he could afford a cook, never mind the "staff" Amelia was apparently envisioning.

"You should have told me," Boone said, close to her ear so he wouldn't be overheard. "And the fact you didn't makes me believe that you knew I'd be angry."

Amelia grinned. "What a silly thing to be angry about. How awful to find your wife is well-to-do."

"This is more than 'well-to-do,' and you know it." All Boone could think about at that moment was the shack he'd grown up in, the fact that he hadn't owned a pair of boots until he was ten years old. Amelia had grown up in this luxury. He'd known, of course, that she was used to a finer life than the one he could provide her, but this was far beyond what he'd imagined. And she didn't seem bothered a bit by it. He remembered her standing in his kitchen, staring mutely at the stove, and he suddenly understood how very lost she must have felt.

About as lost as he felt at the moment, he realized. And yet, Amelia had hardly complained. She'd gamely learned how to light the stove, how to wash laundry, how to be the wife of a poor Texas doctor. He stared at the servants, at the pure wealth they represented, and took a long, bracing breath.

He felt her hand on his arm, and looked down to see Amelia smiling up at him. "Don't you dare get angry with me, Boone. Look, the stables." She pointed to a long, two-story stone structure set back from the house. "Edward, do you think Boone could have a horse to ride?" Amelia asked. "I so miss riding. Did you know there were no sidesaddles in Small Fork? Not one. If a lady wants to ride, she must do so like a man. I wanted to try but never got the chance. It's just as well. It looks quite painful to me." She grinned widely. "You two will simply have to go out for a ride tomorrow and look at the grounds. I'll come, too."

Amelia clapped her hands together. "Oh, I cannot tell you how wonderful it is to be home."

"She's only slightly deliriously happy," Boone said to Edward.

"I'm over the *moon*," Amelia said, laughing. "And Boone is, too. Or so he says."

Boone shook his head, not quite recognizing the vibrant woman next to him. She was talking a mile a minute, smiling and fairly hopping up and down in her excitement. It was difficult to remain angry when she was bubbling with happiness next to him. "I'm over the moon," he confirmed solemnly. He pushed aside his misgivings. This was what he wanted, a life as different from the one he'd had as he could get, and a happy wife. He'd lived his life in fear, and he'd be damned if he was going to carry it with him his entire life.

Amelia knew she was probably worrying too much about Boone, but she couldn't help feeling terribly guilty for forcing all this on him. It didn't matter how many times he told her he was glad to leave Texas, she couldn't quite believe him. She wished for once he would do something just for himself, and be damned to the rest of the world. She wished he could be carefree, laugh without restraint. Love her without restraint.

It was perfectly awful loving him, knowing he

didn't love her. She'd made the mistake once of thinking physical love was the same as emotional love for a man. Boone was a different person entirely when they were making love. He was full of abandon and almost playful. But he always left her alone in bed, claiming that he couldn't sleep or was fearful his nightmares would awaken her. On the ship, she would awaken to find him on the floor, sometimes thrashing about in the throes of a nightmare. He wouldn't tell her about them, and she'd stopped asking.

As they walked up together to their room, Amelia prayed their life would change now they were in England. He certainly seemed happy to be here.

"You should rest before dinner," he said as they reached the landing, where generations of Hollings earls graced the walls, their portraits looking sternly down at them. Edward had not yet gotten his portrait done, and Amelia intended to request that he smile for his. What an unhappy lot her ancestors seemed.

"Your room, missus," the maid said with a little curtsy. "And the doctor is next door," she added, looking from one to the other. "Is that awright, then?"

"That's fine," Boone said, his cheeks turning red, making Amelia wonder if he were bothered by the separate rooms.

"We can have them move you to my room without a problem, Boone."

"No, it's probably better," he said, not looking at her. "You know I don't sleep well, and you need your rest."

"I don't mind your dreams," Amelia said hesitantly, and watched as his cheeks grew even ruddier and his jaw clenched in irritation. "I grew quite used to them on the ship."

"It's better," he repeated, then walked to the next door down where the little maid waited.

"Better than what?" Amelia muttered to herself as she entered her room with a frown. This wasn't her room, her old room. It was the best guest room in Meremont, which only made Amelia feel more depressed. She wanted her old room, her old life, she thought rebelliously. A life without a grumpy husband who didn't love her, and probably never would.

After the maid left, Boone went to the window and looked out, giving another curse when his eyes met the vast expanse below him. The gardens were immaculate, and the sea shined painfully blue in the distance. The room was large, luxurious, and masculine, with a heavy canopied bed and dark russet bedding. A large, intricately carved wardrobe that looked like it was from the Middle Ages dominated one corner of the room, and a fireplace, with a small fire already lit, gave the vast space a homey feel. Everything he looked at reminded him of everything he could never give Amelia.

He closed his eyes against the hurt he'd seen in her face when he'd said he wanted to have his own room. The truth was, he couldn't sleep with her, not with the violent nightmares that had been plaguing him of late. They'd always been bad, always terrorized his sleep. He would have thought he'd have outgrown such things as nightmares about the beatings he'd received, but for some reason they'd only gotten worse. And now, in his dreams, he'd begun to fight back, begun to pummel his father. Until he was dead.

They were bloody, horrendous dreams that he awoke from feeling depressed and sickened. In his dreams, he was worse than his father, slowly choking the life out of him, relishing the old man's terror. He'd awoken from one such dream grabbing his pillow in his fists, twisting viciously, as he'd twisted his father's neck in the dream. And Amelia had lain sleeping next to him, oblivious to the fact that it could have been her beneath his hands and not simply a pillow.

My God, he'd already struck her once, leaving an ugly bruise that made him sick to see. She'd shrugged it off and laughed, told him not to be silly. She knew he didn't mean it, and of course, he hadn't meant to hurt her. But he had hurt her, and next time it could be much, much worse.

The dreams were a shameful reminder of where he'd come from, a past from which he could not escape. He'd thought that perhaps having Amelia sleeping next to him would give him solace, but it only seemed to make things worse. Perhaps her soft breathing, her subtle movements triggered something in his sleeping brain that awoke the fear and violence lying dormant there.

He wanted to be with her, wanted to hold her in his arms, but he could not take the chance of hurting her. She would regret their marraige even more if she knew the extent of the brutality in his dreams. Boone was beginning to believe that whatever demons had made his father the way he was also lived inside of him, and simply waited to escape.

"Something's wrong," Maggie said that night as she pulled a brush through her long, dark curls.

"You saw it too, then."

Maggie turned to her husband, surprised he'd noticed that not all was right between Amelia and Boone. "They don't hate each other."

"They don't look at each other. I've never seen a couple not look at each other as much as those two."

Maggie looked at the reflection of Edward, smiled at him. "I hadn't noticed that specifically. I suppose not every married couple is as in love as we are."

"Or as Rand and Elizabeth are."

Maggie gave Edward a troubled look. "I do get the distinct feeling that they are not deliriously happy. At least Boone is not. And it's more than that he is feeling a bit out of place here. I can't quite put my finger on it."

Edward came up behind Amelia and put his hands on her shoulders. "Remember when you returned to England?"

"The first time or the second time?"

"Either time. I loved you so much, I couldn't bear to look at you. It hurt too much."

"I do remember. And I remember doing the same," Maggie said, her brow furrowed. "But we weren't married then. Each of us was just pretending we weren't madly in love, so that the other wouldn't know . . ." Her voice trailed off and Edward raised an eyebrow.

"Precisely."

"Do you really think they are madly in love but afraid to let one another know?"

Edward shrugged. "It's either that, or they truly don't love one another."

Maggie turned and swatted him playfully on the arm, and he bent and gave her a long kiss in apology. Pulling back, he smiled at his beautiful wife. "If they do love each other, it shouldn't take too long before they figure it out."

Maggie still looked worried. "What if one is not looking at the other because they are in love, and the other is not looking because they are not."

It took a moment before Edward could figure out what Maggie was saying. "Ah. Unrequited love."

"Oh, that would be horrible. Who's the unrequited one, then? Boone or Amelia?"

"Boone. Women are entirely more fickle about love than men. And remember, the poor sod was already half in love with her before they were even married."

Maggie stood and wrapped her arms around Edward's neck, nuzzling her face against his chest. "I'm so glad we figured it out. Imagine if we hadn't. Imagine if one of us was too proud to admit how stupid you were being."

Edward let out a laugh and gave his wife a sound kissing as punishment for her teasing.

"I do hope the ball we planned to introduce Boone to society isn't a mistake. He's so very shy."

"Mmmm."

"Lord Hollings, you are not listening to me at all," Maggie said in mock anger.

"How can I possibly care about a ball when my

wife is standing in my arms?" he said, his hands beginning to drift just where she wanted them.

Maggie let out a soft sigh of pure pleasure. "It's too late to cancel, the invitations are out, and . . ." She squealed as he lightly nibbled at her ear. And that was the end of that particular conversation.

# Chapter 18

The next few days were spent settling into their new life, looking at homes for let or purchase, and for Boone, meeting his future patients. Dr. White led him 'round to the patients that he visited the most—the Fitzfields with their twelve children, Mrs. Delvin, who had been bedridden for two years, and Mrs. Langley, who, Dr. White suspected, was simply lonely.

He found the village charming, the people warm, but a problem came up that he had not at all anticipated. He could only understand every other word they were saying, which Dr. White found rather delightful.

"Me conker's 'l swerlen, if'n ye noticed," one old gent said. "Me conker." He'd looked at Dr. White helplessly until he translated for him.

"He has a swollen nose. No doubt from visiting the pub, eh, Sully?" The old man gave the doctor a sheepish look and tipped his hat to both men before heading down the street—probably to visit yet another pub.

Amelia kept busy touring houses and finding none to her liking. They were either too austere, too small, or too far away from the town center.

Discouraged, Amelia returned to Meremont with Maggie.

"I think we've been to every available home in Hollings," she said as the women walked up the shallow steps to Meremont's front door.

"You know you can stay here as long as you want," Maggie said.

"I know, but I'd like to be in our own place for the holidays. And I think Boone would too."

They walked into a little sitting room, and Maggie pulled a rope for tea. "I'm famished. I swear I've become a proper English lady having tea each day."

"It is the thing I missed most when I was in Texas," Amelia said feelingly. "That and trees."

Maggie was thoughtful for a moment before asking, "Do you think Boone misses Texas?"

Amelia shrugged. "He doesn't say he does. But I don't think so. I have noticed that he looks more tired of late, as if he's not getting enough rest. He doesn't sleep well."

"Are you worried?"

She shook her head and stared into her tea. "I don't think he's ever slept well," she said, and left it at that. She wanted to add that Boone seemed happy, happier than he'd ever been. Yet more distant.

That was why, the next day, when Boone arrived home early, she made it her mission to drag him outside for a walk with her.

"Shall we go down by the beach? It's a lovely day

and the tide is low so we'll have plenty of beach to walk on."

Boone smiled. "All right."

Amelia gave a little happy jump, making Boone smile even more broadly. She adored it when he smiled, she thought as she hurried to fetch her coat and gloves. The sun was shining, but it was a windy day and down by the sea it was always cooler.

As the wind buffeted them, making their cheeks pink, Amelia said, "Now you know why all my gowns were wool."

Boone pulled his collar up. "I like it." Seeing her look of disbelief, he said, "I do. But, it does get warm in the summer, here, doesn't?"

"A bit," Amelia said, laughing. She picked up her skirts and ran to the bluff, then disappeared from view. Boone let out a shout, only to find Amelia peering back up at him from a safe shelf over the crashing surf, laughing with abandon. "Sorry," she said, between laughs, then proceeded to expertly scale down the steep path to the rocky beach below.

Boone followed her, liking the way she confidently lifted her skirts and navigated the path with ease. When they reached the bottom, she flung herself against him, laughing.

"Your lips are like ice," he said, kissing her.

"I know. Isn't it wonderful?"

They walked hand in hand, looking at the seagulls hanging from the sky, surfing the wind. Tiny little plovers skittered in the sand in front of them searching for food.

"This is nice," Boone said, breathing deeply of the salty sea air. He'd never spent much time near the water. It was bracing and invigorating, and again he was struck by how different this place was from Small Fork.

"You must have felt very strange in Texas," he said, gazing out onto the white-capped sea.

"I did."

He looked down at her, realizing how very strong she'd been in such a strange land. She'd complained of the heat, but in a goodnatured way. How shocking it must have seemed compared to this damp coolness. "You were very brave," he said, wishing he could say something more, but feeling foolish.

"No more brave than you," Amelia said, kissing his cheek. She swallowed and looked out at the sea. "I'll always be grateful to you."

*Grateful.*

They walked a bit further up the beach, then looked back, surprised how far they'd come.

"I believe if we walk up this path, we'll come to a road and the walking will be a bit easier."

So the two began trudging up the walk, happy to find a set of sturdy stone steps and a wooden railing that had been carved into the cliff. "My goodness, it's been a while since my legs have gotten this much exercise."

Boone reached the top first, and held his hand to hoist her up the last few steps. They both turned toward the road . . . and that was when they saw the home they would live in for the rest of their lives.

It seemed a bit magical, that they would turn and see the house, abandoned and overrun by ivy, a crooked "For Sale" sign tacked to a white picket fence badly in need of whitewashing.

"Oh, my," Maggie breathed.

It wasn't a large house by any means, but one that welcomed them, as if it were calling out to their very souls. The two-story clapboard house had a slate roof and tiny little turrets, as if it were trying to be far grander than it was. A balcony stretched along the top floor, and French doors looked out to the Irish Sea. At the very top of the house was a widow's walk. If Boone had conjured up the perfect house, he couldn't have done better.

They looked at each other and smiled, feeling one of those rare moments that married couples share when they know, deep in their hearts, they are thinking precisely the same thing at the same moment.

"Welcome home," Boone said, and they both ran across the road to get a better look at the old place.

"Oh, it's lovely," Amelia said, standing on the front porch and gazing out to the sea. "I can't believe our agent didn't point it out to us. Perhaps it's in disrepair." They stood side by side and peered through the window, each putting their hands on either side of their heads to block the glare of the sun. Inside, the walls were whitewashed, and a large fireplace dominated what must have been the main parlor. Sheets covered the furniture, but they could see the wide-plank floors and old-fashioned wall sconces. It was absolutely charming.

They walked around to the back, stepping over a garden gone to weeds, as well as discarded wagon wheels, and even the rotted carcass of an old rowboat.

"It doesn't look as if anyone has lived here for years. I wonder why," Amelia said. The house was larger than it appeared from the front, stretching back into an overgrown lawn. No neighbor's house was visible, giving the place absolute privacy.

"Maybe it's haunted," Boone said. "By an old sea captain." He looked at the widow's walk built onto the roof.

"Oh, I should love to have a ghost or two," Amelia said, clapping her hands together.

It was moments like this when Boone had to use all his restraint not to drag her into his arms and proclaim his undying love. She was so beautiful standing there in her simple day dress, her windswept hair a mess, her cheeks flushed from the wind and sun. She'd long ago taken off her hat, as it was futile to keep it on in the strong wind that blew in from the sea, and so strands of her hair whipped across her face. He reached out and tucked one strand behind her ear, swallowing heavily.

"I think I'll come to you tonight, if you don't mind," he said, his voice sounding low and gruff.

"I don't mind." She turned to look back at the house. "I wish it could be ours now. I wish we could sleep here tonight."

"You don't think it's too small?"

"Goodness, no. You should have seen the stone mausoleums that agent was showing me. They had about as much warmth as a sanitarium. But this . . . this is a house for a family." She blushed prettily, and Boone's gut wrenched.

"Do you think you're . . . ?"

Amelia was momentarily confused, then realized what he was asking. "No, not yet. I'm quite sure. But someday, we'll have children and they'll grow up here and run down to the beach."

"Only when they are old enough."

"Yes, and we'll build sand castles and explore and collect seashells."

"How many children?"

"Six," she said with a decisive nod.

"Six? That's a half dozen."

"Yes. A lovely number. And if we have to make the place larger, we can always add on."

"Six children?" he asked again.

"Yes," Amelia said, hugging herself and gazing up at the house. "Six little rosy-cheeked, well-behaved, beautiful children. The boys shall look like you and the girls like me."

"That would probably be best," Boone said indulgently.

Amelia grinned happily. "Let's go speak to my agent and tell him to find the owner so we can arrange a purchase."

"Don't you want to see the inside first?" Boone asked.

"Not at all. If it's something we don't like, we can fix it. But we'll never find another home like this. It's calling to me, Boone. It's the strangest thing. It's almost as if it were waiting here all this time, waiting for us to find it here. We can make it happy."

Boone looked at the house skeptically and followed Amelia back to the front of the cottage.

"Look," she said, pointing at the house. "It's smiling."

Boone tilted his head and realized that the house, with its symmetrical shape and gracefully curved porch, did indeed look like it could be smiling.

\* \* \*

Two weeks later, Amelia sat in her brother's library and breathed deeply. Oh, that *smell,* that wonderfully familiar smell of books and beeswax and leather. Could there be a more wonderful smell on this earth? She hugged herself, her eyes still closed, as she scooted down further into the overstuffed chair where she'd decided to curl up with a book for the afternoon.

Why, it was almost as if she'd never left at all. Other than the fact she now was married, of course. The cottage would not be ready for another few weeks, and was in far worse condition than it first appeared. The place had been empty for fifteen years and needed to be completely modernized. Amelia couldn't wait to move in, but in the meantime, enjoyed being home.

Boone had been kept inordinately busy with his new patients, who, after a bit of reticence, were eager to meet the handsome young American doctor. Especially the women, Amelia noted with some displeasure. Boone claimed to be completely oblivious to the fact that nearly every woman in the village, whether a toddler or in her dotage, suddenly developed some sort of illness.

"At least they all pay in silver," had been Boone's only comment. Indeed, after a career spent collecting eggs and beef as payment, real currency was a bit of a novelty.

Her brother entered the room, pausing for a moment when he saw his little sister once again taking up space in his library. "Here again, are we?"

Amelia wrinkled her nose at him.

"Don't you think you should spend a bit more time doing something else?"

"Doing what? Other than needlework, there's not much for me to do until the cottage is ready. I was hoping Aunt Matilda would be arriving soon with the children. I do miss them."

"They'll be here soon enough," Edward said dryly. "And as you do nothing more than read and visit with Maggie, I don't see why you cannot spend a bit more time getting the cottage ready. Surely you must need curtains and such."

Amelia gave him a level look. "I've already ordered them. It took approximately twenty minutes. Other than putting on a pair of coveralls and picking up a hammer, there's not much for me to do to get it ready. I fear if I did, I would do more damage than good, anyway. Boone works all day. I hardly see him. Who knew there were so many sick people in Hollings? Sick women, that is."

"Jealous, are you?"

"Of course. The women of Hollings see far more of my husband than I do." Even at night, after the rare times they made love, Boone would leave her bed for his. And every time she pretended it didn't matter, even though it broke her heart.

"I have to work, just like your husband does. As a matter of fact, I have several meetings this afternoon which require privacy." He stared at her expectantly. "I'm afraid you'll have to leave."

Just then, as if planned, the butler announced the arrival of her brother's counsel.

"Don't you have friends to visit?"

"Of course," Amelia said, forcing herself to sound cheerful.

The fact was, the one visit she'd made to an old friend had been a disappointing affair, strained to the point of being exceedingly uncomfortable. Betsy Gardner was now Lady Havershaw, as she'd married a local baron, an older man who'd been widowed and was trying to add a boy to his brood of five girls. Betsy had taken on a sour look, like someone who was terminally unhappy with life. Amelia couldn't remember her being quite so disagreeable before. They hadn't been best friends, but Amelia remembered a few afternoons discussing parties and eligible bachelors together. Perhaps the only thing they'd had in common back then was that they were both unmarried.

And Amelia had the distinct feeling, as difficult as it was to fathom, that Betsy somehow felt superior to Amelia, simply because she'd married a doddering old baron. Betsy had said nothing overt, of course, nothing Amelia could repeat and show as proof, but the visit had not gone well.

"Perhaps I can go visiting," Amelia said, warming to the idea. After all, Betsy wasn't the only old friend she'd had in the area.

She asked a footman to have a carriage made ready and hurried to change, thankful to have a maid again who could help her into her nicer dresses. She put on a lovely sky-blue day dress that reminded her, for some reason, of the distinct color of the Texas sky at midday. Oddly, it made her smile to think of it.

Within twenty minutes she was handing her card to a solemn butler who worked for one of her friends, Mrs. Beatrice Turner. Beatrice and Amelia had gone to Prout Finishing School together, often commiserating on the complete inanity of much of what they were required to learn. Beatrice had married a very nice gentleman, the heir to a successful shipping enterprise.

Their home was vast and built to impress, containing many modern conveniences, such as electricity and modern plumbing, that many of the older homes in the area did not yet have. Bringing the ancient homes of England up to modern standards was never an inexpensive task. Amelia had been to the home once before leaving, and found it and her friend delightful.

"Madam, if you will," the butler said, bowing slightly and leading her to a sitting room off the marbled entry hall that boasted one of the most impressive chandeliers Amelia had ever seen. Why, it looked large enough to hold a half dozen people swinging upon its great arms, and she smiled, picturing several members of the aristocracy twirling about on it.

Amelia was surprised and delighted to find the sitting room filled with women she knew, women with whom she'd shared many hours during her London Season. It did not take long to realize they were not nearly as delighted to see her as she was to see them.

"Amelia. What a surprise," Beatrice said in a tone that to Amelia sounded rather forced. How very odd.

"Yes, well, I've been back for more than two weeks and haven't had a chance to visit old friends, except, of course, for Betsy," Amelia said, trying valiantly to sound normal.

"Yes, Lady Havershaw mentioned it," Beatrice said.

"It's so wonderful to see everyone." She meant it. It was wonderful, and yet not. Something was strange, though she couldn't quite put her finger on it.

Beatrice indicated that she should sit, and Amelia did.

"We heard you were married," said Beatrice's younger, unmarried sister Emily. And someone actually shushed the girl.

Taken a bit aback, Amelia nodded. And smiled. But this time her smile was far more brittle. "Yes. I'm certain some of you have even met my husband. Dr. Kitteridge."

They let out polite murmurs of agreement.

"It's lovely to be home again. Texas is very different from England. Much warmer. In temperature."

The women simply stared.

"Did I interrupt a conversation? Please continue." And to a woman, they blushed, making Amelia instantly suspicious that she had been the topic of their conversation. She supposed it was natural enough that they would talk about her return, but it certainly was not natural that they should act so strangely toward her now. Not long ago, she would have ignored them, gone on with a smile on her face. But she was either far braver than she'd been or far less patient with their petty behavior, and so she challenged them. "You were discussing me, weren't you?"

She could tell by their reaction that she was right. "How lovely," Amelia said brightly, clearly surprising them and gaining a bit of satisfaction. "What would you like to know?"

"We've heard rumors," Emily blurted out, and Beatrice glared at the young woman. "Well, we have," she said, pouting.

"Rumors? I'm certain only half of them are true," Amelia said, full of charm even as her throat began to burn. Bravery, it seemed, was a fleeting thing. She'd never, in all her life, been the object of censure, and she realized this was only but a tiny glimpse of what her life would have been like if she had returned to England without a husband.

"We are all very concerned about you," Betsy said, her brown eyes darting to the other women. "We'd heard that Mr. Kitteridge, your fiancé, *former* fiancé . . . Oh, it does get confusing." She fluttered a hand in front of her face as if her sensibilities were so strained, she had to cool herself. "That Mr. Kitteridge was, shall I say, uncommonly common."

"Yes," Amelia said quietly. "I suppose by the ton's standards he was. Of course, none of us realized it when he was here."

"We were a bit shocked by your sudden attachment to him," Beatrice said, looking about the room for encouragement. "We all were. But you were so completely convinced he was something other than a charlatan, we all kept quiet."

"Is that right?"

To a woman, they all nodded.

Amelia passed a hand across her forehead. "I don't see what that has to do with the present. I've returned, married to a perfectly respectable man. A physician."

"We're sure he's very nice," Beatrice said, speaking

for all the women in the room, who were bobbing their heads as if attached to the same piece of string. "But surely you must agree that you will now be moving in a different circle from the rest of us."

Not knowing what else to say, Amelia's face turned red. "I'm not quite certain what you mean. My brother is an earl, a rather powerful one. And I call the Duchess of Bellingham a personal friend."

"She's an American, though."

"But still a duchess," Amelia said, aghast at the snobbery she was witnessing. She stood abruptly, knowing that the anger coursing through her body would end up in tears, which would only cause her more humiliation. She didn't want to give these horrid women the satisfaction of seeing her cry, even if they were tears of anger. Angry tears were still tears, after all. "I daresay my life will not be diminished by the loss of such dear friends," she said, her tone scathing. "Good day."

"We didn't mean to offend," one of the women called out, and she actually heard a soft snicker from another.

Amelia didn't cry until she was beyond the gate of the home, one she now found ugly and pretentious, a monument to false pride and ill-conceived priorities.

Maggie was going over that week's menu when Amelia came storming into the house, her cheeks tear-stained, though any tears that had fallen were long gone.

"What happened?"

"Those snobbish, horrible women I thought were

my friends think they're too good for me now," Amelia said, her voice shaking with anger. "I hope none of them were invited to the ball."

"I fear they probably were. And they likely accepted," Maggie said, putting the menu aside. "What did they say?"

"That we'd no longer be moving in the same circles," she said, mimicking the patronizing "concern" in their voices. "They actually said that. To me. My brother is one of the most powerful earls in the kingdom, and they have the nerve to say that to me. Honestly, I hope one of them gets ill and Boone must treat her, and I hope he gives her nightshade. Why, Boone is twice the man any of those ninnies is married to. Betsy married that old codger Havershaw and she has the nerve to suggest I've married ill? I wish I was still in Texas. I'd go over there right now with a rifle and . . . and . . ."

Maggie listened to her speech open-mouthed, then began to laugh. "So. It's you, then."

Amelia looked at her sister-in-law as if she'd gone mad. "Me, *what,* then?"

"You love Boone."

"Of course I do," she said, as if Maggie were daft.

Maggie clapped her hands, delighted. "When did this happen?"

Amelia looked at her hands, memories washing over her. She hadn't told Maggie or Edward about Julia's murder, had not wanted them to worry, and she hadn't wanted to discuss it. Her friend's death was still a raw wound, still incredibly painful. "Right after Julia died," she said softly, then related the entire horrible incident to Maggie.

"After the funeral, we went to her little house and

Boone had put back all her glass bits. There must have been more than a hundred of them, hanging just the way she'd liked it. I knew, of course, what a singular man Boone was, but I didn't know the true depth of him until that moment." She took a deep breath, and said fiercely, "He's twice the man of anyone I know. Except, perhaps, Edward. He's intelligent and wonderful and kind."

Maggie continued to smile. "But he doesn't know you love him, does he?"

Amelia lifted on eyebrow and looked away. "No," she said quietly. "He doesn't. And nor will he."

"Why ever not?"

She closed her eyes briefly, for the truth was too painful to bear. "Because, he doesn't love me. We all mistook his penchant for doing the right thing for love. He is kind to a fault. Did you know the only reason he was still in Small Fork at all was because Julia needed him? He ran the store to please his old friend, he stayed in Small Fork for Julia. And he married me for pity."

Maggie furrowed her brow. "Do you really believe that?"

"Yes," Amelia said. "I do. He said as much."

That seemed to deflate Maggie a bit. "I see."

"And now those horrible women are treating me as if I'm less than they are, less than I was only a year ago."

"I'm finding the ton is a fickle lot," Maggie said, "and these women are hardly the cream of society. They are the kind of women who will ride your coattails when it is convenient for them to do so, but will drop you when it is not. Surely you know better than to take stock in anything they say."

"You are right, but it still infuriates me." Amelia was thoughtful for a moment. "I suppose they were never great friends anyway. Hardly more than acquaintances."

Maggie smiled at the younger woman. "There. See? You must grow a thicker skin. Believe me, I know how awful it can be to be the victim of gossip. New York society isn't much different from the aristocracy here. If it weren't for Elizabeth, I would never have met your brother, never mind married him. My father's arrest doomed me to a life of poverty."

"You're so lucky to have a friend like the duchess," Amelia said.

"She's your friend, too, and no doubt can secure an opening to society for both you and Boone."

Amelia smile impishly. "It would be wonderful to show those women what for. I believe I shall start at the ball, by making certain I dance with the duke and my brother. Perhaps I can even convince Boone to take to the dance floor. I don't care if he steps on my toes a hundred times."

# Chapter 19

Boone looked at his reflection and grimaced. He felt completely foreign wearing this formal suit with its tails and black vest. His new, crisp white shirt was heavily starched and uncomfortable, and the tie around his neck looked silly. He was used to the simplest of tie knots, but Lord Hollings had insisted he borrow his valet and do up a proper knot.

"I look like a waiter," he'd said to the valet.

The proper young man had replied, "Only if you deport yourself like one. I would suggest you dress each evening, and then on occasions such as this, you will feel more comfortable."

Boone's only response was to tug at his stiff collar, which earned him a look of disapproval.

"And don't forget your gloves," the valet had admonished.

Boone tugged them on and gave himself another look. Not too bad. Not horrible. Certainly not as horrible as attending this ball would be. As soon as Lady Hollings had informed him of the ball, he'd felt slightly queasy each time he allowed himself to think about it. No doubt Amelia would want to dance, and he would not be able to. So he'd have to suffer on the sidelines and watch her dance with men who were born to this world, who felt comfortable wearing evening suits. No doubt he'd have to talk to people as well, people he'd never met who would be curious about him. Just the thought of being in a room full of strangers was enough to bring him into a cold sweat. But the look on Amelia's face when her brother had made the announcement had been priceless. She looked like a child about to be given a sweet.

It was likely only the first of many balls he'd have to suffer through, so he might as well get used to it.

A knock sounded on the door and he called for whoever it was to enter, expecting to see the valet checking up on his latest victim, only to hear a female gasp.

"You look stunning," Amelia exclaimed, rushing over to him and grabbing his hands. "Cunningham did this, didn't he," she said, referring to the valet. "He's turned you into a proper English gentleman." She lifted a hand to his hair, which he'd allowed Cunningham to cut. "You will be the most dashing man in the room. Now. How do I look?"

Words could not describe how beautiful Amelia looked at that moment. She twirled about, laughing, her skirts shimmering and swirling around her. It was, by far, the most revealing gown he'd ever seen her in, and it hit him hard that other men would be holding his wife in their arms while they danced, and would be able to look upon her at their leisure. He couldn't very well forbid her to dance, although he wished he could.

"Don't you think you should wear a shawl?" he suggested, and from her frown, he knew it was the wrong thing to say.

She looked down at herself as if she wasn't the most beautiful woman in England, as if that gown didn't make him think of ripping it off so he could make love to her. "I don't like the fact that other men will see you wearing this. I don't think you know what you do to a man. You're so damned pretty, it hurts my eyes just to look at you. If I can't keep my hands off you, how will anyone else?"

Apparently that was the right thing to say, for Amelia smiled. "Because my very big, very handsome, very possessive husband will be scowling at them fiercely."

"I suppose you'll have to dance if they ask."

"I will. But I'll wish it were you. Dancing is far easier than it looks. I do wish you would give it a try. I told Maggie just the other day that I'd suffer broken toes if I could dance with you. I'd be the envy of every woman in the room."

"Only those who enjoy embarrassment and intense pain," he said with a self-deprecating laugh. "I wouldn't wish that upon anyone, particularly not my wife." Boone had never danced in his life, he sure wasn't going to start tonight and humiliate himself and his new wife. "I'm already so nervous I can hardly walk, never mind dance," he said with an honesty that surprised them both.

"I'm nervous, too," Amelia said. "How will I ever decide whom to dance with first?"

Boone took a deep breath and looked rather ill.

"You truly are nervous, aren't you?" Amelia asked, full of concern.

"I've never been to a ball before," he admitted.

"It's like a big party with overdressed and over-stuffed people milling about pretending they are more important than they are," Amelia said. "The married men, after an obligatory dance or two, generally play cards or billiards, smoke cigars, and drink fine French brandy. At midnight, we gather to eat, then dance again. It's really great fun if you'll just relax a bit. You'll be fine."

"I don't dance, drink, gamble, or smoke," Boone pointed out dryly.

Amelia laughed. "Then you will simply have to watch me having fun."

And that's what he did, suffering from the side-lines watching Amelia dance with partner after partner, laughing and smiling and generally glow-ing like an overbright gaslight.

He did try to talk to people, but after a few incon-sequential sentences, had nothing more to say. After exhausting the topics of cowboys and indians, and leaving his listeners greatly disappointed that he hadn't much knowledge of either, other than mending broken bones, he was left standing there watching Amelia have fun.

"She adores dancing," Maggie said, coming up beside Boone.

"I can see that," he said, scowling. Amelia at that moment was dancing some lively number that re-quired her to bounce around the floor while her partner, some young buck, stared at her all-too-vis-ible attributes. "Does she have to dance that fast?" He'd wanted to say "bounce" but thought better of it.

"It's a polka," Maggie pointed out, laughing.

At that moment, Amelia's partner took her in far too close for propriety and Boone took a step onto the ballroom floor, his fists clenched. As if realizing what he was doing, he took a calming breath and tried to relax. My God, he thought, it's pure torture watching her with other men. He hadn't thought it would be so difficult. If she'd looked bored or anything other than delighted, it might not have bothered him so much. But she seemed so entirely happy, far happier than he'd ever seen her. Except for the day on the ship when they reached Liverpool. "I'm not sure I like balls. I have to tell you, I'm about to take every man in this room and drag them out for a brawl."

Maggie smiled and shook her head. "You really must learn to dance, Boone. There is a very well-attended Christmas Ball coming up in December."

"Sounds like pure torture," he said.

"Only if you allow it to be," Maggie said, laughing. "Amelia will certainly be invited and will want to go. Lady Rotherham's Christmas Ball is always the event of the Little Season, so you must learn how to dance."

"I'd feel foolish," he said, watching the buffoon on the dance floor totter about with his wife.

"How do you feel right now?" Maggie asked gently.

"Like I want to take her from that dance floor, and . . ." He flushed. "I'd better learn to dance before I kill someone."

Maggie studied him for a long moment before saying, "I see. I can teach you. Five years of brutal lessons from a very demanding dance teacher made me quite the expert. We were not rich. But my mother made certain I was trained as if we were. She'd always dreamed of an advantageous marriage for me. It was her number one priority."

Before Boone could accept her offer of dance lessons, a small group of women approached them and Maggie became decidedly chillier, more like the countess she was. The three women gave her the tiniest of curtsies to which Maggie nodded regally. It was fascinating, really, this odd hierarchy that everyone thought was so important.

"Lady Hollings, what a wonderful crush tonight," one of the young women said, but she was looking at Boone.

"Allow me to introduce to you Dr. Kitteridge," Maggie said, sounding almost reluctant. "Dr. Kitteridge, Lady Havershaw, Mrs. Turner, and Miss Eldridge. They are all neighbors of ours."

"Dr. Kitteridge," Lady Havershaw said, her eyes flaring just the tiniest bit in recognition. "So lovely to meet you. We're all friends of your wife. How wonderful that she still has a chance to enjoy these events. Why, the last time she had such a delightful time was at last year's Christmas Ball, where she met your brother. It was quite a spectacle," she said. Then, as if she realized how that sounded, she quickly added, "I mean meeting such a celebrated man as your brother. I do believe they danced all night."

Boone smiled and nodded even though he hadn't known a thing about how Amelia and Carson had met. It shouldn't bother him that Amelia had been at a ball with Carson, that his brother had no doubt danced with her. But it did, like a burning ache in his gut. He could picture his brother, bigger than life, eating up the attention, drawing the notice of a beautiful young girl who would one day feel forced by circumstance to marry a man she did not love. "She enjoys dancing," he said, not knowing what else to say.

"And you don't enjoy dancing?"

"No, ma'am, I don't."

The girls tittered, then Lady Havershaw hastened to explain. "You sound just like your brother. 'No ma'am,'" she repeated, giving a decent imitation of a Texas accent.

"You met my brother?"

"Oh, yes. We all did, but once he saw Amelia, he didn't look at any of us . . ." Her voice trailed off in what seemed like a rather calculated way. "My goodness, it's so nice to meet you, Doctor. We'll be certain to call for you if we get the sniffles."

Boone stared curiously after the three women, who walked away, their heads together, their mouths flapping furiously. Only the youngest one looked back and gave him a worried look. "Why do I get the feeling they were trying to cause trouble?"

"Because you are an excellent judge of character," Maggie said darkly. "Those are the kind of small-minded individuals that make life here so difficult for us."

"Us?"

"Americans," Maggie said. "You might as well know that there are some members of the ton who look down upon Americans as second-class citizens. Or worse."

"Why?" Boone asked, clearly baffled.

"Because we don't have blue blood. There are

many people who believe Edward married far beneath himself when he married me. Even my friend Elizabeth, who is from one of the wealthiest families in America, has seen some criticism—from her own mother-in-law even. The dowager treats her like a servant. It would be amusing if I didn't know how much it bothered Elizabeth. For generations, the English aristocracy only married among themselves or to foreign members of the aristocracy. It's only in our modern age that it's become more acceptable to marry outside your rank. It seems so silly, but that's the way it is," Maggie said, as if she truly didn't care.

The lively music ended, and Boone watched Amelia chatting with her latest partner before being escorted off the dance floor and toward where he stood. "And Amelia. Was she expected to marry someone in the aristocracy?"

Maggie hesitated. "It did cause a bit of talk when she went off to Texas to marry Carson. But at the time we all thought he was a wealthy ranch owner who could allow Amelia to continue to live the life of privilege she'd become accustomed to. A sort of *Texas* aristocracy, I suppose." Too late, Maggie seemed to realize what she was saying. "But she was extremely fortunate to find you, and . . ."

Boone forced a smile and raised a hand to stop her. "I understand," he said. And he did. He was beginning to understand things all too well.

Amelia didn't think she could dance another step. She was happy, but exhausted, and feeling slightly guilty that she had abandoned Boone for as long as she had. She was about to look for him when she was waylaid by Emily, Beatrice's younger sister, who looked delightful in a modest white lace dress. The girl had come out only last year.

"Mrs. Kitteridge," Emily called out.

"Good evening, Miss Eldridge," Amelia said coolly.

The girl worried her hands. "I feel simply awful about the way my sister treated you at her house. I wanted you to know that I was not party to that, not at all, and that I'm so very sorry to have been in the room at all."

Amelia immediately warmed to the sincerity of the girl's apology. "Apology accepted."

"I don't know why my sister puts on such airs. You might think she was married to a duke instead of that odorous Lord Havershaw," she said, giving a mock shudder. "Have you *seen* him? Honestly, my sister sold her soul just so she could marry a title. Now she acts as if she's better than everyone. But the truth is, I believe she's simply jealous. She was jealous of you last year when Mr. Kitteridge showed such keen interest in you, and now she's jealous because, well, because Dr. Kitteridge is simply the most handsome man any of us has ever seen." Emily's youthful enthusiasm was refreshing after being faced with the dour looks from her old friends. "It was so romantic the way he couldn't keep his eyes off you while you were dancing. All of us, *my* friends at least, were enthralled. We all vowed to forgo the title hunt and marry only for love."

Amelia looked at Emily and knew she was looking at herself a year ago, when she'd believed in romantic love, that marrying the right man could make all one's problems go away. She felt old and weary compared to the girl standing in front of her—even though she was only a year older.

"I appreciate your coming over to tell me," Amelia said. "And it's wonderful to know I can have a friend in Hollings."

"Oh, you do," Emily said, smiling widely.

"Now, if you'll excuse me, I think I've neglected my wonderful husband long enough. He's been very indulgent letting me dance the night away, but I confess I'm about to expire from exhaustion."

"I'd love to visit with you. I've always dreamed of going to America, of seeing a real live cowboy. I was too young to attend last year's Christmas Ball, so I never did get a chance to see Mr. Kitteridge." As if realizing she was entering forbidden conversational territory, Emily pressed her hand against her mouth. "I never do know when to keep my mouth closed," she said, blushing.

"You will learn," Amelia said, laughing good-naturedly. "And perhaps someday I will tell you the entire sordid tale."

Emily's eyes widened. "Is it truly sordid?"

"I shall endeavor to make it so," Amelia said with a wink.

It took her only a few minutes to find Boone outside, staring glumly toward the well-kept lawns of Meremont, even though it was far too dark to see much of anything. It was cool, but the air felt wonderful after the heat of the ballroom.

"I'm sorry I spent so much time dancing," Amelia said.

"I don't mind."

Amelia's shoulders slumped. He should mind. A

man who loved his wife certainly would have minded. "I've never danced with so many men in one evening," she gushed, watching his expression carefully for even one sign of jealousy. Even though that had not been her intent while dancing, a small sign of jealousy would have been heartening. "During my first Season, I had to be more careful with whom I danced, but as a married woman, I can dance with anyone I please."

"Except me."

Was that a glimmer of anger? Good. "Yes, but you don't mind. There aren't too many husbands who would be so completely understanding. I'm so very lucky."

"Lady Hollings mentioned a Christmas Ball."

"The Rotherham Ball," Amelia said, a feeling of dread hitting her. She would most certainly be invited, but would certainly not go. It was at that ball one year ago that she'd made such a fool of herself with Carson. It was at that ball she'd convinced herself she was falling in love. She absolutely would not attend. "I think we should send our regrets if we do receive an invitation."

"I want to go."

Amelia looked at Boone with complete surprise. "It's a terrible crush and not at all fun. The people who attend are old and . . . and boring. And there's dancing all night. Dancing and more dancing. I'm afraid I won't see you all night if we attend."

"I want to go," he repeated, this time with such steel in his voice, Amelia was startled. "I enjoy watching you dance."

She let out a rather unladylike snort of disbelief. "I've had my fill of dancing. Some of the people who go to such balls aren't very nice," she said, feeling desperate to somehow convince him that she did not want to attend without telling him the real reason why. "It's not like in Texas where everyone accepts everyone else. It's different here."

"Are you saying you're ashamed of me?" For some reason, Boone seemed to be purposely antagonizing her, which was completely unlike him. He was being ridiculous, and she told him so.

"If you must know, last year I made a spectacle of myself at the ball."

"Oh?"

"It's of no consequence now," she said, thinking it was better not to bring Carson into their conversation when Boone was already acting so jealous. "I'd just rather not attend such an event. I'm not part of that world any more."

"Then you *are* ashamed of me." He'd been looking out to the gardens, but he faced her, his expression stony.

"No, you ninny, I'm ashamed of myself."

"You have to face them sometime," he pointed out with maddening, cold logic.

"People can be cruel, especially members of the ton. They delight in other's failures," she said. "Why, some women I thought were my friends hinted that I wouldn't be welcomed in the same circles simply because you don't have a title or means. There are some people who think less of me for marrying you and are rather delighted by my fall. That's all. I told you it was silly."

"Is that what you think?" he asked.

"Honestly, Boone, right now I think I should punch you in the eye for being so completely stupid." Instead, she punched him in the chest, then stalked off.

In two steps, he caught her and grabbed her arm, spinning her around to face him. She stared at his hand holding her arm.

"Well, at least you're touching me," she said scathingly.

He dropped her arm as if scalded, his cheeks turning ruddy.

"Do you know how long it's been since you've touched me?" she asked. "Do you?" She shook her head, horrified at the pleading tone of her voice. "I know you didn't want to marry me any more than I wanted to marry you. But we *are* married."

He reared back slightly as if she'd hit him again. "Perhaps we shouldn't be," he said with dead calm.

She gasped, and he looked incredulously at her, as if surprised that she would even react to such a cruel statement. "Do you mean that?" she whispered, her heart aching in her chest.

"Why can't you tell me the real reason you don't want to go to that ball?" he asked with deceptive softness. "Why can't you tell me that it's where you met and fell in love with Carson?" He stepped away from her, his gray eyes as cold as the Irish Sea on a stormy night. "I'm an idiot. I fully admit it. And I'm jealous; I'm crazy with it. I don't like men dancing with you, and I don't like that you met Carson at that damned ball. I don't like the fact that he kissed you, touched you, before I did. I don't like the fact that you're probably thinking of him when I touch you."

Amelia winced and made a sound of denial and Boone stepped forward, some madness consuming him. Maybe it was watching his wife in the arms of other men all night, maybe it was the way she smiled up at them, maybe it was the way they stared down at her, their eyes filled with unguarded lust. Maybe it was that he knew he wasn't good enough for her, and never would be.

*You piece of shit. You little piece of shit.*

Maybe it was that he loved her and knew she would never love him. He didn't know what drove him at the moment, only that he couldn't stand the thought she didn't love him, couldn't take one more false smile, one more touch that meant nothing beyond the satisfaction of some carnal need. She was backed against the wall, looking up at him as if she'd never seen him before. She looked frightened, and he reveled in that fear. He wanted her to be afraid. He wanted her to feel something, anything for him other than pity or gratitude.

"Boone, don't."

He put his hand on her throat, gently. So gently he shook from it. His other hand braced the cold stone, and he curled it into a fist, scraping his fingertips on it until they hurt, a voice screaming in his head: *Love me, love me. Please God, make her love me.*

"You're scaring me." He felt her swallow against his hand, felt her fear.

He blinked and dropped his hand, pushing harshly away from the wall. My God, what was wrong with him?

"I have to go," he said half to himself. "Somewhere."

Amelia was silent, staring at him, tears coursing down her face. She had cried before, but she'd never cried because of him, because of his cruelty. He took a step toward her and she winced.

"I don't know where to go," he mumbled.

"Just go away," she said, turning her face from him. "Just go away."

# Chapter 20

Amelia pressed herself against the wall, shivering, tears streaming down her face. How had everything gone so wrong? She'd never seen him so angry, never seen his gray eyes so cold. She dashed away the tears and took a deep, shaky breath, her heart slamming against her chest when she heard the French door to the terrace open.

"Amelia?"

"Oh, Edward," she said, throwing herself into her brother's arms.

"What's wrong? I just saw Boone and he looked like death. Did he hurt you?"

Amelia shook her head, still clutching her brother's lapel. "No. But we had a terrible row and he said awful things to me. He actually said that we shouldn't have gotten married at all. He was cruel and Boone is the kindest man I've never met. I've never seen him like that."

"All couples fight," Edward said, patting her on her back.

"Not like that. I think he's leaving me. I told him

to go. Oh, Edward," she sobbed. "I have to find
him. He was so unlike himself. I don't know what
to do."

"For now, you have to get yourself together. Chin
up, right? You can't let everyone at the ball see how
upset you are."

Edward handed Amelia a handkerchief and that
almost made her start crying all over again, for it
only brought back memories of how kind Boone
had been to her when Carson had broken her
heart. She'd dampened more than one of Boone's
handkerchiefs. She dabbed at her eyes, then blew
her nose with gusto.

"Just leave it out here for now. We'll retrieve it in
the morning," Edward said, looking at the sodden
cloth warily.

Amelia nodded and gave him a brave, watery
smile. "How do I look?"

"Like you've had a terrible row with your husband," Edward said dryly. "But if you smile enough,
people may overlook your red eyes. I'll escort you
around the perimeter and get you to your room.
Then I'll look for Boone once everyone clears
out. It's nearly three, so I imagine some have already left."

When they returned to the ballroom, it was clear
that many of the guests had already departed, for
which Amelia was grateful. She smiled and nodded
and clung to her brother's arm, nearly collapsing
from released tension when they finally reached
the hall that led to Meremont's guest suites.

"I'll find him for you. Don't worry." He kissed
Amelia's forehead, before turning down the hall to

Boone's room, ready to choke the life out of the man who'd made his little sister cry.

But Boone wasn't in his rooms. He wasn't in the house at all.

Boone sat on the floor in the cottage and watched the sky lighten, his entire body numb. It was a blessing, finally, to stop feeling. To stop wishing that someone could love him. He sat like a child would, legs slightly splayed, his back against one wall, his palms facing up as his hands rested on his thighs. When Edward knocked on the door, he didn't answer, simply shifted his eyes to the door and waited. He was so damned tired.

When Edward entered the room, he stared at his brother-in-law without interest, and if Edward decided that Boone needed a beating for frightening his sister, he'd just take it. Just let him pummel him over and over like a ragdoll. He didn't care.

"You look like hell," Edward said, coming over to where he sat. He dragged a nearby chair closer and took a seat. "Amelia's quite upset. What happened?"

"I think we both realized this was a mistake."

"What is a mistake?"

"Forcing Amelia to marry me. Thinking I could make her happy. I can't. And she deserves to be happy, to with a man who can make her happy. I thought it would be enough, me loving her. It's not. It's killing me. Eating me up inside. Driving me crazy, making me say and do things I shouldn't." His hands curled into fists. "You wouldn't understand."

Edward let out a chuckle and Boone glared at him. "You are an idiot, I will give you that," Edward said. "The first time I proposed to my wife, she said no. And I would have died for her. For a long time, it hurt like hell. When you believe the person you love most in this world doesn't love you, it is hell. So, yes, I understand." Edward pulled out a flask and offered it to Boone, shrugging when the other man shook his head. He took a drink, then capped the flask. "Do you know for certain Amelia doesn't love you?"

"Yes," he said tiredly. "I'm sure."

Edward smiled and shook his head. "I'll let the two of you figure it all out. I just wanted to make sure you were still in England. I'll tell my sister you're here, if you don't mind."

"Please don't."

Edward let out an impatient breath. "You don't strike me as a particularly stupid man, but I've been wrong before." With that, Edward sat up and left the house without another word. Boone didn't move, just followed his brother-in-law's departure with eyes that burned from weariness.

Amelia was waiting for her brother when he returned, and rushed at him the moment he walked through the door, pulling him into the privacy of his library. "Did you find him? Is he all right? Is he planning to leave? Oh, for goodness sake, Edward, tell me."

"May I take a breath?"

"Edward."

"He's at your cottage. He's fine. And I don't know if he's planning to leave or not," he said.

"Oh." She walked over to the nearest chair and slumped into it, completely deflated. "Is he really fine?"

"Actually, no," Edward said, and Amelia's heart wrenched. "Let me give you some brotherly advice. Go to him, Amelia. Tell him how you feel. Please, for God's sake, end the poor man's suffering."

Amelia stood up and began pacing. "If I tell him I love him and he doesn't love me, then I'll be devastated, Edward. Truly devastated."

Edward busied himself at his desk for a time. "Bring him food," he said, without looking up from his work. "He looked hungry and there's not a morsel to eat in that house. If you don't return today, I won't be alarmed."

"Then you think . . ."

"Just go, Amelia."

Amelia grinned and hurried to the kitchens to see what the cook could gather up for them. Running to her rooms, she fetched a warm cloak, and ran back down the stairs to the kitchens to pick up a basket filled with food. "Thank you so much, Mrs. Morrison," she said, and fairly skipped out of the kitchen.

He loved her. He must love her. Else why would he get so jealous of her dancing, why would the thought of Carson kissing her make him angry? As she walked, she repeated over and over those words, he loves me, he loves me. But when she reached the cottage, she stopped, her heart pounding in her chest. What if he wasn't there? What if he was still angry? What if the man she loved didn't love her?

She opened the door without knocking, almost expecting him to be there waiting for her. She could hear a banging noise coming from the kitchen and followed it. "Hello? Boone?"

The banging stopped and he emerged from the back of the house looking so disheveled, so utterly, breathtakingly handsome, that Amelia actually felt her knees weaken.

"Hello." She lifted the basket. "I've brought food."

He stared at her, his eyes shifting briefly to the basket, before coming back to her face. He was still in the same clothes from the ball, but they bore little resemblance to the elegant suit he'd been wearing. He wore only the shirt, with collar removed and cuffs rolled up, and slightly untucked from his trousers. A smudge of dirt marred the now-wrinkled shirt. He looked completely exhausted, his eyes red-rimmed and hollow.

"May we talk?" Amelia asked softly, even as her heart pounded painfully.

He let out a long breath and nodded, silently walking over to a sofa and taking the protective cloth from it, folding it neatly before sitting, making Amelia smile. She placed the basket on a table, then sat at the opposite side of the sofa, as if they were a newly courting couple observing proper etiquette.

Amelia took a deep breath, feeling that all-too-familiar sensation of a burning throat that indicated tears were far too close. She swallowed and steeled herself for what she had to say. She would not cry, no matter what he said. No matter what he forced her to say. She lifted her chin and clutched her hands together almost painfully.

"Do you know when I fell in love with you?" she asked, as if she were asking him what he'd like for lunch.

He looked at her sharply, disbelievingly, then looked away as if he were angry. But Amelia would not stop now. She would come and say what she had to say. Then, if he didn't love her, she would leave. "It was after Julia died and you hung all those little bits of glass. I remember thinking that there was not another man on earth who would have done that. That's when it happened."

Amelia stared at Boone's stony profile, watching as the muscles in his jaw worked, over and over, as his hands clenched, as his breathing became oddly harsh. Finally, he looked at her, his eyes so tortured, Amelia nearly let out a sound of dismay.

"What?" he growled. "What did you say?"

"You were not listening?" Amelia asked, baffled and slightly miffed, having just laid her heart at his feet.

"Say it again," he said, and that's when Amelia saw that his eyes glittered with unshed tears. "Say it again," he whispered, his voice shaking with raw emotion.

"I love you. With all my heart."

The tension suddenly left his body and he squeezed his eyes shut, pressing the heels of his hands against them. "Again," he said.

Amelia let out a watery laugh, tears now falling freely down her face. "I love you. I love you," she said, moving next to him and pulling him close. "I love you, Boone Kitteridge. I love you. I love you."

He laughed, his face transformed. "Again," he said, laughing and kissing her.

"Not until I hear it from you," Amelia said, between kisses.

"I fell in love with you the day you walked into my store wearing that fancy yellow dress and looking like moonbeams were shooting from your hair."

"Oh, Boone."

He kissed her then, a rare, beautiful kiss, filled with anguish and relief and all the love he'd been holding back for months. He kissed her mouth, her cheeks, her chin, as if to make up for every time he'd wanted to kiss her but had held himself back. Amelia felt that wonderful, familiar warmth growing, making her body languid and alive.

"Shall we try out our new bed?" she asked with an impish smile.

He gave her one last drugging kiss, his tongue moving against hers, as she let out a whimper of need.

"Come on," he said, standing and holding out his hand. And then he ran for the stairs, all signs of exhaustion gone, tugging her along behind him as he took the steps two at a time, Amelia giggling breathlessly as she tried to keep up.

He dove for the bed, taking her with him, landing on his back and pulling her down on top of him. "Say it again," he said, smiling and looking so boyish Amelia laughed aloud.

"Are you going to be a pest about this, Boone? I do hope I don't regret telling you."

"Say it," he growled.

"I'm sorry, I don't have a clue what you can mean."

He pulled her down for a long kiss that stole her breath, moving his hands to her backside and pulling her hard against his arousal. "Amelia," he said with a warning tone.

"I love you," she said, kissing him between each word. "I love that you are the kindest man I've ever met. I love that you never, ever think of yourself first. I love that your hair curls when it rains. I love that your eyes look blue when you wear blue, and gray when you wear everything else. I love that you folded that sheet before sitting down on the couch. I even love that you scowl whenever I'm being extraordinarily nice to you. Like now." She moved her hand and stroked the length of him. "Why are you scowling?"

He smiled. "I'm just not used to it."

"I shall endeavor to be so nice to you that you will get used to it," she said pertly. She sat up on him and began to undo her buttons, loving the way his eyes followed her progress, the way his hands lay restlessly at her waist, the way every once in a while he moved his hips upward as if he couldn't take one more second of not having her.

She turned her back just enough so he could unlace her stays while she unhooked her chemise, letting out a sigh of pleasure when he kissed her neck and moved his hands to her breasts, eliciting such intense pleasure, she cried out. "I do like that," she breathed, moving against him, feeling a strange power when his erection grew even harder.

He turned her to face him, and he took one nipple into his mouth, suckling, sending such intense exquisite sensations between her legs she thought she might reach release at that moment. Amelia, her dress still gathered at her waist, moved against Boone in an almost involuntary way, as if driven by a carnal need she could not control. She wanted release. Wanted it. Now.

"Touch me," she said. "Oh, God, Boone, please."

In one movement, she was on her back and Boone was struggling to take off the rest of her clothes, cursing at her shoes, pulling off her drawers and underthings until she was naked before him. For some reason, she felt even more wanton lying there naked while he was still fully clothed.

"Touch me," she repeated, unnecessarily. For he was lost in her, drinking her in, touching her at the apex of her thighs, moving against the slick heat of her. "Oh, touch me, touch me," she said, over and over, even as he did, even as he put a finger inside her, moved a thumb against her. Kissed her.

Amelia, panting, lost in a haze of arousal, looked down to see Boone kiss her there, between her legs. Felt his tongue, oh, goodness, his tongue. *There*. "Yes," she said, moving her hips uncontrollably, feeling herself losing her grip on reality, feeling her body shake with intense pleasure. She convulsed around his finger, against his mouth, letting out a scream, and was still pulsing with her release when he put himself inside her. Amelia nearly giggled when she realized that one of Boone's pant legs was still on. He shucked it off even as he mouthed one nipple, as if impatient beyond reason to have her.

He moved against her, then stopped. Suddenly. "Say it," he said, grinning down at her.

"I love you."

"I love you, too."

He moved again, his face straining to hold back his release. "Again," he groaned.

"I love you," she whispered, and continued to

whisper in time to his thrusts, until he threw back his head in ecstasy, until he lay beside her completely spent.

"God, I'm tired," he said against her neck. "But I'm even more hungry. Come on." He threw his shirt at her and she pulled it on, loving that it smelled like him, of outdoors and Boone. He pulled on his pants and held out his hand to her, bringing her back down the stairs that only a few moments ago, they'd run up.

They ate cold chicken, standing barefoot in their kitchen, while Amelia heated up a crock of rich vegetable soup Cook had included. Afterward, they dressed and walked the beach, returning to make love again, this time more slowly, appreciating each other's bodies until they were both extremely knowledgeable about what made the other happy.

As the sun went down, they lay together in their bed, so completely exhausted they could hardly move. Boone lightly stroked Amelia's hair, and every once in a while gathered the strength to move his head and kiss her smooth shoulder. "I should get up," he said.

"No. Stay a bit longer." Amelia pulled him against her, resting her head on his shoulder, one arm draped across his torso. "Just a bit. You're so warm," she said sleepily.

"Mmm." It was all he could muster. She was so soft, so warm, and he was so very, very happy, that he drifted off to sleep before he could think about getting up, before he could feel that panic in his gut that he might hurt her.

\* \* \*

Boone awoke to the strange sensation of a woman softly sighing next to him, to the sun just coming up and making the water on the Irish Sea glow a soft rose, to birds chirping in the oak tree outside their window. As he watched Amelia, her eyes drifted sleepily open, so brilliantly blue, his breath caught in his chest.

"Good morning," she said, and snuggled closer.

"Mornin'," he said, sounding gruff compared to her quiet greeting.

She moved her head just enough so she could give him a kiss, soft, soft lips against his, and he felt as if his heart was going to explode, it was so full. He was sleeping with his wife, the women he loved, who apparently loved him. It was a miracle, that's what it was. And he'd slept through the night without a single dream that he could remember.

Boone realized, lying there, that he'd never felt quite so rested in his life. He wanted to run ten miles, swim in that cold, cold sea until his lungs burst. He wanted to make love to his wife until she screamed in pleasure. He wanted to yell from every rooftop in England that he was in love.

That he was loved.

Instead, he kissed his wife on her downy cheek, closed his eyes, and drifted back to sleep.

# Chapter 21

Amelia snuggled into her overstuffed chair in her favorite room of her brother's Hanover Square town house, a copy of the *Illustrated London News* on her lap, happily reading Anthony Hope's short story in the Christmas supplement that came with the *News* each year. She adored the Christmas season, and had decided that she was not going to let something as silly as Boone's stubbornness about attending the Rotherham Christmas Ball ruin it.

"Isn't it time you got dressed for the play?" Maggie called from the door. She was wearing a lovely dress of rich blue satin, with dark blue velvet trim accenting the deep neckline. It was embroidered with an intricate vine of delicate leaves made from gold and pearl beading that trailed from her trim waist to the gown's hem.

Amelia glanced at the clock and jumped up. "Goodness, I had no idea it was so late," she said. "Where is Boone?"

"Getting a last fitting at Edward's tailor, poor

man. They should be home any minute and ready to go. I'm so looking forward to seeing *A Christmas Carol* on stage. I never have, you know."

"I haven't either, except if you count a production I did with the children two years ago," Amelia said. "I was all three ghosts and Aunt Matilda's oldest was Scrooge. I'm afraid it was highly unrecognizable, but we had a grand time."

Amelia picked up her skirts and ran to the door. "I'll never be ready in time. Look at my hair," she said, running down the hall to her rooms. Fortunately when she arrived, her maid was already there with her dress laid out, looking completely relaxed.

"Do your best," Amelia said, turning her back so that the maid could begin unhooking her dress. Within minutes, she was in her gown and sitting as her maid efficiently put up her hair into a simple but elegant style.

"All done now," the woman said, securing one last strand of seed pearls into her hair.

"My goodness, Mary, how you did this in such a short time, I'll never know," Amelia said, gazing at her reflection. She was a vision; even Amelia knew it. Her gown was an emerald green silk with a gently rounded neckline trimmed in tiny beads that matched a row of pearls along the hem. A rich, embroidered swirling pattern on the skirt gave the creation a festive look that matched the evening's event. She'd gotten used to a far more ordinary girl looking back at herself, one who wore dresses that buttoned up the front, and did her hair in a hastily pinned bun. She'd never complain about not having servants, but could fully appreciate their worth. She adored her simple life, but it was wonderful, once in a while, to enter the tonier world of her brother.

"Honestly, Amelia, no matter how good I think I look, you always have to look better," Maggie said from the doorway with a mock frown.

"And no doubt Her Grace will outshine us both," Amelia said, referring to the Duchess of Bellingham, Maggie's best friend.

"Of course," Maggie said without rancor. "I do have to tell you that I'm a bit worried. The men haven't returned home yet, and we should be leaving soon if we are to make the curtain."

Amelia stood and looked out the window at the gaslit street below. "A carriage just arrived. It must be them." A moment later, two men disembarked. "They're here. Shall we meet them and stun them with our beauty?"

"I think we shall," Maggie said, holding out her arm. The two women marched down the hall toward the entrance arm-in-arm, only to have Boone blast by them.

"Boone. Hello," Amelia said, watching as he climbed up the stairs two at a time. It wasn't until he reached the landing that she saw the blood. "Boone. What happened?"

She started to follow him up the stairs but her brother stopped her. "There was an accident." At Amelia's expression, he quickly added, "He's not injured. He saved a man who was, though. It was remarkable." Edward shook his head and almost seemed in a mild state of shock. Maggie grabbed his arm. "Edward, what happened?"

He looked at each woman, a strange smile on his face. "You both know Lord Wallace." The women nodded. "He was struck by a carriage, then another ran over his arm. We didn't see it happen, but Boone heard him screaming and jumped down from our carriage. It hadn't even stopped yet. He ran to the scene, pushed everyone aside, and proceeded to stem the bleeding." He swallowed, suddenly looking slightly ill. "The blood was . . . copious. It was a miracle, really, that we came upon him in time. His own physician is caring for him now but he credited Boone with saving his life."

Amelia turned and ran up the stairs to find her husband stripping out of his brand new blood-soaked frock coat. "You're all right?"

"Of course," he said, looking down at his ruined shirt. "But I'm afraid I've nothing suitable to wear to the theater tonight."

Edward's valet entered the room and let out a small sound of despair at the sight of his clothing, then immediately left the room. "Squeamish?" Boone called out, and Amelia shushed him.

"Not everyone can bathe in someone's blood without fainting," Amelia said, laughing. She sobered, gazing at her adored husband. "Edward told us what happened. Apparently I'm married to a hero."

Boone shook his head. "I did what I was trained to do, that's all. Edward said you know the man? Lord Wallace?"

"Yes, he's quite an important political figure. He's a viscount. Do you think he'll live?"

"Most probably. His physician seemed competent enough. But his injury was bad and there's always a chance of infection." He pulled off his stained shirt. "You look beautiful. Maybe no one will notice I'm not dressed."

"Surely you're going to wear more than that," Amelia said, giving his body a long and longing look.

"Sir. I have a solution," Cunningham said, entering the room. In his hands he held a fine, newly pressed suit. "You and Lord Hollings are of a similar build, and I have obtained his permission to use this. I'm afraid I cannot replace your frock coat," he said, looking over at the fur-collared coat mournfully, "but the weather is unusually warm tonight so perhaps you do not need it."

"Oh, Cunningham, you have saved the night." Amelia gave her husband a quick kiss on his cheek and departed the room.

Word of heroic deeds spread just as quickly as misdeeds in the ton, and it wasn't long before everyone knew that Lord Hollings's personal physician and brother-in-law had heroically saved the life of Lord Wallace. By the time they got to the Lyceum, the first act had begun, but everyone forgave their late arrival. Their appearance in the private box drew what seemed to be undue attention, raised opera glasses, and whispered murmurs. Suddenly, just as old man Scrooge was listing the failings of the poor, a man in a box across from them stood and began clapping. Loudly. And staring directly at Boone.

Another man joined, and then another, until it seemed the entire place was standing and applauding, and the poor actors were left on stage to wonder what on earth was happening.

"Stand and acknowledge them, Dr. Kitteridge," Edward said.

Face red, Boone stood and gave a slight self-conscious bow, an action that brought forth a rousing cheer. Even those who no doubt didn't have a clue what was happening, raised their voices. And when Boone sat, it all died down, and the play continued as if nothing had happened.

Boone was equally moved and horrified by the acknowledgement. He leaned over to Amelia and said, "Good thing Cunningham found me a nice suit to wear."

Amelia stifled a giggle, and grasped Boone's hand. She didn't let go until intermission.

At intermission, Boone was surrounded by the highest members of the ton, all of whom couldn't wait to thank him for saving Lord Wallace's life. Details of the accident had lost a few facts along the way, but no one would hear of Boone humbly saying he'd only done what any doctor would. Amelia stood by him, beaming up at the man that the entire world now knew was special. Spying Emily Eldridge in the crowd, Amelia pulled away and went over to the young woman.

"Oh, it's so exciting, isn't it? I heard Lord Wallace's arm had nearly been taken completely off and Dr. Kitteridge sewed it back on," she gushed. "It's so thrilling."

"I don't think it was quite that dramatic," Amelia said with a laugh, "but I am quite proud of him. He came home covered in blood. It was positively gruesome. I do hope Lord Wallace is doing well."

Amelia looked over at Boone, fearing he'd be uncomfortable with the attention. He stood, inches taller than the rest, looking solemn and handsome, a calm presence amidst the clamor. How different he was from Carson, whose smile and flamboyant mannerisms now seemed so superficial. He'd welcomed the hero-worship, encouraged it even, when he'd done nothing to deserve the accolades showered upon him. And there was Boone, a true hero, looking rather uncomfortable to be the recipient of such adulation. What a silly, stupid girl she'd been a year ago, she thought.

Next to her, Emily sighed. "He is the most handsome man, Mrs. Kitteridge. You are the luckiest of women."

"And he's very devoted," Amelia said, pointedly.

Emily gave Amelia a mock pout, then grinned as if she couldn't even pretend to be grumpy. But her frown turned genuine when her older sister Beatrice joined them, acting as if she hadn't insulted Amelia to the core the last time they'd met. "You must tell me all about it," she said, smiling coolly just as the lights flickered, announcing the beginning of the second act of the play.

Amelia gave a rueful look, as if she were sorry she wouldn't have the chance to speak to Beatrice about the incident. "Perhaps we can talk tomorrow at the Rotherham Ball," Amelia said, thinking to herself that she would avoid such a conversation if at all possible. She was not one to easily forgive.

"Oh," Beatrice said, flushing slightly. "We've decided not to attend."

"Because we weren't invited," Emily put in. Beatrice flashed her sister a look that would have frightened a meek girl, but Emily simply smiled.

"I suppose you were right, Beatrice," Amelia said.

"Right?" the other woman asked, confused.

"We *are* moving in different circles now. Perhaps I can visit you when we return."

Beatrice suddenly looked as if she'd eaten a lemon. "Yes. That would be lovely."

Emily gave Amelia an impish look, then left with her sister. Whoever said revenge wasn't gratifying apparently hadn't met Beatrice Turner.


The Rotherhams had outdone themselves, creating a ballroom so filled with Christmas cheer it appeared a veritable forest of holly, mistletoe, and green boughs. Hanging from the ceiling were crystal snowflakes that glittered in the gaslight, sending tiny bits of light throughout the room, making it almost appear as if it were snowing.

Entering the ballroom on Boone's arm, Amelia looked up and felt a sharp melancholy tug in her heart.

"Julia," Boone said, softly.

"I was thinking the same thing. It is lovely, though, isn't it?"

As they walked into the room, they were greeted warmly by some of the ton's highest-ranking members, and Amelia knew it was because of Boone's newfound popularity. All her fears that he would not be accepted were obviously unwarranted.

"My goodness, what a crush already," Amelia said, craning her head to see if she could spot anyone she knew. Her brother and sister-in-law had gotten swept away in the moving mass of ball-goers, and now she could not find them. She did spy the Duke and Duchess of Bellingham in one corner, looking incredibly regal standing together. The duchess looked as if she'd been born in the world of the aristocracy, even though she was an American. And Amelia had to admit, Boone, with his fine black formal suit and quiet confidence, could easily have been mistaken for a member of the ton.

The tradition of putting up a Christmas tree only on Christmas Eve had been ignored. Each corner of the room was filled with a freshly cut tree, and the pine scent mingling with expensive perfumes and cologne was nearly overpowering.

"Oh, look, Boone, we've got four berries," Amelia said, looking down at the sprig of mistletoe each married couple had been given as they entered the ballroom. With each sprig came instructions that they should only give one kiss per berry. As each kiss was made, a berry was removed.

Amelia was looking down at the little sprig smiling, and when she looked up, Boone gave her a quick kiss.

"Boone, you've wasted a berry," Amelia said, laughing.

"I don't think sneaking a kiss from my wife is a waste," he said, and tried for another.

Giggling, Amelia turned, only to run into her brother.

"How many berries do you have?" she asked Edward.

"We had two, but they're gone already," Maggie said with exasperation. "I'm sending Edward for another."

"I'm afraid that's cheating, and I'll have to report you to Lady Rotherham," Amelia said with mock sternness.

Just then, the orchestra struck up the "Grand

March," and en masse, the ballroom floor cleared, revealing the Rotherhams' stunning starburst mosaic medallion in the center of the floor.

"We didn't have this at our ball," Amelia whispered to Boone, who watched, puzzled, as couples promenaded around the ballroom floor. "As guests of honor, we would have been first in line."

"I'm forever grateful," he said, using a rather bad English accent. Amelia giggled and lost another berry when he kissed her cheek. "I just can't help myself. You're so beautiful tonight."

Amelia blushed. She adored the dress she was wearing, a deep red velvet that revealed creamy shoulders and dipped low enough to show a hint of her breasts. It was the simplest of designs, but the most elegant of anything she owned.

"Now we only have two left and hours and hours to go before the ball is over."

After the "Grand March," the crowd applauded, their claps muffled by the gloves each wore. If there was one thing Boone detested about formal wear it was these silly white gloves he was forced to wear. When he'd complained to Amelia, she explained that his sweaty, manly hands would ruin the ladies' gowns, so it was better to sweat inside his gloves.

"But my hands wouldn't be sweating if I didn't have the dang things on," he'd pointed out logically.

"How many men are on that dance card of yours?" he asked now.

She hid it from view. "It's full," she said, watching as the first dancers took up a lively reel.

"Then why aren't you dancing?"

"Because it's full," she said again, holding up the

elaborately decorated little book. "It's the only polite way a lady can decline a gentlemen's request to dance."

"I want you to dance," Boone said.

"The last time I did, you were a jealous boor," Amelia cheerfully pointed out.

"That was before."

"Before what?"

She was looking at up him, her eyes sparkling, and he just couldn't help himself. He wasted another berry. "Before I realized how much you love me," he whispered in her ear.

The Duke of Bellingham strode up to her at that moment and bowed gracefully. "I wonder if you would honor me with a dance, Mrs. Kitteridge. If that is acceptable, Dr. Kitteridge," he said with a small bow.

Amelia pretended to look at her completely empty dance card. "Of course, Your Grace, I would be honored." She held out a gloved hand and gave Boone a secret smile, and Boone watched her dance off in the arms of another man.

It didn't bother him at all, for he trusted their love completely. But watching her dance, her graceful turns, her smiling face looking up at the duke, he wanted to feel her in his arms, even if it meant humiliating himself on the dance floor. Suddenly, he was glad of those gloves, for he could feel his hands begin to sweat. It wasn't lost on him that he could stem the flow of a spurting artery with more calm than he could dance with the woman he loved.

Amelia didn't dance every dance, and he didn't stand on the side scowling at her dance partners, either. He was frequently pulled away from his spot to talk with men who wanted to hear in detail how Lord Wallace was faring. The man would recover, though he was still weak from blood loss. For the first time in his life, he felt confident and comfortable in his own skin, talking with men on all matter of subjects.

As the night wore on, his anxiety grew about the last waltz—"The Blue Danube." As compositions went, it was one of his favorites. He just prayed he wouldn't make a complete ass of himself. Whenever a waltz came up, he studied how the other men held themselves, the steps they took, the confidence in their demeanor.

He watched, smiling, as Lord Hollings danced a polka with Amelia, brother and sister laughing as they threw themselves wholeheartedly into the steps. A hand touched his arm.

"You'll do fine," Lady Hollings said, looking up at him. "You know the steps. In fact, you're a finer dancer than many of the men out there, including the earl. You were a much better student than I."

Boone knew he did not look like a man about to dance with his beloved wife. Likely he looked more like a man about to face an executioner. He'd step on her toes. He'd hit someone else. As the polka wound down, he took a shaky breath.

"You look like you're about to be ill, Dr. Kitteridge," Maggie said, a smile in her voice.

"You'd make a fine doctor," he said grimly.

As brother and sister approached, Boone stepped forward and bowed slightly in front of his wife.

"May I have the honor of your hand for this dance?" he asked solemnly.

Amelia looked at him, tears glittering in her eyes,

all the love she felt for him clearly showing for everyone to see. "Oh, Boone, you don't have to," she said.

"Yes. I do." He held up a gloved hand and she took it, gazing at her husband as if he were allowing her to walk on water.

The first strains of the waltz began and she braced herself, her heart breaking for this man she loved so much, who'd put himself at such risk for her. And then, the most amazing thing happened.

He was wonderful. Not just adequate, but wonderful. He led her around the dance floor like a man who'd been taught by the finest of dance tutors, and she narrowed her eyes suspiciously. "Dr. Boone Kitteridge," she said, "you know how to dance, don't you?"

He smiled down at her. "Only the waltz," he said, twirling her about with newfound confidence. "And only with you."

And then Dr. Boone Kitteridge did something that would be talked about for years. He stopped dancing and used up their last mistletoe berry, right there on the dance floor, right there for all to see. It seemed as if the entire room let out a collective sigh, for few had ever witnessed anything more shockingly romantic than Dr. Kitteridge kissing his wife in the middle of that Christmas waltz.

Did you miss Jane's
other books in the series?
Go back and read those as well!

## MARRY CHRISTMAS

A Christmas wedding to the Duke of Bellingham.
Any other socialite in Newport, Rhode Island,
would be overjoyed at the prospect, but Elizabeth
Cummings finds her mother's announcement as
appealing as a prison sentence. Elizabeth has not
the slightest desire to meet Randall Blackmore, let
alone be bartered for an English title. Her heart
belongs to another, and the duke's prestige, arro-
gance, and rugged charm will make no difference
to her plans of elopement.

Against his expectations and desires, Randall Blackmore has inherited a dukedom and a vast estate
that only marriage to an heiress can save. Selling
his title to the highest bidder is a wretched obliga-
tion, but to Randall's surprise his intended bride
is pretty, courageous, delightfully impertinent—
and completely uninterested in becoming a duchess.
Yet suddenly, no other woman will do, and a
marriage in name only will never be enough for a
husband determined to win his wife in body, heart,
and soul . . .

# A CHRISTMAS SCANDAL

Dashing, debonair, and completely irresistible, Edward Hollings has all of Newport buzzing—and to Maggie Pierce's surprise, she alone has caught his eye. But when the handsome earl returns to England without proposing, a devastated Maggie knows she must forget him. Life only gets worse for Maggie, as all her dreams of happiness and love come crashing down around her. When Maggie receives an invitation to go to England for the Christmas birth of her dear friend's baby, she accepts—vowing to keep her devastating lies and shameful secrets from the one man she has ever loved.

Edward vowed he'd never marry, but he came dangerously close with Maggie. She's beautiful, witty, indescribably desirable—and Edward can't forget her. When Maggie visits mutual friends for Christmas, Edward can't stay away. In fact, he finds himself more attracted to her than ever—a desire fueled even more by Maggie's repeated snubs. With the love he never thought he'd find slipping away, Edward is determined to make Maggie his own, no matter what the cost . . .

# More by Bestselling Author

# **Janet Dailey**

# More by Bestselling Author

# Lori Foster

# More by Bestselling Author
# Hannah Howell